Fiona Leitch is a writer wit written for football and mot illegal raves and is a stalw commercial, even appearing as the Australasian face of a cleaning product called 'Sod Off'. After living in London and Cornwall, she's finally settled in sunny New Zealand, where she enjoys scaring her cats by trying out dialogue on them. She spends her days dreaming of retiring to a crumbling Venetian palazzo, walking on the windswept beaches of West Auckland, and writing funny, flawed but awesome female characters.

Her debut novel, *Dead in Venice,* was published by Audible in 2018 as one of their Crime Grant finalists. Fiona also writes screenplays and was a finalist in the Athena Film Festival Writers Lab, co-run by Meryl Streep's IRIS company.

Also by Fiona Leitch

The Nosey Parker Cozy Mysteries

Murder on the Menu

A Brush with Death

A SPRINKLE OF SABOTAGE

A Nosey Parker Cozy Mystery

FIONA LEITCH

One More Chapter
a division of HarperCollins*Publishers* Ltd
1 London Bridge Street
London SE1 9GF
www.harpercollins.co.uk
HarperCollins*Publishers*
1st Floor, Watermarque Building, Ringsend Road
Dublin 4, Ireland
1

This paperback edition 2021
First published in Great Britain in ebook format
by HarperCollins*Publishers* 2021

Fiona Leitch asserts the moral right to be identified
as the author of this work
A catalogue record of this book is available from the British Library

ISBN: 978-0-00-843660-5

This novel is entirely a work of fiction. The names, characters and incidents portrayed in it are the work of the author's imagination. Any resemblance to actual persons, living or dead, events or localities is entirely coincidental.

Printed and bound in Great Britain by
CPI Group (UK) Ltd, Croydon CR0 4YY

Chapter One

'I'm ready for my close up, Mr DeMille.'

Daisy and I were in the kitchen eating breakfast but turned round at the sound of Mum's voice.

'What the—' I spluttered, almost choking on my tea. Daisy's mouth dropped open and a piece of half-chewed toast fell out. Germaine, our Pomeranian fur baby who had been lurking under the table hoping for scraps, took advantage of the distraction and gobbled it up.

My seventy-year-old mum stood in the doorway, clad in a floor-length black gown covered in sequins, several of which were barely hanging on by a thread. She had a bright-pink pashmina around her shoulders and lipstick that matched it. Long diamanté drops dangled from each ear, earrings that I recognised from my own stash of costume jewellery that hadn't been worn for years. I thought she'd probably been going for a neatly coiffured up-do with her hair, but it looked like a magpie had made a nest on the top of her head, shoved in a cheap stolen tiara, and then squirted it with a liberal application of hair spray to stop it moving.

Daisy recovered her senses before I did. 'That's a … a bold look, Nana,' she said, with a diplomacy that belied her tender years. Mum beamed at her and I swallowed hard; I couldn't let her leave the house looking like this. It was 8.30 on a Saturday morning in sleepy Cornwall and she resembled a woman of geriatric easy virtue.

'You look very… That dress is… It's quite…' I was lost for words, which doesn't happen very often. When you're a copper – which I had been, in a previous life – you come across all kinds of bizarre scenarios where what you say can be the difference between defusing the situation peacefully or making it all kick off. However, none of those previous cases had involved my mum. I fell back on a line that was the last resort of bewildered police officers the world over. 'So what's going on here, then?'

Mum attempted a look of affronted dignity, but just ended up looking constipated. 'It's the casting today, isn't it?' she said, in a voice that clearly suggested I should know what she was talking about. But I didn't.

'What casting? What are you going on about?'

She tutted as if you really couldn't get the domestic

staff these days and extracted a leaflet from the gold lamé evening bag she was clutching. I took it from her and read it aloud for Daisy's benefit.

"Ever wanted to be in a movie? Now's your chance! Extras wanted for period drama filming in October at Polvarrow House, Penstowan Cross. Good rates of pay. Casting session Saturday 27th September from 10 a.m." I looked at Mum. 'So this is why you're dressed up like Audrey Hepburn coming down from a bad acid trip, is it? This is why you got me to take you home yesterday, to pick your outfit up?' Mum had her own house, but she more or less lived with us now that we'd moved back to Penstowan, enjoying the idea of independence without any of that tedious having-to-clean-your-own-bathroom business.

'I *was* going more for a Downton Abbey look,' said Mum reproachfully. 'The film people popped in to the coffee morning on Wednesday.' The local church held an OAPs' coffee morning every week, which was a hotbed of gossip, scandal, and discussion about, I dunno, surgical stockings, heartburn tablets, and funeral insurance. What else would they have to talk about? 'They asked us to put the word out as they'll need a lot of extras. I told them my daughter would bring me along.'

'Would have been a good idea to tell *me* that,' I grumbled, but I didn't really mind. I didn't have anything much planned for the day.

Daisy turned to look at me, excitement in her eyes, and I knew what she was going to say before she even opened her mouth.

'Yes, you can come too,' I said, 'although I can't promise they'll need anyone of your age.' I turned the leaflet over in my hand; there were more details about the movie on the back. 'It says here it's a period fantasy drama – whatever *that* means – with a top-notch cast including—' I sucked in my breath and looked at Daisy with wide eyes. 'Zack Smith!'

Daisy looked like she would fall off her chair. 'Zack Smith? Oh my God, you're joking! He's *amazing*.'

'Who the heck's Zack Smith?' asked Mum, hobbling further into the room and slipping off her high-heeled but wide-fitting shoes.

'You remember that thing we watched the other night, with the soldier who got involved with MI6 and they had him hanging from the London Eye with his shirt off?' Daisy blushed slightly. She would be thirteen in a couple of weeks and I'd known it was only a matter of time before she discovered boys, but it appeared to be happening already.

'The fat bloke with long hair?' Mum screwed up her face, trying to remember.

'No, Nana,' said Daisy impatiently. 'You're thinking of the wrong film. The one where they chase him through the underground and then trap him on the London Eye, and then he jumps into the river and escapes. The young black guy with the six-pack.'

'I never quite worked out how he ended up without his shirt on,' I said. 'Apart from the fact it showed off his abs, which obviously made quite an impression on you.'

'No!' Daisy protested hotly. 'So what if it did, anyway? I bet you fancied David Hasselhoff or someone cheesy like that when you were my age.'

'The Hoff? How old do you think I am?' I asked, offended. 'It was Mr Darcy…'

'Yeah, you do know he's a fictional character, right?' Daisy looked at me as if I were some kind of weirdo. Which was probably fair enough.

'They did it on the telly,' I explained. 'Colin Firth coming out of the lake with a wet shirt on was a very special moment in my formative teenage years.'

'Ooh now, that Colin,' said Mum. 'He's a lovely-looking fella. I wouldn't mind sharing my electric blanket with him.'

'Mum!' I said, exasperated.

She laughed. 'You can't tell me you'd rather curl up in bed with a good book than with Mr Darcy himself! I'd even get a trick hip fitted for him.'

'Honestly, you're— What do you mean, a trick hip?' The minute the words left my mouth I regretted it; I did *not* want to know what a trick hip was, not coming from my own mother.

'You know Margery? Married to Alf the butcher? The one with the facial hair?' I nodded. Poor Margery did indeed have an unfortunate amount of chin fluff, far more than her pasty-looking husband. 'She had a new hip done a couple of years ago but it never healed right. She told me it pops out of the socket when they…' She gave me a meaningful look and a nod.

Daisy and I looked at each other, aghast.

'I feel nauseous,' said Daisy, laying down the piece of toast in her hand with a pained expression. 'I may never eat again.'

'Always a good idea to keep the man in your life happy,' said Mum. 'How do you think she got her new dishwasher?'

I hadn't been to Penstowan Cross for years. It was one of those nothing places you only went to if you lived there. It was basically a remote country crossroads, on the four corners of which sat a church, a rundown pub, an even more rundown garage (one petrol pump for cars, one for tractors), and a handful of houses. It was a toss-up whether the pub or the church attracted more visitors, but neither did as much business as the garage, and all three had seen better days. None of the four roads that made up the cross led anywhere particularly interesting, apart from (or maybe including) the one that led back to Penstowan itself. And of course the one that took you to Polvarrow House.

I piled everyone, including the dog, into the car and we set off.

'Margery and Alf,' began Mum. Daisy and I shuddered at the thought of the gymnastics Margery had apparently done to get her new dishwasher. 'They live out this way now, on the new estate.'

'What new estate?' I asked. The crossroads lay up ahead.

'The new owners of Polvarrow sold off some of their land, didn't they?'

'I dunno, did they?' Mum seemed to forget sometimes that I'd been away for the best part of twenty years, and the ins and outs of life in her little bit of Cornwall didn't tend to make it onto the London evening news.

'Yeah, they've proper brought the area up,' said Mum. She wasn't kidding.

The pub had had a massive makeover. The paintwork was fresh, tables were dotted about cheerfully on the grass verge out the front, and I could see round the side that the beer garden was looking, well, like a beer garden, rather than a Cold War-era No Man's Land. Hanging baskets decorated the front of the building, still full of flowers despite it being very much autumn. The old garage had been taken over, rebranded with in-your-face corporate signage, more pumps (with higher prices), and an on-site supermarket. And despite the fact that you can't really give a church a makeover as such, it still managed to look brighter and more welcoming; a place to gather and give thanks, rather than to confess terrible sins and get a dose of hellfire.

I turned the car towards Polvarrow House. I'd only been to the house once before, when my ex-husband Richard, a.k.a 'that cheating swine', and I were planning our wedding. I'd had these big ideas of having the reception at a country house, and on a trip down to visit my parents (on my own, as usual) I'd heard that the owners were thinking of making it a wedding venue to help with the costs of running the house. I hadn't mentioned it to anyone – to be honest, I was torn between having the big dress and the fancy wedding, and just going off somewhere hot and getting married on the beach (in the end we did neither) – and I'd taken myself off for an afternoon to have a look around.

It had been *awful*. The house had looked decent enough(ish) from the outside, although the grounds were slightly wilder than I had expected, with none of the neatly clipped box hedges or striped lawns that I'd imagined; but once inside, the full extent of the disrepair and neglect the building had fallen into became all too apparent. Instead of the beautiful period decor I'd been hoping for, handprinted wall coverings, plaster mouldings, and gilding, there was woodchip wall paper – that weird embossed paper that you put up and then paint over. It had been painted over in a kind of stale-tobacco yellow; or maybe it *hadn't* been painted over and it was down to generations of heavy smokers. The furniture was a bizarre mismatch of old antique pieces, most of which needed re-upholstering, and flatpack stuff from Ikea. There was a strange, musty, and unpleasant smell emanating from somewhere, and the thought of inviting my guests to sit down and eat something that had been prepared in that mould-ridden cesspit of a kitchen made my insides go all squirmy. No thanks. I had quickly made my excuses and left, but not without seeing the look of utter helplessness and despair on the owners' faces. I felt sorry for them, lumbered with this monstrous house, but not *that* sorry. I hoped the new people had worked their magic on their own home as much as they had on the village.

We drove past the entrance to the new estate, which was all grass-verged cul-de-sacs, internal garages, and identical boxy but neat detached houses, then turned into the long driveway towards Polvarrow House. The wrought-iron gates stood open, painted glossy black with a curly *PV* motif picked out in gold; there was no sign of the rust that had blighted them on my previous visit.

We headed along an avenue of elm trees, their leaves beginning to colour into that almost lime-green that would turn to yellow then bronze as autumn established itself more fully on the landscape. To the right, a narrow strip of neatly trimmed grass was bordered by huge shrubs – ancient rhododendrons and azaleas by the look of it, although I'm hardly a horticultural expert and they are just about the only plants I can ever recognise. Beyond them lay the back gardens of the new houses, bordered by black iron railings.

The avenue curved left, away from the housing estate, and we were greeted with our first view of Polvarrow House itself, looking rather more salubrious than when I'd last been there. There were box topiary balls in big stone planters lining the driveway, and the ornate carved fountain that had been cracked and covered in green moss the last time I'd seen it was now shooting plumes of water into the air that landed with a gentle plashing sound in the pool below.

'Wow,' said Daisy, and I had to agree.

'It's beautiful, isn't it?' I said.

'I didn't mean the house,' she said, and then I saw what she was looking at.

It looked like Hollywood – or the behind-the-scenes part of it, anyway – had come to Cornwall. There was a whole village of tents, motorhomes, and trucks parked on the gravel at the side of the house. There didn't seem to be any filming going on, but it was still a hive of activity – movie people with clipboards walking around looking important, talking into mobile phones, and gesticulating wildly. I pulled up next to a friendly-looking older man who was just about the only person standing still, and wound down the window. He bent down to speak before I could say anything.

'Hello! Are you here for the casting?' he said. All three of us nodded. 'Lovely! Just follow the drive round to the back and park up, then follow the signs.' He stepped back with a smile, and indicated where to go.

We drove around to the back of the house. The car park was rammed, and I recognised a few cars. We parked up and got out of the car. I had managed to persuade Mum to change into something a little less eccentric, tempting her with the promise of a visit to the local garden centre afterwards. She always enjoyed pottering around and looking at the plants, even though she had brown fingers like I did and rarely bought anything. They also have a particularly good café there, and I had learnt long ago that my mum would do pretty much anything for a toasted teacake and a nice cuppa.

We followed the signs for 'Casting' back round to the front of the house and towards a big marquee tent. The friendly man we'd spoken to earlier stood outside and smiled as he saw us.

'You found somewhere to park? Marvellous!' he said enthusiastically.

'Are you the director?' asked Daisy. He laughed.

'Oh, good Lord no,' he said. 'I'm nothing to do with all this. I'm David Morgan, the owner of Polvarrow.'

'You own this place?' I said. 'It's beautiful. I came here once, years ago when the last owner was still here, and it was in a right state.'

He nodded. 'Yes, they were lovely people but I think the repairs had just got on top of them. It's very expensive, running a place like this.'

'But worth it.'

He turned and looked proudly at the house. 'Yes. Yes, it is.'

We all admired Polvarrow House for a moment, then—

'Nosey!' We turned to see my oldest friend in the world, Tony Penhaligon, standing in the doorway of the tent, clutching a piece of paper. He waved it at us. 'Come to put your name down?'

'Don't tell me *your* mum dragged you along here too?' I said, as Germaine rushed over to him, tail wagging. She was always pleased to see him. He dropped onto his haunches and started to make a fuss of her.

'Nobody dragged me,' he said, laughing as Germaine

snuffled at his hand, then at his pockets. 'I'm sorry, gorgeous, no treats for you today.'

'I wasn't expecting any,' I said. He straightened up, eyebrows raised.

'You do know I was talking to the dog?'

I sighed. 'Yes. I'm used to her getting more attention than me. So what, you really want to be in this film?'

'Yeah!' Tony nodded enthusiastically. 'I always wanted to be up on the big screen. Don't you remember, all the school plays…?'

'Ooh yes!' said Mum. 'I remember. You did *The Wind in the Willows*.'

'Guess who I was?' Tony turned to Daisy, who was trying to calm the dog down.

'The wind,' I murmured.

'You were just jealous because I got the lead role and what were you? Oh yeah, the old washerwoman!'

'You did have to go on stage in front of everyone with your face painted green,' I pointed out.

'So jealous…'

'Do we have to audition?' said Daisy. 'Do they make us do a screen test, like you see on the telly?'

'No,' said Tony. 'You just fill in the form and wait for them to call you. They give you a once over to make sure you look right—'

'Look right?' I asked.

'It's a period drama, innit? No tattoos or nose rings.'

Tony winked at Mum. 'Better cover up them tattoos of yours, Shirley!'

Mum giggled. I rolled my eyes. Tony had always been able to wrap my mum round his little finger, much more so than I could, which was hardly fair.

'And that's it?' said Daisy. She'd been excited but a little nervous at the idea of having to get up and perform in front of everyone, I thought, and she looked relieved. Tony nodded.

'That's it. Nothing to worry about. Here.' He led us into the tent. Just inside was a long table covered in forms and mugs full of biros. A bored-looking woman sat behind it, scrolling through her phone. She barely looked up as we entered. Along the side of the tent were a couple of rows of seats, most of them full, while at the other end stood another table, this time with a man and a woman seated behind. He called, *'Next!'* and the occupant of the seat nearest to them stood up and handed over a completed form, then waited awkwardly in front of them. Everyone in the seats stood up and shuffled along to the next chair.

Mum and Daisy both took a form and went to sit down while they filled them in. Tony looked at me expectantly but I shook my head.

'Nope. I have no desire to see myself on the big screen.'

'Really? I don't believe you.'

'I don't!'

'You just don't want to get cast as a washerwoman again.' Tony grinned and I aimed a slap at him, which he dodged easily. 'No, look, think about it. It's really easy. All you have to do is stand around and go 'rhubarb, rhubarb' or whatever. They pay you a hundred quid a day and feed you, just for standing there in a costume.'

'A hundred quid?' It was tempting, but ... no. 'You don't need the money, though, do you? The shop's doing all right?' Tony ran the town's only department store, which had been owned by his family for several generations.

'The shop's doing fine, I just want to be a movie star. Good job I've got a nice boss.' He looked at me seriously. 'How much work you got on at the moment?'

'Enough,' I said, but I didn't actually have any. My catering business was slowly picking up, but it was the wrong time of year for weddings or outdoor events, and Christmas party season wouldn't start for another couple of months yet. Truth be told, I was living off my savings, and they wouldn't last for much longer.

'Really?' Tony lowered his voice. 'Come on, Jodie. This is easy money. I worry about you...'

'You really don't need to.'

'Yeah, I do. I don't want you running out of money and moving back up to London; I've got used to having you around again.' He smiled. 'I need you here to bail me out if I get into trouble. Not that I'm planning another disastrous wedding or anything.' My first job back in Penstowan had been catering for Tony's nuptials with his then-fiancée Cheryl, and to say it hadn't gone according to plan would be an understatement. His ex-wife's body had turned up in the venue's shrubbery, and Cheryl had done a runner in fright, making it look like Tony had done away with both of them.

I looked at him. 'You'd better not be. I don't think Nathan would want me under his feet on another murder investigation.'

'Oh, I dunno. I think he enjoys it...' Tony looked around as the man behind the table called, 'Next!' again. 'All right, at least come and sit with us.'

We joined Daisy and Mum. They were excited and chatted with Tony but I sat there thinking, *a hundred quid a day, just for standing around in a costume?* I could actually use a hundred quid a day. It was Daisy's thirteenth birthday in a couple of weeks and I knew what I wanted to get her, but wasn't sure if I could really afford it. And the Gimpmobile – my catering company van, so called because of its previous owner's, um, *interesting* retail business – had developed a clanking noise that couldn't even be drowned out by having the radio on full-blast, which was normally my go-to repair strategy. I hoped it was just a temporary malaise and not a death rattle, but I feared it was the latter.

I nudged Tony. 'Are you sure that's how much they're paying?'

'Yup. I asked.'

'How many days will they need us for?'

'I dunno, but they're only here for two weeks. Apparently they've already shot most of the film up in Scotland.' He chuckled. 'I thought you weren't interested?'

'I wasn't.' I lowered my voice. 'But Daisy needs a new computer, so I wanted to get her a fancy one for her birthday. She's getting into photography and I want to get her all the software, and it's really expensive.'

'Then do this, for God's sake! It'll be fun! We'll get to hang out together!' Tony jumped up and grabbed another form, then sat down and thrust it into my hands. 'Fill that in and stop being daft.'

So I stopped being daft – how could I turn down that amount of money, just for putting on a posh dress and standing around looking posh in a posh house? – filled in the form, and waited my turn. The casting people finally got to us, looked the four of us over, nodded, and sent us away with a promise that they'd be in touch with a shooting schedule. Even Daisy was told she'd get a call, although they'd probably only need her for one day.

'So that's that, then,' said Mum. 'I'm ready for my toasted teacake, Mr DeMille.'

Chapter Two

It was just over a week later that I got the call. Daisy was at school and Mum wasn't needed on set (I was already getting the lingo down), so I left her dog-sitting and made my way to Polvarrow House.

'*YES!*' My friend Debbie pounced on me the minute I got out of the car. She was a loud (very loud) Mancunian, and she'd married my high-school crush (who was still a lovely bloke, although not quite the stud muffin at forty that he'd been at sixteen), but she was a lot of fun and I'd been very happy when she'd moved down to Penstowan with Callum and their two children after Tony's ill-fated wedding a few months ago.

'Tony said you were signed up for this,' she said, pulling me in for a quick hug and then releasing me, smoothing out the material of her dress. 'This is gonna be a right laugh, innit? What do you think of the threads?'

She gave me a quick twirl. I had to admit she looked *amazing* in her costume. It was a long silk gown in a peacock-blue-green shade – my favourite colour. It was an Empire cut, the type that fits tightly under your boobs and then flares out, hiding any chubby bits. And it enhanced a couple of areas that on Debbie really didn't need enhancing. I nodded towards her impressive cleavage.

'You could park a bike in that,' I said, and she giggled.

'I know! Good, innit? I sent Callum a selfie and he was all for rushing over here and loosening me corsets.'

'So when're you getting into costume?' I said, and she laughed again.

'Mate, we are going to have *so* much fun... Go on, go and get your frock on!' She pushed me towards a large trailer that was parked next to the old stable block.

The trailer was a scene of organised chaos. The wardrobe mistress, a woman in her fifties with a mass of frizzy hair, tiny glasses on her nose, and a tape measure around her neck, ploughed through a crowd of extras who were all squirming into their dresses and zipping each other up.

'Don't tug at it; you'll rip the fabric,' she said to one

woman, whom I recognised from the local supermarket. 'Breathe in.'

'If I breathe in any more I'll turn blue,' muttered the woman under her breath. I smiled at her sympathetically.

'Then at least you'll match the dress,' said the wardrobe mistress. She turned to me. 'Name?'

'Jodie Parker,' I said, reaching out for a dress that was hanging on a rail near me. She snatched the dress away.

'Hold on...' She consulted the clipboard in her hand, then looked me up and down with a thin smile. 'Ah yes, you're not with this lot. Over here.' She led me away from the rack of beautiful silk dresses to another one that looked like a rail of potato sacks.

You have got to be kidding me, I thought, as she handed me my outfit...

'Oh dear Lord!' Tony was the last person I wanted to see while I was in this get-up, so of course he was the first one I met when I left the tent. I scowled at him.

'Don't say a *word,*' I growled. He wiped the smile off his face, but it didn't stay off for long.

'I'm sorry, I just... I can't believe you got the washerwoman part again!' He laughed, but it was more sympathetic than mocking.

'It's not fair,' I grumbled, fully aware that I sounded

like Daisy being told she couldn't stay up past 9 p.m. on a school night. 'I mean, have you seen Debbie? She looks gorgeous. That dress of hers—'

'I didn't think you were a dress person?' asked Tony reasonably enough, as he'd only ever really seen me in jeans and T-shirts, as an adult anyway.

'I'm not. I'm not a flipping potato-sack person either, though.' I flopped down on a bench. 'I am never going to live this down. All you lot are the aristocracy and I'm a maid.'

Tony smiled and sat next to me. 'If it's any consolation this isn't the most comfortable outfit I've ever worn.' He tugged at the neckline of his shirt. It had ruffles on it.

'That *is* a smashing blouse you're wearing,' I said, giggling.

'Yeah, I can see this style really catching on down the King's Arms on a Friday night. All the lads coming in for a pint after being out fishing all day, they go wild for a frilly shirt.' He smiled at me and I felt better, even though the fabric of my horrible brown dress felt like hessian and I could already feel it chafing under my arms.

'You do realise I'm going to take loads of photos of you in that blouse – and those trousers! How tight are those trousers?'

'My meat and two veg feel like they've been vacuum-packed,' said Tony, getting to his feet to show me exactly how tight they were. Good Lord, they *were* rather tight. I swallowed hard. What had I been saying? Oh yes.

'I'm going to take loads of photos of you in that get-up and whenever you annoy me, a new one's going online...'

We sat and watched as members of the crew scuttled back and forth across the grounds, darting in and out of the trailers that were parked along the gravel drive. Tony pointed to one.

'See that big one there? That's Faith Mackenzie's trailer.'

'Faith Mackenzie? I didn't know she was in it. Who else?'

'Well, Zack Smith's the main draw, isn't he? I bet you knew *he* was in it.' I nodded vigorously and he grinned. 'From what I can make out he's the young pretender to the throne or the rightful heir or something – you know how these things work. Faith is the evil queen, and she's married to Jeremy Mayhew.'

'Who's that? The name rings a bell.'

'He was in that cop show years back, *Bagnall*. The one up North. Last seen in *Game of Thrones*, where he died a hideous death.'

'Didn't everyone?' I said. 'I know who you mean. I thought he'd died of alcohol poisoning or something years ago.' Mayhew was a Liverpudlian actor, handsome in a craggy-faced kind of way, what they used to call a 'man's man' – basically, a heavy drinker with a short fuse and a sexist attitude to women. Faith had reached that age where she had officially been declared a National Treasure, having started life as a model, then acted in a few minor Hollywood movies in the Eighties before becoming a staple of British television and, more recently, a long-running cast member on an even longer-running soap opera. 'How do you know all this, anyway? This is only our first day on set.'

'I talk to people.'

'You mean you're as blooming nosey as I am!'

Tony grinned and shook his head. 'I ain't nosey, I'm a people person. And then there's the love interest, because you've always got to have a love interest. Another one I've never heard of, Kim Tacky-something. Japanese, I think…'

I thought hard. 'Kimi Takahashi? She was in that superhero movie a couple of years ago, with the machines that turn rogue.'

'*Terminator*?'

'No, no, much more recent than that, it was a kids' film. Daisy was obsessed with it. She played a toaster or something.' Tony burst out laughing. 'I'm being serious! She was like, *the soul* of this four-slice Breville sandwich press—'

Tony put his hand on my leg to steady himself as he laughed hard. I normally wouldn't even have noticed, but those snug breeches had had a rather disquieting effect on me. 'Stop it, you're killing me,' he gasped. 'Oh God, these trousers are so tight. One big sneeze and this crotch is *toast*.' And that started me off too.

We got a few strange looks, this weirdly dressed couple having hysterics on a bench while all around us were people getting on with their jobs, but if anything, that made it harder to stop.

But we did stop – eventually – and Debbie came to join us, looking at our red faces and watery eyes curiously. Not long after, we were called onto the set – the grand ballroom.

Polvarrow House hadn't had a grand ballroom when I'd last visited, but it did now.

'Wowsers…' I said, as we were herded into the room, and even Debbie, who wasn't easily impressed, whistled through her teeth.

'Bloomin' 'eck!'

The room was light and airy, with huge windows along one side that looked out onto the grounds. The last time I'd seen this room it had been in dire need of a repaint and had been crowded with furniture. Now it had all the period details I'd been hoping for: a huge marble fireplace at one end, with white plaster cornicing and decorative mouldings on the ceiling. There was a massive mirror over the fireplace and someone had gone crazy with the gilding, but when I looked closer I could see that a lot of it was just gold paint; the film crew had done a few temporary alterations to make the room even grander than the bones of it suggested. There were heavy gold velvet drapes at the windows, and lights and candles everywhere, reflecting off the white marble and the gilding; the room felt dressed for night-time.

'Right, hello everyone!' A businesslike but smiling young woman stood in front of the assembled extras. 'My name's Lucy. I'm the first AD' – a woman in the crowd of extras raised a hand – 'first assistant director. I'm kind of the liaison between our director, Sam Pritchard, and everyone else.' The woman put her hand down. Lucy smiled again. 'Okay, so as you can see, we're at a ball. We're going to meet our handsome young pretender to the throne, the lovely Zack, in this scene. There will be some dancing going on but all you lot have to do is stand around and mingle. Look like you're having a good time, but remember, this is set in a kind of parallel eighteenth century, so nothing too rowdy.' She fixed Tony with a mock-stern look. 'Remember, you're not down the pub with the lads!' Everyone laughed politely and Tony gave her a little bow, grimacing slightly as his trousers creaked under the strain. She turned to look at me and my fellow housemaids; there was also a tall, gangly lad in a tight footman's uniform who was squirming about uncomfortably. *Chafing,* I thought to myself. 'Now, you guys just have to stand around the room, as if you are ready to serve at a moment's notice. So be alert, but don't stare directly at anyone; you're the help, remember.' I nodded along with my fellow servants, but the rebellious little voice inside me didn't feel very agreeable; I was still sore about the costume.

The walkie-talkie clipped to Lucy's belt crackled and she answered it, holding up a hand to stop us talking as she listened.

'Okay, if you can all just wait here…' she said, hurrying away.

We stood and waited. And waited. My feet started to hurt and the room was beginning to get hot. Everyone else seemed to have important things to do – playing out cables and taping them down with duct tape to prevent trip hazards, fluffing up furnishings and moving them a tiny but significant couple of centimetres to the left, then back to the right, then, no, back to the left, adjustments to the camera – but we extras just stood there. Waiting.

'Flipping 'eck, this is boring,' said Debbie, yawning. Tony tugged at the crotch of his trousers. Some crew members want around and turned off the big spotlights to stop them overheating. And then they all just stood there waiting too, chatting, and I got the impression that all this hanging around wasn't an unusual occurrence.

'Blow this for a game of soldiers,' I grumbled, heading for a chair by the fireplace. The gangly footman looked scandalised, until most of the other extras followed suit, finding themselves somewhere more comfortable to sit or stand. Tony pulled a chair across the room, earning a glare from one of the cushion-fluffing crew members but ignoring it. He positioned it next to mine and motioned for Debbie to sit in it, then perched himself on the arm of my chair, lowering his tightly-clad nether regions slowly down until they were almost level with my eyes. I carefully turned away.

The crew started to look at watches and phones. There were mutterings and discussions. Maybe this amount of waiting *wasn't* normal. I watched a group of them by the camera, and it looked like they'd just nominated a junior crew member to go and find out what was happening when Lucy the first AD came rushing back in.

'Sorry, everyone, let's break for lunch,' she said, and turned to leave. One of the camera crew called out to her amidst a chorus of groans.

'What's happening, Luce?'

'Nothing. Faith's just had a little bit of an accident…'

Chapter Three

Of course my ears pricked up at her words. To my mind 'a little bit of an accident' was quite often code for 'flipping great disaster', especially when spoken in the tone of voice and accompanied by the facial expression currently being employed by Lucy. I followed Tony and Debbie out of the room, wondering what type of 'accident' could have put the kibosh on the morning's filming.

'Let's get something to eat,' suggested Tony. Food always sounds like a good idea to me, although when someone else is cooking it doesn't always live up to my standards. *Shame they didn't hire me to do the catering,* I thought. My cooking is always going to be better than my acting. I wondered if Polvarrow's kitchens were in a better and more hygienic state than on my last visit.

But I didn't get the chance to find out because we were directed outside to an area by the old coach house where a classic Airstream motorhome was parked – one of those really long silver bullet-shaped retro caravan things, pure 1950s Americana. *Of course,* I thought, remembering one of my fellow catering students. He'd told me that when he graduated he was going to set up his own mobile catering business specialising in film and TV shoots, because they don't always shoot at locations with kitchen facilities; certainly not ones capable of cooking for a large number of people, all day, for days at a time. The facilities I remembered here definitely would have struggled to cope. A flap in the side of the caravan was open, forming a counter, and inside I could see a fantastic custom-made kitchen. Lining the counter were trays of pasta, another of sausages and burgers, tofu, rice, vegetables – it looked like there was something to suit all diets, no matter how faddy, in this hot buffet. Further along the counter were trays of salads and filled sandwiches. The radio was playing loudly and the chef, an olive-skinned guy in his thirties, was singing along to it, either completely unaware or just unbothered by the queue forming outside. He turned around, still singing, holding a tray of the most delicious-smelling curry and added it to the buffet. Then he plonked down a big pile of plates and smiled at the line of hungry film people.

'*Buon appetito*!' he said. 'Grub up!'

The food looked and smelt fabulous, and I definitely liked the look of that curry. But there was a long queue of people ahead of us and I knew we were in for quite a wait as they all helped themselves.

'Hmm...' I murmured quietly to myself, but not quietly enough because Tony looked at me sharply.

'I know that 'hmm',' he said. 'What you thinking?'

'I'm just thinking I might have a little wander around...'

My little wander around took me across the gravelled yard, back towards the bench where Tony and I had earlier had hysterics. There were several people gathered around the large trailer that he'd pointed out to me as being Faith Mackenzie's on-set home. I recognised her co-star, Jeremy Mayhew, whom I was used to seeing in gritty contemporary dramas where he was invariably clad in jeans and a leather jacket. He was well-built and stocky, and he looked weird in breeches and knee-high riding boots, although at least his shirt was less frilly than Tony's (I supposed that too many frills would detract from his character's evil nature). I'd seen him in a repeat of a ludicrous cop show from the Eighties once and he'd been pretty hot in his younger days, but years of heavy drinking had led to the tell-tale red-veined cheeks and nose of an alcoholic. He was still kind of attractive in a craggy-faced, hedonistic way – like the sort of bloke who could show you a good time, as long as you were happy with debauchery and a kebab rather than dinner and a night at the opera.

Next to him was a younger man, who was tall and slim and wearing a baseball cap. I guessed he was around my age (forties), but he had a youthful air about him, and the superhero T-shirt and black-rimmed glasses he was wearing made him look like a fairly typical film nerd. Going by the way the people around him deferred to him, though, he had to be someone important. Lucy was also amongst the group, and every now and then she would turn round and make sure that no one was paying them too much attention; she was obviously trying to play down whatever was happening. A van with the words *24 Hour Locksmith* and a padlock and key logo on the side pulled up nearby and a man – presumably the locksmith – jumped out, reaching into the back for a bag of tools. Lucy rushed over to him, talking quickly, and led him to the trailer. The small crowd parted and the man with the tools stood and looked at the door.

'You are *so* nosey…' I jumped as Tony joined me, carrying two hot dogs in long buns. He gave one to me. 'Onions and ketchup but no mustard.'

'Thank you.' I took it from him and took an enormous

bite, getting ketchup on my nose. He shook his head and reached out a finger to wipe it off.

'Mucky pup. Can't take you anywhere. What are we looking at?'

I didn't answer straight away. We watched as the locksmith took out a special tool and started to very carefully unpick the lock.

'Faith's got herself locked in,' I said. Tony laughed.

'Nothing too dramatic, then.'

'No...' I took another bite of sausage. 'Who's that bloke in the baseball cap?'

Tony squinted. 'I think that's Sam Pritchard. The director.' He swallowed a lump of sausage. 'Funny, innit? I've seen all his films but I couldn't pick him out of a line-up even if my life depended on it.'

'Mmm...' I watched as the director (if that was indeed who it was) spoke to Lucy and then hurried away. 'How do you lock yourself inside a caravan though?'

'What do you mean?' Tony watched the scene with rather less interest than me.

'Well, it's a caravan, not Fort Knox. It's only going to have a Yale lock or something, isn't it?' I'd done my fair share of caravan cleaning, growing up as a teenager in a holiday town. Most of my friends had had summer holiday jobs doing the same thing. 'When you go inside and pull the door shut behind you it locks, yeah? So no one can get in from outside without a key.'

'Yeah.' Tony sucked up a straggly slice of fried onion that was threatening to escape from his bun.

'But all you do if you're inside is turn the little knob thingy and it opens. So why doesn't she just open it?'

Tony looked at me. 'Your sixth sense tingling again, is it?'

I shrugged. 'It's the police training. It never leaves you... Maybe she's collapsed. Maybe she's been taken ill and can't get to the door.' We watched as the locksmith stopped picking the lock and bent down to stare very carefully into the keyhole. Jeremy, who had stayed close by, stepped up to the door and spoke, directing his words towards the caravan, before stepping back again.

'Hmm,' I said. 'So much for that theory.' I felt Tony turn towards me in surprise. 'He didn't knock or shout or anything, did he? So the person inside the caravan – presumably Faith – is probably just on the other side of the door. And neither Lucy nor the director seems particularly worried, just a bit stressed. So Faith isn't lying unconscious or anything like that.' I looked around. 'No one's panicking enough for her to be ill. These all look like technical crew, not medical staff.'

'Well, that's good, then, isn't it?' said Tony, losing interest.

'Yeah, so why doesn't she just open it?' I watched as the locksmith turned to the first AD and gestured to the lock. She stepped forward again and put her eye to it, but she obviously couldn't see anything as she shrugged. The locksmith gestured to the door and it looked to me like he was out of ideas.

I started forward but Tony grabbed my arm.

'Hang on, what are you doing?'

I smiled. 'I'm just going to offer my assistance. And find out what's going on.'

'So, *so*, nosey...'

I strode across the gravel and stopped next to Lucy and the locksmith, who were still talking.

'...mechanism's buggered,' he said, and then stopped as they both looked at me.

'I'm a bit busy,' said Lucy. 'What is it? A problem with your costume?'

'No...' I started, and then stopped. 'Does it *look* like there's a problem with my costume?' I tugged self-consciously at it.

Jeremy Mayhew had stopped to give me a really obvious once over, but turned away (I was slightly offended by the speed with which he'd decided I wasn't worth more than a casual glance) and spoke to the door again.

'Look at the lock one more time, darlin'. You see that little knob? Just give it a turn—'

'For Christ's sake, Jeremy, I know how to open a bloody door! I haven't locked myself in!' I recognised Faith's voice from inside the caravan; she sounded just like her character off the telly. And ready to explode.

Lucy was still staring at me, waiting for me to explain myself.

'No, sorry, I was just coming to see if Ms Mackenzie might like someone to bring her some food if she's stuck in the caravan?' I said, in my most helpful voice. 'I could get her a plate from the food truck.'

'Oh, yes please!' said Faith, before Lucy could react. 'Why didn't you think of that, Lucy?' The first AD glared at me, like it was my fault the caravan had a dodgy lock.

'I'll get someone…' Lucy said, but Faith's disembodied and slightly exasperated voice interrupted her.

'No, let her do it. She's already here and willing. What's your name?'

'Jodie,' I said. 'Is there a window we can talk through? Might be easier than shouting through the door…'

'Round the back,' said Faith. I walked around to the back of the caravan. There was a wide window which I guessed must run the length of the lounge area, but it was too high to look through from ground level and heavy net curtains had been hung there for privacy. I looked around; there was a plastic storage crate nearby. I tipped out the cables that were inside and carried it over to the window, standing on it just as the net curtains moved and the window was opened a little way.

Faith Mackenzie, ex-model, movie star, and doyenne of the soap opera, peered out. In her late fifties (or maybe early sixties – no one knew her real age), she looked like a much younger woman. She had great skin, lovely hair, and a slim figure, all of which pointed to someone who spent a lot of time (and money) taking very good care of their appearance. I couldn't imagine her ever leaving the house in less than full make-up, and definitely not in track pants and a T-shirt unless it was to actually go and exercise – not popping down the road for a pint of milk and a packet of biscuits, which was the only time these days that my exercise gear got a workout. She also had a nice smile, even now, when she must be thoroughly bored and starting to get impatient.

'Cooee!' she said. 'Hello, Jodie, wasn't it? Thank you for thinking of me.'

'Oh, it's nothing,' I said airily. I have to admit I was a little bit starstruck; I'd never really been into soaps, but since Mum had more or less moved in with me we'd started to watch all of them together. And although Faith was obviously on a break from filming her role in *Mile End Days*, her episodes were still showing and we'd actually watched her playing pub landlady Clara Brown the night before. Clara was a mouthy cockney matriarch, not someone you'd want to get on the wrong side of, and it sounded like her role in this movie was basically the same but with a posher accent.

I cleared my throat. *Oh my God I'm talking to Clara! Mum'll have a fit.* 'So, what's going on in there? Are you all right?'

She rolled her eyes, but at the situation rather than me, I felt. 'The blasted door is stuck. They tried to tell me I'd locked it by mistake, but I haven't. They all think I'm some menopausal old biddy. And if Jeremy tries to talk me through opening a door one more time, I swear to God…'

I laughed sympathetically. 'Well, I just heard the locksmith say the lock mechanism's broken, so hopefully that'll shut him up. I don't suppose you can climb out of this window, can you?'

Faith sighed. 'I actually *am* a menopausal old biddy, and a National Treasure. There's no way I'm squeezing out of a caravan window. Can't someone just break the door down? There must be a ton of strong young men out there.'

'Which way does the door open?' I asked. 'Inwards or outwards?'

'Outwards.'

'Then someone would need to kick it down from inside. I don't suppose you fancy trying that either,' I said, and she laughed.

'Not really.'

'Fair enough.' I looked at the window again. 'Does that window open any further…?'

'You want me to do *what?*' Tony looked as if his flabber had been well and truly ghasted.

'You can get through that window. Go on, you always wanted to be a hero.'

'Did I? Don't remember that.'

'All right, but you *did* always want to be an actor, and if you get on the right side of Faith you might get bumped up to a speaking part.' I gave him a shove. 'Go on.'

'Jodie…'

I put on my most sincere face. 'I believe in you, Tony. And more to the point, I'm not big enough to bash the door in myself or I'd do it.'

He looked at me for a moment, and then laughed.

'All right, I'm going in.'

Faith looked out of the window at our approach. Lucy had ignored me upon my return to the caravan as I was carrying a tray of food lovingly dished up by Gino, the singing food-truck man. The movie star's face lit up hungrily, which I at first put down to the plate of pasta salad I was carrying but then realised with a shock that it was Tony she was staring at. Hmm. Maybe this wasn't such a good idea after all.

'Here's your food,' I said, reaching up. Tony, being taller, took the plate from me and handed it through the open window.

'Miss Mackenzie,' he said, with a slight bow. *Yeah, all right, don't overdo it, Tone,* I thought. *She ain't royalty; she's just playing it.* She smiled.

'Please, call me Faith,' she said, taking it from him. She had a lovely smile and she shone it, full beam, on Tony. Hmm…

'Now, if you'd like to stand aside, Miss … Faith, I'm coming in too.'

'Ooh, are you here to rescue me or are you dessert?' she giggled, with an eyebrow raised in a suggestive fashion. It suggested something to me, anyway. *Hmm…*

Tony laughed. 'We'll start with getting that door open,' he said. He stepped up on the plastic crate, then pulled himself up so that his torso was level with the window sill. I thought for a moment that he wasn't going to fit after all – he had put some weight on since I'd back, as I'd been feeding him a bit too often – but the tight trousers were evidence that he'd been taking more care of himself lately, and he managed to wriggle through until just his legs were sticking out. *He's been working out,* I thought approvingly.

I could hear muffled laughing from inside the

caravan, and then Faith must've taken hold of his arms and pulled because he suddenly disappeared from view.

'Dammit!' he cried.

'Are you all right?' I asked, concerned.

'Bloody trousers…'

Faith laughed and I suddenly had a vision of Tony sitting on the caravan's couch next to a ravening Faith in just his pants. What if he couldn't get the door open? They'd be stuck in there together for goodness only knows how long, and I didn't fancy his chances against her. *If he even puts up a struggle,* I thought. I jumped up on the plastic crate and tried to haul myself up.

Tony looked out of the window. 'I'm fine, I just split my— What are you doing?'

I looked up at him nonchalantly, or as nonchalantly as it was possible to when you're hanging onto a window ledge with one leg stretched up as far as it will go, while also wearing a hideous maid's costume. 'I thought you might need a hand.'

'Don't be daft. Go round the front and warn them that I'm going to try and kick the door down.' His head disappeared again and I stood there for a second, absolutely furious with myself for suggesting it, with Tony for agreeing to it (although that was also my fault because I'd badgered him into it), but most of all with Faith for being a much more attractive prospect for any man than a penniless single mum with a failing business and a muffin top currently straining against a brown hessian shift dress. Not that I cared.

The locksmith was packing up and Lucy was in discussion with a couple of crew members, while Jeremy stood around looking manly but ultimately useless.

'We could try and take the door off its hinges and lift it off,' said one of them, doubtfully.

'No need,' I said. 'You'd better stand back.' Lucy looked at me, but before she could speak there came a howl from inside the caravan, like a cross between a constipated Bruce Lee and a banshee, and the door burst open. Tony's momentum carried him through the doorway after it and he hurtled into the air, missing the steps that led from the door down to the ground and careering into me. I staggered back under his weight but he somehow managed to stay upright and hold onto me at the same time, pulling me into his arms before I ended up on the grass.

'Oh, my hero!' Faith stood in the doorway. She held a suspiciously flattering pose, half-turned to the side and draped against the door frame, with the light streaming through the open window behind her providing a warm glow, almost an aura, around her. She made sure everyone had seen her at her best (or was that just me being mean?) before stepping out of the caravan and rushing over to Tony. 'Are you okay?'

'Yes,' said Tony, unceremoniously letting go of me. 'No bones broken.'

'Oh, I'm *so* glad. It was *so* good of you to come and rescue me.' She threaded her arm through his. 'Do come and have some lunch, we must keep your strength up.'

For WHAT? I thought. I glared at Tony. 'I'm fine too, thanks for asking.'

Faith turned to me with a smile on her face, but I no longer trusted it. 'Of course, Jodie, thank you for your help. Now, let's get some lunch.' And with that she led Tony away.

Chapter Four

I pulled my jeans and hoodie back on and left the wardrobe caravan without looking back. The morning had been imbued with far less Hollywood glamour than I'd been expecting.

With Faith now released from her caravan incarceration, filming could start, but so much time had been wasted that the director had decided to film a different scene and do the ballroom one the next day. My band of domestics had been let go, but Debbie had been asked to stay and had been given *another* gorgeous dress to wear. It also appeared that Tony was Faith's new favourite person on set (even if he was just a lowly extra) and I thought it was only a matter of time before my jokey prediction of him being given a couple of lines to say came true.

Bloody film people, I muttered to myself. I was glad to be out of it. I was in such a hurry that I jumped in the car and shoved it into reverse without looking properly.

'Oi!' There was a shout and someone banged against the side of the car with their hand. I swore under my breath and looked up as they came over to the driver's window … straight into the (rather dreamy) eyes of Zack Smith…

I wound down my window, blushing, mortified. 'I'm so sorry, I didn't see you…' *How could anyone not see HIM?* He held up a hand to stop me.

'It's all right. It weren't me; it was this little one.' He bent down and picked up a dog, one of those small, yappy, long-haired, rat-looking things – a Pekinese, I thought. Not a patch on my Pomeranian. 'My co-star's dog. I said I'd walk it for her while she's in Make-Up but between you and me, it's a right bloody nightmare. And I can't get the hang of this…' He was holding the same sort of lead I had for Germaine – the extendable type. The dog wriggled and yapped in his arms and he put it down, glaring at it. 'It keeps running off and I can't stop the lead getting longer.' The dog made a dash for it again and he reached down to grab it by the collar. It was dark-pink leather and covered in glittering diamanté stones.

I opened the car door, making him step back, and reached out for the lead.

'I've got the same sort for my dog,' I said, reeling the

nylon leash in and clicking the locking button on the plastic housing. 'Here. You just click this on and off to lock it to the length you want.' I smiled, remembering that I'd had exactly the same problem with Germaine when I'd inherited her. She'd belonged to Tony's late ex-wife, she of the body-in-the-shrubbery, and I'd somehow ended up with her; reluctantly at first, but it hadn't taken long (about five minutes of staring into her cute, foxy little face) for me to fall in love with her. 'These little dogs are usually pretty intelligent and they tend to be good at escaping. What's her name?'

'It's called Princess.'

'Stop calling her 'it'!' I said. 'You wouldn't like it if someone referred to you as 'it'.'

He smiled. 'No, I wouldn't. You're right. I just ain't used to dogs. You part of the movie?'

'I'm an extra, but I'm not sure I'm cut out for this sort of thing.'

'Too much hanging about?'

'How did you…?'

He laughed. 'It's the first thing everyone says when they come on set. 'I didn't realise there was so much waiting around.' Basically, it's minutes of proper full-on action surrounded by hours of boredom. But you're escaping?'

'Only until tomorrow. I need the money.' *And I might need to rescue my best mate from Faith Mackenzie.*

'Ha! Don't we all. See ya, and cheers for this.' He waved the lead at me, then stepped back so he and Princess the Pekinese were out of the way. I got back in the car and drove away, feeling like the morning hadn't been *all* bad after all.

I drove into town to get some bits from the supermarket. Seeing Zack with the dog had reminded me that my own four-legged friend was running low on biscuits, and come to think of it, the two-legged occupants of the house didn't have any either. I grabbed a basket, then thought better of it and got a small trolley instead (you *always* need more at the supermarket than you think). As I pushed it along the fruit and veg aisle, I spotted the familiar (and handsome) figure of DCI Nathan Withers ahead of me, perusing the apples.

I suddenly decided to make an apple crumble.

'Hello, stranger!' I said, reaching for a bag of Granny Smiths. Nathan started in surprise, then looked at me.

'Sorry, I was miles away,' he said, smiling at me.

'So I see. Where've you been? I haven't seen you around for ages.' Ooh, that sounded like I'd been looking out for him. Which I had, but I wasn't going to let him know that. 'Not that I've been looking or anything…'

He smiled wanly. 'It's nice to know somebody missed me. I had to go home. I only got back last night.'

'Home? You mean Crosby? Is everything all right?'

'Not really. My dad's in hospital. Heart attack.' Now that I was looking at him properly, rather than just gazing at him lustfully, I could see that he was pale and seemed tired.

'Nathan, I'm so sorry! Is he going to be all right? How's your mum taking it?' He looked so sad for a moment that I wished I hadn't asked. 'Sorry, you don't have to talk about it. I'm being nosey.'

'You, nosey? Never.' He smiled again, and this time it looked more genuine. 'It's nice that you're concerned.'

I looked in his trolley. It was full of ready meals for one and bags of pre-prepared frozen rubbish. 'I'm so concerned that I'm going to make you a decent meal tonight,' I said. 'I mean it. Finish your shopping then come round, if you're off duty?'

He hesitated for a second, then nodded. 'Thanks, Jodie. It's just really hard being so far away, innit?'

I put my hand on his arm, but it felt completely inadequate. I really wanted to pull him in for a hug, but that's the problem with unresolved sexual tension: it makes the most innocent, heartfelt gesture feel a bit inappropriate. And I really was thinking about him with my heart this time, not my other bits…

Mum opened the oven door and sniffed.

'You've done a proper job on dinner tonight,' she said. 'What's all this in aid of?'

'Nothing,' I said, a tad too defensively. 'I just fancied cooking something nice.'

It *was* nice too. I'd picked up some lovely salmon and hoki fillets at the local fishmongers (we actually had a fishmonger! After years in London, with no option but to buy everything from the massive supermarket nearby, it felt like a luxury). I'd softened leeks in some butter and wilted some spinach along with them, then made a rich, creamy sauce, adding a few strands of saffron that had been steeping in a spoonful of hot water. I cut the fish into chunks and stirred it, along with the veg, into the sauce and let it simmer while I mashed potatoes, adding butter, milk, and a handful of cheese. Then I piled the fish mixture into a pie dish, topping it with the mash and another handful of cheese on top. It was smooth and velvety, and perfect comfort food.

'If I can't cook for paying clients, I'll just have to cook for you and Daisy,' I said. I turned to Daisy, who had just come into the kitchen with the dog following at her heels. 'Lay the table, will you, sweetheart?' She gave a big dramatic sigh – apparently I treated her little better than a slave, what with making her lay the table occasionally and wash up the dinner things – and then pulled out the cutlery drawer. 'Oh, you'd better lay four places,' I added casually. All three of them (Germaine included) looked up at me, and I felt my cheeks starting to redden.

'Tony coming round, is he?' asked Mum.

'No, Nathan.' Mum opened her mouth to say something so I leapt in quick. 'And before you say anything, it's not a date – not with you lot here – he's just had some bad news from home and I want to make sure he's okay.'

Mum and Daisy exchanged meaningful looks.

'And you can stop looking at each other like that!' I said, hotly. 'He's just a friend.'

The doorbell rang. *Saved by the bell.*

'I'll get it,' said Mum, a glint of mischief in her eye.

'Oh no you flipping won't,' I said, standing in her way. 'And remember what I said. He's had some bad news and he needs looking after.'

'He needs cherishing.' Mum grinned. I ignored her and went to let our dinner guest in.

Nathan stood on the doorstep holding a bottle of wine, a box of chocolates, and a bunch of flowers. He smiled with uncharacteristic shyness, which made my heart do a little flippy-floppy thing in my chest, and held up the wine.

'I wasn't sure what to bring, so I made sure I covered all the bases,' he said. I laughed.

'Mum'll have the wine, Daisy will eat the chocolates, and I'll have the flowers,' I said.

'Really? I was kind of picturing you getting drunk and scoffing all the soft centres.' He grinned.

'Dammit, you know me too well…'

He followed me into the kitchen, where Mum and Daisy were dutifully waiting. It was so obvious that they'd been told to be on their best behaviour that it was embarrassing.

However, once we were all seated at the table, tucking into the fish pie, the atmosphere became more relaxed and we chatted easily. Whenever Tony came round for dinner (he was never exactly invited, he just quite often happened to be there doing an odd job for me right around the time we normally ate…) we'd known each other for so long, and my parents had known his parents for years too, it just felt like having another member of the family at the table. Increasingly though, at other times – like today, with the tight trousers – I wasn't entirely sure *what* it felt like. But he could always gossip with my mum and with Daisy, too; he had a really nice way with her, despite not being a dad himself. He was certainly a better male role-model than her own useless, absent father.

But with Nathan it was bound to be different. We'd only become friends (initially, enemies) a few months ago, when I'd insinuated myself into a murder investigation, and we'd worked together on a few cases now. He'd laughed when I'd first called myself a private investigator (which I'd only done because he'd been arrogantly winding me up), but he'd come to respect and sometimes even ask for my input. I'd been a good copper; I'd never been CID, like him, but that had been through choice, because I'd loved being on the beat and talking to people out on the streets (and quite often running after and handcuffing them). I'd left the force to stop Daisy worrying about me, the way I'd worried about my dad when he'd been Chief Inspector of Penstowan Police Station, but there wasn't a day that went by when I didn't miss it. Well, maybe I didn't miss it *every* day, but I missed it more often than I'd expected to. But Daisy was happier, so I didn't regret leaving one bit.

Nathan chatted away, much more like his usual self than he had been in the supermarket, but then Mum and Daisy were at the table and he probably didn't want to unburden himself in front of the whole family. He had seconds of the fish pie, but pushed his plate away when Mum offered him thirds.

'No thanks, Shirley, I am stuffed,' he said. 'That was lovely. Fish pie's one of my favourites.'

'I know,' I said absentmindedly, then cursed myself; this was supposed to be a casual dinner among friends, not a full-frontal culinary attack on a potential lover. 'I mean, I was planning to cook fish and you know how some people are funny about eating fish, so I was a bit worried and then I remembered you saying how much you liked fish pie—' *Stop talking, Jodie!* Daisy gave me a funny look, but Mum, bless her, leapt in and distracted Nathan's attention from my inane babbling.

'Jodie said you'd had some news from back home,' she said. My gratitude at her distraction evaporated instantly. I glared at her.

'I'm sure Nathan doesn't want to talk about it,' I said, sending her the telepathic message that I would slip a laxative into her bedtime cocoa if she didn't change the subject. But I didn't need to break out the Ex-Lax.

'It's fine,' said Nathan, smiling at me. 'Yes, my dad had a heart attack on Sunday morning. Quite a big one. But he's had a stent fitted and he's doing all right.'

'What's a stent?' asked Daisy.

'One of the things that causes a heart attack is when your arteries get clogged up,' explained Nathan. He was so calm about it, not at all angry with Daisy for asking, and it reminded me of another dinner conversation when she was about five. She'd asked her dad to explain what made thunder and lightning and he'd curtly told her to google it, probably because he didn't want to admit he didn't know. 'They can get clogged up with fat, stuff like that, if you don't have a very good diet. Your mum makes sure you eat healthy food, but my dad likes his doughnuts a bit too much.'

'I hate doughnuts,' said Daisy. She obviously wanted to say something supportive but wasn't sure what.

'I quite like them. I'm a police officer, aren't I? We're *supposed* to sit in our cars and eat doughnuts.' Nathan smiled at her. 'Anyway, the doctors go in and clear all the crud out of your arteries, and then they slide the stent in. Once it's in place, it kind of inflates and it holds your artery open, so it doesn't get clogged up again.' He shrugged. 'Something like that, anyway. I'm not a doctor.'

'So he's recovering in hospital?' I asked. He nodded.

'Yes. I went up there after the attack to make sure he was okay, and I stayed with my mum until he was through all the surgery. I would have stayed longer but she told me not to waste my holiday on her.' He laughed softly. 'Who else am I going to waste it on?'

Me, I thought automatically, but then I could hardly bugger off to Torremolinos for a week of passion with him and leave Daisy at home with Mum.

I shook my head to clear it of thoughts of romance on the Costa del Sol and began to stack the empty plates up.

'Well, you know where we are if you want some company,' said Mum, and my heart swelled. Yeah, she was a bit dotty, she could talk the hind leg off a donkey, and she was always embarrassing me and dropping heavy-handed hints at random men about my lack of a husband, but she was warm and lovely and had a habit of taking in waifs and strays. Nathan was too blooming muscular and good-looking to be a waif but he must get lonely, so far away from his family. Although God knows there had been a few times when I wanted to be far away from mine…

'Anyway,' I said, changing the subject before we all turned into the Waltons or something. 'I haven't told you about my day yet. I'm an extra on that film they're shooting at Penstowan Cross,' I explained to Nathan. I turned to Daisy. 'I only met Zack Smith.'

'No!' She looked at me with wide eyes. 'What happened?'

'I nearly ran over his dog. Well, she's not actually his dog; he was walking her for a friend. Long story.'

Nathan laughed. 'Why does that not surprise me?' He looked at me with a smile on his face that was warm and genuine enough to make the memory of Tony's snug breeches fade away to nothing.

'Ooh and Mum, I spoke to Faith Mackenzie. She got locked in her caravan and Tony had to climb in through a window and break the door down.'

'Oh, Tony's in it as well, is he?' Nathan's smile faltered for a moment, or did I imagine it?

I nodded. 'Yeah. Faith seems to have taken a fancy to him. She'll probably lock him in with her next time.' I laughed, but I suddenly wasn't sure I found it that funny.

'How do you lock yourself in a caravan?' asked Nathan, amused. 'Locked out, yeah, but *in*? These celebrities aren't the brightest, are they?'

'That's exactly what I thought!' I said. 'Not the bit about her not being very bright – I had quite a long conversation with her and that woman knows *exactly* what she's doing—' Ooh, that sounded catty. What was the matter with me? 'They had a locksmith and everything, but he couldn't pick the lock. He couldn't even get his tools inside the mechanism.'

'Superglue,' said Mum. We all looked at her; that was random, even for her.

'What about it?'

'In the lock. You probably won't remember. One of your dad's friends, Vinnie Butler—'

'He sounds like a right hardcase,' Nathan muttered to me, and I smothered a giggle.

'Vinnie had these caravans on his farm, over near Crackington Haven. The year we had the solar eclipse down here.'

'I think they had that *everywhere*, Nana,' said Daisy.

'Yes, I know they did, cheeky madam!' said Mum, rolling her eyes good-naturedly. 'We had a lot of tourists come down for it, because we got a better view of it than the rest of the country. It was 1998, or maybe 1999 – a couple of years before you went off to London. So Vinnie decided to set these caravans up and rent them out for the week to tourists, only, the week before, someone went round and sabotaged all of them so he couldn't.'

'By squirting superglue in the locks…' I looked at Nathan meaningfully.

'Do you think someone screwed with the lock on purpose, then? Why would they want to do that?' he asked.

'Eddie reckoned Vinnie must've upset someone. There were a lot of campsites nearby; I suppose they thought he was taking trade off them,' said Mum.

'No, I mean the caravan today. To scare Faith, maybe?'

'If that was the intention it didn't work,' I said, remembering the predatory gleam in her eye when she saw Tony. 'I think it would take a lot more than that.'

'So what did it achieve?'

'Other than wasting a morning's filming and irritating a lot of people? Nothing.' I stood up. 'Pudding?'

Chapter Five

Nathan stayed for most of the evening. He helped me wash up the dinner things – my slave, Daisy, was taking advantage of a (not particularly) rare night off and hiding away upstairs – and Mum asked him about his parents, how old they were, what his mother was like... It was a pretty thorough grilling, but to be fair, it didn't feel awkward or as if Mum was pumping him for information, and Nathan seemed quite happy to talk.

At 9 p.m. he got his coat on. I picked up the lead and whistled for Germaine, who had seemingly been fast asleep in her bed. She was at my feet in seconds, making me suspect she had been awake all along, just waiting for me to get my behind in gear and take her out.

'I'll walk you to your car,' I said, and he laughed.

'It's literally outside your door, but okay.'

He said goodnight to Mum, called up the stairs to Daisy, and then we left the house.

It was chilly. The day had been bright and sunny, and not too cold – a perfect autumn day, in fact – but now there was a distinct nip in the air, a reminder that winter would be with us before we knew it.

'This is me,' said Nathan as we drew level with his car approximately thirty seconds after leaving the warmth of my house, and we both laughed. He shook his head. 'Nah, come on, I'll walk the dog with you.'

'Are you sure? I'm just taking her down the road so she can have a pee.'

He nodded. 'I've spent the last week either driving for hours at a time up and down the motorway or sitting by a hospital bed. It'll be nice to stretch my legs properly.'

Germaine scampered on ahead, sniffing at lamp posts and the patches of weeds that had sprung up along the grass verge. She had a specific routine that never ever varied. She had certain places that she had to investigate thoroughly, just in case tonight was the night she would grace them with her pee; but she invariably ended up doing her business in the same spot, right at the end of the street. Sometimes she would even go so far as to cock her leg experimentally, as if calculating the angle of urination, but she would always find it wanting and move on to the next area. Strictly speaking, as a female dog she didn't need to cock her leg at all, but I'd read somewhere that bossy female dogs do it to mark their territory. Germaine was involved in a long-running feud with the fat old Labrador a few doors down, and I reckoned she was showing him whose manor this was. I'd seen a few hen parties do much the same thing outside South London nightclubs on my old Friday night shifts in the Met…

'It's hard, being away from your parents when they're getting older,' I said, watching her pounce on a defenceless yellow-flowered weed. Germaine had a thing about yellow flowers. 'I know what it was like when I was living in London, when my dad died.'

'That was an accident, though,' said Nathan. 'It was so sudden, there was nothing you could have done. No chance to say goodbye.'

'No,' I said, turning away to watch the dog. He touched my arm gently.

'Sorry, that was a really daft thing to say. I know how much your dad meant to you.' He sighed. 'My mum's coping really well, and as awful as it might sound, I'm glad it's happened this way round. Is that a terrible thing to say?' He looked at me, his eyes suddenly watery. I shook my head.

'No, it's not. My dad was this big, strong copper, he'd banged up loads of wrong'uns, and was in charge of three stations, but if Mum had gone first he'd have been lost.' I smiled at him. 'Women of our parents' generation are used to looking after everything and everyone, aren't they? Our dads went out and earned the money, but our mums ran the home; they budgeted, they paid the bills, they looked after the kids and made sure everyone had clean pants...'

He laughed. 'That's exactly what I mean. My dad wouldn't even know how to use the washing machine.'

I looked him up and down in mock judgement. 'It's about time you learned how to, as well.'

He held his hands up. 'Woah, Ms Parker, that sounds suspiciously like a sexist comment to me. I'll have you know I am a dab hand at the laundry *and* I know one end of a Dyson from the other.'

'You can't cook, though.'

He grinned. 'That's why I'm friends with a chef. Sorry, a *private investigator* who can also whip up a dessert in less than two minutes. Chocolate lava cake in a microwave? Genius.'

I waved away his praise with a big show of modesty. 'Oh really, it was nothing. I'm hardly going to go to a lot of effort for the likes of you, am I?'

He laughed. 'And that's me firmly in my place.'

'You're welcome.'

We stopped as Germaine finally found the spot worthy of her very special attention and lifted her leg. I turned away – I didn't expect the poor thing to be able to perform in front of an audience – only to find that Nathan was a lot closer than I'd thought, and I almost ended up in his arms.

We smiled at each other. It would have been romantic, but for the sound of Germaine going at it like a canine fire hydrant. Even so…

Nathan's mobile rang and the mood (such as it was) was over before it had even really begun. He pulled his phone out of his pocket and glanced at it.

'It's my mum,' he said, looking concerned.

'Do you want me to leave you alone?' I asked. He shook his head and answered.

'All right, Ma, everything okay?' His Liverpudlian accent came through more strongly than when he spoke to me. 'Is Dad—? Oh, no, no that's cool. Hang on.' He held the phone away from his mouth. 'Everything's fine; she just rang to say goodnight.'

'I'll leave you to it, then,' I said, and he nodded. He brought the phone up to his mouth.

'Yeah, I'm still here. I'm with a friend. Just saying goodbye now…' He grinned at me, and I felt myself going hot. That grin did things to me. 'Yeah, her… Hang on.' He held the phone down again as I turned to leave. 'Jodie! Wait. Thanks for tonight. I really needed to be with someone.'

'I'm glad it was me,' I said, not even caring that it sounded a bit much for two people who were supposedly just friends. I leaned in and gave him a peck on the cheek, then yanked at the lead and dragged poor Germaine away mid-stream.

Daisy was in bed when I got home. I was pleased to see that she hadn't taken major advantage of our dinner guest's presence and attempted to stay up past her bedtime, but had got herself ready and was patiently waiting for me to come back with the dog.

She was sitting up reading one of my old Agatha Christie novels, carefully marking it with a bookmark bought during a school trip in London (from the gift shop at Tate Modern) before laying it on the side table. She'd been taught well: no bending over the corner of the page to mark it or (heaven forbid) breaking the spine of the book. She loved books, just as I did, and just as Mum did. You could tell a lot about someone by the way they read a book, my mum had told me once, and she was right. I'd lent one to a guy I was going out with, years ago. It took ages for him to give it back, and when he did I discovered that he had *WRITTEN HIS NAME IN THE FRONT,* like a monster. I was horrified. He said that it was because he'd taken it to work to read during his break, but I suspected it was because he'd not intended to give it back. Reader, I dumped him. Richard (the cheating swine) had never, in my recollection, even *read* a book, which told you everything you needed to know about him and more.

'Good book?' I asked.

'You know it is; you've read it,' she said, and I laughed.

'True. Lie down then. Time to go to sleep.'

She patted the bed and Germaine jumped up to snuggle against her feet. I'd started out with such good intentions about not letting the dog even come upstairs, and yet here she was sleeping every night on Daisy's bed. She occasionally got up in the night and cuddled up to me as well, and although I hated being woken up, I never minded when it was the dog because it was nice getting some affection, even if it was from someone even hairier and smellier than my ex-husband.

'I like Nathan,' said Daisy abruptly. I looked at her in surprise.

'Do you?'

'Yeah. So does Nana.'

'Nana likes *all* men, particularly if they're good-looking and single.' I leant down to kiss her on the forehead.

'If you ever wanted a boyfriend, I wouldn't mind, you know,' she said. 'I want you to be happy.'

'Oh, sweetheart, I *am* happy!' I blinked furiously. I am *such* an emotional old baggage at times. It doesn't sit well with my police training but there seems to be bugger all I can do about it. I sat down on the bed and held out my arms for a hug. She sat up and actually hugged me back, which doesn't happen anything like enough when your kids hit their teenage years, and then Germaine's nose appeared under my arm as she wormed her way in. We laughed and made room for her.

'How could I not be happy with you two in my life?' I said, kissing her again. 'I've got everything I need, right here.'

I left her to sleep, and Mum went up to bed an hour later. I sat on the sofa, wrapped up in a blanket and with a mug of cocoa in my hands, thinking over the events of the day.

I thought about Tony, busting the door down in Faith's caravan. Had the lock really been tampered with, or was it just faulty? If it was faulty the locksmith should have been able to pick it, but if it had been sabotaged … why? It hadn't achieved anything.

I thought about Zack Smith. He had a nice smile, and if I were twenty years younger I would no doubt have been rendered speechless during our earlier encounter, but I'd reached an age where it was entirely possible to admire the beauty of something without wanting to possess it. Still on the subject of possessing things, I thought briefly about Tony's tight trousers, but quickly steered away from that as it seemed to be leading me into dangerous and unfamiliar territory (I mean, come on, this was *Tony* I was thinking about!).

I thought about Nathan, and about how nice it had been to spend some time with him as a friend, to just hang out rather than be working on (or arguing over) a case. I hoped he wasn't worrying too much about his dad; I really did know what it was like to be miles away when a loved one was sick. Mum's increasing amount of health problems (although they were all fairly minor) had played a big part in us moving back to Penstowan.

Another less welcome thought occurred to me. What if the same worries led to Nathan moving back up North?

But when my eyelids started to droop and I made my way up to bed, the last thought that popped into my head was of his phone call, just before we said goodnight. What he'd said to his mum. 'I'm with a friend… Yeah, her.' *Nathan's told his mum about me,* I thought, and I fell asleep with a warm glow enveloping me that wasn't just down to the duvet.

I woke the next morning to a text message from Debbie, asking for a lift to Polvarrow House. I dropped Daisy off at school and found my fellow but rather more glamorous extra lurking at the gates, having dropped off her own offspring.

She chattered excitedly about yesterday's shoot – she'd stayed on in the afternoon and had actually seen some action. I thought about telling her that I'd had dinner with Nathan the night before, but I knew she'd blow the whole thing out of proportion and make it sound like it was a date or something (and it so wasn't, not with Mum and Daisy there, and with Germaine and her fussy bladder).

We pulled up on the gravel driveway and started towards the wardrobe trailer, where doubtless there was another magnificent gown waiting for Debbie, and another potato sack for me.

'You came back, then?'

We both whirled around at the voice behind us. Zack Smith was standing outside another caravan, having a crafty puff on an e-cigarette. He gave me a friendly smile. He was dressed in a fancier though no less tight version of Tony's costume from yesterday, but whereas Tony had looked like a cross between a camp pirate and an Eighties New Romantic pop star in his, Zack looked like—

'Sex on a stick!' breathed Debbie, mouth open. I nudged her hard and she pulled her jaw up with a snap.

'I told you, I need the money. Where's your friend?' I asked. He looked around quickly, suddenly alarmed.

'What? Oh my God, I've lost it…' He looked back at me and winked. 'Nah, I told Kimi I nearly got it – sorry, *her* – run over by this madwoman and she had a fit. She won't be asking me again…' He gave me a broad smile, and I could see he wasn't exactly upset at having his dog-sitting duties revoked.

'What a shame. It looked to me like you and the dog were starting to become friends.' I smiled. "Princess and Zack'. Got a nice ring to it.'

He laughed loudly. 'Yeah, right. One of them little dogs really goes with the image, you know what I mean?' He finished his smoke and pocketed the cigarette. 'Anyway, better get on. Laters.'

He went into the trailer and shut the door. I headed for Wardrobe, leaving Debbie open-mouthed behind me.

'Wait! How do you—? What was—? Oh my God!'

I smiled to myself and kept walking. I might have a crappy costume but I was mates with the lead.

So yeah, I *did* still have a crappy costume, but at least today Debbie had the dubious pleasure of wearing a stupid Pound Shop tiara that was too big and had to be pinned into her hair with about eleventy billion hair clips to stop it slipping over her eyes. Apparently, director Sam, who as far as I was aware hadn't even made it into the ballroom yesterday, felt that the scene needed 'more sparkle', so every woman and her dog was having their outfit blinged up. Everyone except the downtrodden domestics, of course. We left the caravan, both grumbling about chafing and with her clutching onto her tiara to stop it falling off. She looked like a little girl dressed up as a Disney princess. It might have been mean-spirited and petty of me, but her daft headgear made me feel a lot better. I hoped it would look more realistic on screen.

'Morning, ladies!' Tony looked very chipper. I wondered what he'd been up to last night, when I'd been having dinner with Nathan. I'd half expected a knock on the door, or at least a text, telling me about his afternoon with the stars and asking to be fed.

'They mended your trousers, then?' I snorted.

'That wardrobe woman with the frizzy hair did start having a go at me about the split, but then Faith waded in and told her I was her hero, so…' Tony grinned. I ignored the little voice that said, *her hero???* It was pathetic and didn't deserve any attention. But it still wouldn't shut up.

The sound of raised voices across the gravel courtyard made us all look over towards the stars' trailers. It was a young female voice that held the unmistakeable trace of an American accent mixed with something else that I couldn't quite pin down... A hint of Japanese, maybe? What I could pin down, however, was that the owner of that voice was very, very angry.

'I give you *one job*, that's all, just *one job*, and what do you do?' There was a pause when presumably the person being shouted at answered back, probably in a cowed tone of voice. 'You left her locked up in here? Then where is she? Where's my –' there then followed a stream of terribly unladylike but quite inventive cussing – I mean, I worked on the mean streets of South London for nearly twenty years, so if it shocked me it had to be bad '– baby? Where's my Princess?'

'Oh God, has Zack been dog-sitting again?' I said, shaking my head like the two of us were besties and this was a common occurrence. Tony should know he wasn't the only one who was friends with the stars. Tony looked at me, puzzled, then turned to Debbie, but she didn't answer because the door to the trailer burst open and out flew a harpy – a young and beautiful one, yes, but a harpy all the same.

'And *that's* Kimi Takahashi,' I said. We watched her stride across the courtyard, calling, *'Princess! Princess! Momma needs you!'* 'So, she seems nice and not at all unbalanced...'

Kimi, dressed in a flowing silk wrap and with her hair scraped back from her face, disappeared around the corner of the building. Behind her, in the doorway of her trailer, stood an almost identical but somehow less glamorous version of her – a sister, I guessed, maybe even her twin. She saw me looking at her and stared back, waiting for me to look away, so on principle (of course), I didn't. She gave up and let out a big sigh – I could tell by the exaggerated way her shoulders shrugged up and down – and then followed Kimi.

'So,' I said, enjoying the fact that Tony still looked confused at the casual way I'd mentioned Zack, like we were besties, 'I suppose we should find Lucy and see when we're due on set...'

We wandered about for a bit, nodding to the other extras who were all hanging around looking lost, until we came across Lucy, who was looking harassed. Tony opened his mouth to speak but she interrupted him.

'You haven't seen a dog, have you?' She sounded like she was incredibly fed up but trying hard not to show it.

'Kimi's dog? No,' I said.

'It's a Pekinese.'

'I know. We haven't seen her.'

'We've seen Kimi though,' said Tony with a grin.

'And heard her,' said Debbie.

'*Everyone's* heard her,' muttered Lucy, who obviously felt that the young star was being a bit of a diva. 'Why she had to bring the blasted dog with her anyway... Never mind, keep a look out, will you? And we'll be filming in the ballroom today. Twenty minutes, please.'

She spotted someone over the other side of the yard. 'Glen! Hold up.' And off she went.

'Might as well head over to the ballroom,' said Tony. 'Faith reckons she might be able to persuade Sam to give me a line.'

'Who?' I asked pettily, because I knew who he meant.

'The director.'

'Oh right. A line of what?' I said, thinking, *Faith reckons, does she?* Which was proper daft, seeing as I'd just made it sound like me and Zack were BFFs now. Tony gave me a look, which might have genuinely meant *why are you being petty with me?* or might just have been guilt on my part. 'Sorry, I know what you mean, I was trying and failing to be funny. I hope she does. Let's walk round the long way, shall we? We'll be doing enough standing about as it is.'

We followed the course that Kimi and her sister had taken, round the side of the house to the front where the beautiful facade was somewhat spoilt by the shoot's ramshackle collection of marquees and trucks; the whole production had given rise to a kind of middle-class shanty town. But if you looked away from the house, you could still enjoy the beautiful grounds: a massive lawn, with a croquet area to one side; a medieval knot garden with low box hedges forming an intricate pattern and then in-filled with lavenders and other fragrant plants; and of course the fountain. And further on, there was a large ornamental lake, completely man-made but naturalised with plants and trees around the edge. And something else, in the middle of it.

'Princess! Princess! Help, my baby!' Kimi stood helplessly at the edge of the lake, shrieking, while her sister gingerly set foot into the cold water. She was only a little way from the edge but it was already up to her knees, and she seemed reluctant to go in any further.

'Oh bloody hell, how did the dog get out there?' I said. We ran over to Kimi and before I could even think, Tony had pulled off his shoes and plunged in…

Chapter Six

Tony thrashed through the water, wading out as far as he could and then swimming out to the centre. The daft dog was fighting to stay afloat, weighed down as she must have been by her long, hairy coat, and her struggles were actually taking her further and further out into the water.

Tony eventually reached her and grabbed hold of her, then turned and struck out again for the edge of the lake. By now, most of the cast and crew were watching, though none of them went in to help. Then again, it was 'only' a dog, and Tony was clearly a strong swimmer – one of the benefits of growing up by the sea.

As he reached shallow water he stood up and trudged soggily through the pondweed, scattering surprised ducks before him.

'Oh my…' said Debbie next to me, as I felt my jaw drop.

Tony's white shirt was of course soaked through and now almost transparent, and it clung to a hitherto completely unsuspected set of abs, well defined with what could have been a hint of chest hair, although he was too far away for me to see properly and I may have been imagining it. As he waded towards us I was transported back to the evening of the 15th of October 1995, and I was sitting at home with my mum eating Quality Street (Mum had brought an almost-out-of-date box home from her job at the Co-op) and watching BBC1, unaware that a seminal moment in my young life was about to occur. I unwrapped a Green Triangle, tuning out the sound of Mum's chatter, popped the chocolate in my mouth, and then almost choked. Mum stopped talking. On screen, Mr Darcy strode manfully out of the lake at Pemberley and into the hearts of women (and no doubt a few men) across the nation.

In front of the watching film crew, Tony strode manfully out of the water just like Mr Darcy, the effect only slightly spoilt by the fact that he was carrying a wriggling, bedraggled dog and had a clump of pondweed on his left shoulder. He saw everyone watching and looked around, surprised, then caught my eye and grinned. My heart beat a little bit faster and I was disgusted with it for being so predictable.

As he reached dry land, Kimi ran over and threw herself at him, hugging both the rescuer and the rescuee to her silk-clad chest. I noticed that she was crying – she obviously genuinely loved that dog – but she was managing not to ugly-cry or get snotty. It's not fair how some women can do everything beautifully. I've always managed to do the opposite. Every time I go to the hairdresser (not very often), I'll come out with an amazing hairdo and immediately the heavens will open, the winds will whip up, and I end up looking like I just stepped out of the salon and into the path of a tornado.

'Someone get this man a towel!' Faith barged past me and for a moment I thought she was going to wrestle Kimi for him. I had visions of each of them grabbing an arm and pulling, and poor Tony – poor, soaking wet, *ripped* Tony – being literally ripped … in two, with each woman holding an arm and half a muscular torso (a three-pack?). But there was no need for Faith to resort to physical violence, as one look from the woman who I was beginning to realise wasn't quite as sweet and cuddly as her National Treasure status suggested was enough for the young, beautiful pretender to relinquish her trophy and let go of him.

'Who *is* this guy?' muttered one of the crew behind me. 'Isn't he the one who was sniffing around Faith yesterday?' The man next to him laughed.

'He's just some extra who's trying to bag himself a

speaking part,' he said, and they both sniggered. I saw red.

'*Actually*,' I said, turning on them furiously, 'Tony Penhaligon is the nicest, most decent person you could ever meet. He's always there when anyone needs help, including Faith when she got locked in her trailer and none of you lot had the brains or the brawn to get her out. He'd give you the shirt off his back if you needed it more than him.'

Both men looked taken aback.

'All right, sorry, love...' said one, holding his hands up to protect himself (from what? from me? surely not). But I wasn't so easily placated.

'Pro tip: never slag someone off if there's a possibility their best mate is standing next to you!' I snarled (I hadn't intended to snarl, but it just kind of came out that way). 'Also, I'm not your love. Now, if you'll excuse me...' And I stormed off, not sure where I was going but heading instinctively towards the food truck, horribly aware that I'd probably just made a spectacle of myself.

'Jodie! Wait!' Debbie flew after me. I rounded the corner of the house and stopped, letting her catch up. I could feel my cheeks burning. 'Blimey, they rubbed you up the wrong way, didn't they?'

'You heard what they were saying about Tony,' I said. 'They don't even know him.'

'Not like you do,' she said, smiling knowingly.

'What's that supposed to mean?'

'Nothing, just that you're his best mate. Shall we go and get a cuppa? I reckon our scene's going to get held up again.'

'All right…' I felt myself deflating. We headed over to the truck, where Gino was clearing away the remains of a breakfast buffet; they'd started filming early that morning, before we'd got there. We helped ourselves to tea from the big catering urn and sat at a picnic table.

'So…' said Debbie conversationally. 'That were unexpected.'

'Tony's always loved animals—'

'I don't mean him wading in like a hero, I mean that six-pack.'

'Hadn't noticed it,' I said, stirring my tea. She laughed.

'I believe you. Thousands wouldn't.'

'What's got into him, anyway?' I asked. 'Throwing himself into that lake for that stupid dog! It could have been full of pondweed; he could have got himself all tangled up in it. You saw how deep it was; it could have been dangerous—'

'Would you have been this annoyed with Nathan if he'd done it?'

'What? I dunno. Probably not. It's his job though, innit?'

'And that's your answer, love.' Debbie sat back,

sipping at her tea in a self-satisfied – I'd go so far as to say smug – manner.

'What are you blathering on about?' I shook my head in exasperation. 'Are you saying that Tony's trying to compete with Nathan? Why on earth—?'

Debbie reached out and took my hand.

'You know I love you, right? Don't take this the wrong way, but for an intelligent woman you can be a right div sometimes.'

'I'm not—'

But I didn't get to protest any further because our attention was snatched away from the subject of Tony and what could be behind his sudden heroics by a loud cry of pain and surprise from the other side of the food truck.

Gino lay on the ground, clutching at his arm and howling. His normally tanned complexion was white and bloodless, and he swayed for a moment.

'Uh oh,' I said, 'he's either going to throw up or—' He passed out, but luckily he was already on the floor so he didn't have far to topple, and his head landed by sheer fluke on the soft (but smelly) bag of rubbish he'd been carrying. I squatted down next to him and very gently rolled him onto his side, into the recovery position, being careful not to touch his arm.

'It's all right, Gino,' I said, as he groaned. 'Just lie there for a moment until you feel well enough to sit up.'

'What happened?' asked Debbie, looking around. I nodded towards the stairs that led down from the truck.

'He's fallen down them, I reckon,' I said, as Lucy arrived at high speed followed by some other crew members.

'What the—? Oh, bloody hell!' she said, looking shocked but also exasperated, as if she couldn't quite believe what was happening *now*. I couldn't blame her; the shoot had been eventful thus far, but not terribly productive.

Gino groaned again and sat up, crying out in pain as he moved his arm. I reached out and put my arm around his shoulder on the opposite side, holding him steady and upright.

'I think you've broken it,' I said, noticing the weird position his elbow was in and that the skin around it was already starting to look swollen. No wonder he'd passed out. 'Can you wiggle your fingers?'

Gino looked pale and sweaty. 'I can't even feel my fingers, let alone move them.'

I looked up at Lucy. 'Gino needs to go to the hospital. Right now.' She looked at me for a second, probably debating whether or not to demand who the hell I was, then nodded and took out her phone.

'My truck...' said Gino. I patted him very gently on the good arm.

'Don't worry, if you let me have your keys I'll lock it all up for you.'

'But the food...' he protested weakly. 'I started lunch prep. It'll all go to waste...'

'Jodie's a chef,' said Debbie brightly. 'She can do it!'

Tony and his film-star friend Faith had arrived on the scene, aware that they and Kimi's soggy doggy were no longer at the centre of the drama.

'Jodie's a brilliant cook,' said Tony enthusiastically. 'I hired her to do my wedding.' Faith looked at him, disappointed. I wasn't sure if he noticed, but he followed that up with 'Not that it went ahead...'

The ambulance arrived quickly and Gino was loaded into it. Before they shut the doors and drove away, he called to me.

'Here are the keys to the truck,' he said. He was propped up on a stretcher with his arm in a rough splint to stop it moving. The paramedic had already given him a shot of strong painkiller and he looked much calmer, although still pale. I reached for the bunch of keys he was holding, but he drew them back slightly. 'Do you really know what to do? I'd rather let them eat takeaway than have someone who doesn't know the difference between a *zabaione* and a *crème anglaise* loose in my kitchen.'

'Zabaione is egg yolks, sugar, and marsala, while crème anglaise has cream, milk, and vanilla in it,' I said. 'Okay?'

He looked surprised for a moment, then smiled and relinquished the keys. 'Okay, I'm convinced. Thank you. But I'll be back tomorrow.'

'Of course,' I said. 'Ciao.'

'Ciao…'

The paramedic reached out to shut the door and smiled at me. 'He won't be back tomorrow,' she said quietly. I nodded.

'Thought not.'

Lucy rounded everyone up after the excitement was over, determined to actually get some filming done. But without me, as I was swapping being a pretend domestic for being a real one. It was time to get back to doing what I *really* loved: cooking.

I picked up the bag of rubbish, rounding up the trash that had burst out when it had broken Gino's fall, and dumped it in the industrial-size wheelie bin nearby. Gino must have been carrying it down the stairs and, unable to see his feet or find his footing, taken a tumble. As I headed back to the truck, though, I noticed something strange…

The stairs weren't attached to the vehicle; they were a wooden set, five steps high, that could be picked up and presumably put inside the truck when Gino and his kitchen were on the move. I guessed that the original back door, probably with pull-down steps, had been filled in when the caravan had been fitted out as a mobile kitchen, to maximise space, and it had been simpler to just build this set to use as and when needed. But that wasn't the strange thing.

The strange thing was, the second step down was broken right in the middle, presumably where Gino had put his foot and all of his weight, making it give way and send him tumbling to the ground. He was very lucky he hadn't got a leg caught and twisted in the remaining stairs, otherwise he could have had another broken limb to go with his arm. What made this strange was the fact that the wood looked thick and strong enough to hold the weight of someone much heavier than Gino. So why had it broken?

And that wasn't all. The step had snapped in half, right in the middle. Half of it was still attached to the set of stairs, while the other half lay in the grass. I picked it up and studied it carefully. The end that had snapped off the edge of the stair housing was jagged, with splintered pointy bits sticking out. I held it up against the stair housing and it was easy to see how it fitted together. The other end, though – the bit that would have been in the middle of the stair – was smooth and straight. No jagged bits.

That really was the strange thing. I felt my phone ring in the pocket of my jeans (all phones had to go onto vibrate the minute you got near the set) and looked at the caller display; it was someone who could not have chosen a better time to call. I answered.

'Hi, Nathan, fancy a cup of tea?'

Chapter Seven

Nathan *did* fancy a cup of tea. He couldn't get away just then, but promised to come over and see me in a couple of hours. Which was just as well, because lunchtime was approaching and I had to carry on getting the food ready.

Everything was half-prepared: vegetables peeled, onions and garlic chopped, ovens on to heat. It wasn't immediately apparent what Gino had been planning to cook, but luckily he'd written out a menu for the whole week, and I was able to work out which dishes the mushrooms had been heading for, and that the sweet potato was destined to be roasted in spicy chunks as a filling for Mexican wraps.

I made a creamy chicken and mushroom sauce to go with fettuccine pasta; a lamb curry, chunks of succulent meat with a beautiful rich gravy; a vegan jackfruit and bean chilli (so simple, and the jackfruit tasted just like pulled pork); and lots of fillings for the wraps – guacamole, the roasted sweet potato chunks, salad leaves. I even discovered some 'vegan feta' in the fridge: tofu marinaded in olive brine and herbs to give it that salty tang. I tried a bit, despite never really having been a fan of tofu, and it tasted great, although the texture was less crumbly than real feta.

The beauty of the hot dishes was that they could be kept on the hot buffet counter all afternoon and, if anything, they would taste even better by the end of the day, the flavours having intensified. Whenever I make a curry, I always make enough for two days, and it always tastes even better the day after it was made.

I put everything on the warming plate on the counter and then looked up. There was a queue of people, some grumbling at the wait. Time had flown by and it was already 12.30, and some of them had been here since 5 a.m., setting up lighting, so they were starving.

'*Buon appetito*!' I said, remembering Gino the day before, and everyone tucked in. I opened the back door and gingerly made my way down the steps, watching out for the broken one. It was hot inside the trailer, but out here there was a cool breeze.

I sat on the steps fanning myself for a moment.

'So this is where you're hiding!' Debbie stood in front

of me with her hands on her hips. 'I didn't think I'd have to join all the chavs queuing; I was hoping for some special treatment from the chef.'

I laughed. 'Tell me what you want and I'll grab you a plate. And some for me, too. I'm starving.' I was. It had been hard work, and I'd been so busy that I hadn't noticed my own tummy rumbling until I stopped.

I grabbed us some plates of food (Debbie went for the pasta, while I went for the vegan tortilla wrap – I'd been intrigued by Gino's dish – and I was glad I did because it was *delish*). I was all for us sitting quietly round the back of the trailer but Debbie shook her head.

'I can't sit on those steps in this dress,' she said, reasonably enough. So we headed round to the front and joined the rest of the cast and crew at the picnic tables that had been set out in an open-air canteen.

'Jodie!' Tony was sitting with Faith, looking very cosy, but when he saw us he got to his feet and came over.

'It's amazing how many movie stars these days have got lapdogs, innit,' I said to Debbie, apropos of nothing. She snorted with laughter as he sat down with a rueful grin.

'I can't get away from her,' he said in a low voice. 'She's really nice, but it's getting a bit much. She says I'm her lucky charm.'

I looked at him, trying not to think of the six-pack lurking under his (clean and dry) frilly shirt, and snorted.

'You? Lucky? Does she know about your track record with women?' I saw him stiffen and immediately regretted it. Why was I being nasty to him? He was my best – certainly my oldest – friend in the world. It wasn't like I was jealous of him spending time with Faith or anything – why should I be? And to bring up his past relationships, both of which had ended in disaster, was just mean. Being Mrs Penhaligon, it seemed, wasn't a job for the faint-hearted, but that was hardly his fault. 'I am *so* sorry. I didn't mean it to come out like that.'

'I know you didn't,' he said shortly, but I still felt bad.

'So how come she needs a lucky charm?' I asked, hoping to smooth things over by charging on with the conversation and ignoring it.

He smiled. 'Actors are so superstitious. You know how you have to say 'break a leg' instead of 'good luck', and how you're not allowed to say the name of the Scottish play—'

'Macbeth,' Debbie and I chorused, loudly. A couple of cast members nearby gave us murderous glances and we giggled.

'I thought that were just in the theatre?' asked Debbie. He nodded.

'It is, normally. But everyone's on edge here now because of the curse.'

Debbie and I exchanged looks.

'What curse?' I said.

'It's proper daft,' said Tony, 'but Faith and some of the others have got it into their heads that the production's cursed. You hear about some film shoots being really unlucky, people having accidents, even dying—'

'What a load of rubbish,' I scoffed, but he shook his head.

'No, you should google it. You know *Poltergeist*?'

Debbie and I looked at each other and grinned. '*They're here…*'

'I knew you'd do that. There's this bit in a swimming pool, where all these skeletons pop up—'

'I know the bit you mean. Do you remember, Tone, we got it out of Blockbusters when it came out on video and watched it round mine while my mum and dad were at a dinner party.' I suddenly also remembered that it had been during the two weeks in 1994 when we'd been boyfriend and girlfriend. We'd been fourteen and had held hands and kissed, but no tongues. He certainly hadn't had a six-pack back then. I swallowed. 'It scared the bejesus out of us.'

'Of course I remember…' He looked at me and I knew he was also remembering the first few awkward moments after deciding that we were officially going out together, when we'd sat on the sofa, neither of us knowing what exactly being boyfriend and girlfriend entailed. We'd given up trying to work it out after a while and had just watched the film, throwing Maltesers at each other during the scary bits, exactly as we had done a thousand times before when we were just friends. 'Anyway, they used real skeletons. Real live dead people. Not a good idea. Lots of unexplained accidents, even deaths.'

'That's horrible,' said Debbie.

'And then there was *The Omen*, and *The Crow*, and—'

I shook my head. 'Tony, love, you need to stop looking up rubbish on the internet.'

'It's all true! Anyway, the thing is, these stories spread, don't they?'

'Because people look them up on the internet,' I pointed out, pointedly.

'Well, yeah. But what with Faith getting locked in, the dog escaping and nearly drowning, and now Gino falling down the stairs and breaking his arm...' He leaned in conspiratorially. 'They think this shoot's cursed too.'

Debbie and I stared at him, then at each other, and then burst out laughing.

'Oh, come on! *The Omen* and that, they're horror films with loads of spooky stuff going on, but this film...' Debbie threw her hands up in exasperation. 'The scariest thing about this film is your frilly shirt.'

'Thanks a lot...'

'Honestly, what does this remind you of?' I said.

He looked mystified. 'I dunno, what's it supposed to remind me of?'

I put on a terrible American accent. *''I'd have gotten away with it too, if it hadn't been for them pesky kids!''* He still looked mystified and I felt indignant. 'It's all a bit Scooby Doo, innit?'

'The local sheriff's been dressing up as the ghost of Polvarrow House and terrorising the actors with phantom pasties,' said Debbie, laughing.

'Exactly,' I said. Tony looked at me, his eyes narrowing.

'You know something. What do you know?'

'Nothing…' I didn't really want to mention my suspicions until I spoke to Nathan. But then, if I was right, I should warn them… I looked around to make sure no one else was listening, and then beckoned the two of them closer. 'I think maybe someone *is* trying to sabotage the shoot.'

Nathan looked at me keenly. 'What makes you say that?'

The cast and crew, including Debbie and Tony, had finished lunch and gone back on set. A few stragglers hung around, chatting, but other than that Nathan and I had the picnic tables to ourselves.

I held up the broken-off piece of step. 'What do you think of that?'

He studied it, then looked up at me. 'That's a

suspiciously clean break, if we're meant to believe that it broke under someone's weight.'

'Someone sawed through the middle of the step, didn't they? Not all the way through – someone might have noticed that – but just enough that when a certain amount of weight was put on it, or someone stood right on the cut, it would split in two.'

'Do you think someone was out to get Gino?' Nathan put down the wood and picked up his mug of tea. I shook my head.

'I don't think so. Why would they be? He's the caterer; everyone loves him because he feeds them. And it's a bit of a hit-and-miss method, isn't it? There'd be no telling when it would break, or even if it would be Gino who stood on it. There are probably other people who come up and down those stairs – delivery people maybe, I dunno. And when you add to it the other things that have happened… You heard about the lock on Faith's caravan—'

'We should have a look at that.' Nathan grinned. 'I mean, *I* should have a look at it. *I'm* the copper round here. I keep forgetting… And you think someone let the dog out deliberately?'

'Yes. I think they may have even chucked her in the lake.' Nathan looked horrified. 'I know, that's a really nasty thing to do. But Kimi's sister didn't leave Princess alone for very long. How she managed to get the door open, get all the way over to the lake, *and* end up swimming in the middle of it, in that short a time… I just don't think a dog of that size could cover that much ground in so little time, especially not without being spotted.'

'Which leads on to the next question,' said Nathan. 'How could someone do that without *them* being spotted? We're in the middle of a busy film shoot; there are people everywhere.'

'I was thinking about that,' I said. 'When we saw the dog, most of the crew were in the ballroom, setting up for filming. Not all, of course: the make-up and wardrobe staff were in their trailers, and there would have been some cast members with them getting ready. The rest of the main cast would have been in their trailers, and the extras were either getting dressed or heading for the ballroom.'

'Would they have passed the lake?'

'No. We only did because I was feeling rebellious and wanted to have a walk about before having to stand in one spot for hours wearing a potato sack.' Nathan raised an eyebrow. 'That's another one of my long stories. Put it this way, they obviously don't think I'm leading-lady material.'

'That's a travesty. So who else was near the lake when you spotted the dog?'

I thought hard. 'There were a few crew members; I

don't know who they are. And the bloke who owns the house.'

'Hmm... I'll have a quiet word with him, see if he's seen anyone lurking who shouldn't be here. Even if there weren't many people about, you'd think someone would have spotted a person carrying a dog.'

'Not if it's someone who was meant to be there,' I said. Nathan nodded.

'Yes. A crew member. But I don't understand what the point of these little 'accidents' is. They haven't really caused any problems, have they? I mean, apart from Gino breaking his arm. They haven't stopped filming.'

'No, but they've made everyone uneasy. Ridiculously so.' I told him about the curse and he laughed.

'These creative types, they do let their imaginations run away with them,' he said. 'No common sense.'

'Much better to be a completely unimaginative copper,' I said, and he grinned.

'You said it. At least there's one thing we can be sure of: it's not the local sheriff dressing up as a mummy. I know Sergeant Adams likes to dress up when he's singing in the fishermen's choir, but I think I'd notice if he'd gone full-on Ancient Mariner on us. But if a gang of teenagers and their weird talking dog turn up in a psychedelic van, let me know...' I laughed; I was glad Nathan was on my wavelength, and I wasn't the only one who could see just how Scooby Doo the situation was. Nathan stood up. 'I'd better go. I've got a ton of paperwork to do. Obviously I can't do anything about any of this unless someone wants to make a formal complaint. So far, apart from causing Gino to hurt his arm, it comes more under the heading of 'annoying pranks' than any real crime.' He looked around, but by now the last of the crew had left and we were alone. 'Still, be careful, yeah? Keep an eye out and let me know if anything else suspicious happens.'

'Wait,' I said, as he turned to go. 'Why did you call me earlier? Was there something you wanted?'

He smiled awkwardly. 'No, no, I just wanted to thank you again for last night.'

'No worries, I really enjoyed it.' *Fancy coming round tonight as well?* I thought, but I didn't say it because that might come across as desperate.

'Me too.' Nathan looked at me for a moment, and I thought he was going to say something else. But he didn't. 'I've really got to go. I'll see you later.'

The rest of the day was busy but uneventful. I had kept some food on the hotplate for any cast and crew who wanted dinner, but the shoot wrapped for the day at 5 p.m. amid mutterings about 'the light'. Apparently the ballroom scene was done – it may have taken most of the day, but according to Tony there were only six lines of dialogue and the whole scene would probably only last about two minutes on screen – and they were ready to move on to an outdoor scene, but it would start to get dark before they'd even set up.

I decanted the leftover curry and chilli into Tupperware containers – it saved me having to cook dinner when I got home – and washed everything up, conscious that it wasn't my kitchen and that I needed to leave it in good condition. I'd just taken out the keys and locked up when I heard movement behind me. I whirled around, my heart pounding, to find Zack standing behind me.

'Sorry,' he said, a rueful grin on his face, 'didn't mean to startle you. Do you know what's happening with Gino? Is he gonna be back tomorrow?'

I took a deep breath as my heart rate returned to normal. All this talk of curses must have got to me. 'I don't know,' I said. 'To be honest though, I doubt it. It looked like his elbow was broken, which is really nasty. He couldn't move his fingers or anything. Looks like you'll have to put up with my cooking for another few days.' *Or the rest of the shoot*, I thought; a broken elbow would take some time to heal.

'Bugger,' said Zack.

'Oh, come on, my curry wasn't *that* bad,' I said,

affronted. He laughed, a big booming laugh that made me smile along with it.

'Ha! Nah, I dint mean that,' he said. His accent was pure South London, and I wondered if he'd grown up around the area I'd worked in. Coppers hadn't always been very popular round there – in some cases with good reason. Maybe I wouldn't mention that I'd been in the Met. 'Nah, Gino was going to help me with something.' I raised an eyebrow. *With what?* 'I'm meant to be holding a dinner party tomorrow…' He saw the look of surprise on my face and laughed again. 'Yeah, I know, it's not something I do a lot of, cooking fancy stuff, but it's Kimi and Aiko's birthday tomorrow and I wanted to do something special for them. Gino said he'd ordered the ingredients for me and he was going to help me out.' He looked at me. 'I don't suppose you fancy it? I'll pay you. I was going to pay Gino.'

I wasn't sure I fancied being around movie stars after hours if I could help it. Zack was nice enough, and I loved that laugh of his, but Kimi seemed like a right diva, and if the rest of his co-stars were there… Well, I'd gone right off Faith after that business with Tony (not that I was jealous or saw her as competition or anything), and Jeremy Mayhew, who I'd admittedly only seen outside her trailer, had so far done nothing to dispel my image of him as a sexist old drunk.

Zack saw the expression of doubt on my face but he

was clearly desperate because he said, 'Please? It'll only be two, three hours work max, and I'll pay you two hundred quid.'

Two hundred? That just happened to be the price of the photography software I wanted to get Daisy for her birthday…

I smiled at him. 'It would be my pleasure.'

Chapter Eight

So the next morning I found myself at Polvarrow House at 7 a.m., making breakfast for the crew and for Daisy. Mum had spent a rare night in her own house the night before, so Daisy had been forced to come with me. I planned to feed her and let her have a nosey around the set (like mother, like daughter) before packing her off to school in a taxi.

She was slightly disappointed.

'Where's all the actors?' she said, as she sat at a picnic table picking at a bacon butty. The other tables were quiet – just some crew members wandering over to grab a sandwich before going off to set up lights and props. Nearby, serious-looking men strode around doing technical-looking things with screwdrivers and duct tape, while behind them David Morgan, the owner of the house, strode through the courtyard. I thought at first that he was just watching the comings and goings, but he looked angry, and he was clearly looking out for someone amongst the crew. He did not look like the excited, smiley-faced man who had welcomed us to the casting session the other Saturday.

'Mum?' Daisy sighed. 'I said, where are the actors? I thought I might bump into ... some of them.'

I grinned. 'I think Zack likes to have a lie-in. You'll have to come back after school.'

'Can I?' She looked at me, excited, and I nodded.

'I'll still be here, working. You could go back to Nana's, of course, if you'd rather do that...'

'No!' Daisy said immediately, and then she laughed. 'I mean, no offence to Nana, but...'

'I'll get the taxi to pick you up after school,' I said. 'I've got to help Zack with this dinner-party thing, so you'll definitely get to meet him.'

'Oh my *God!*' said Daisy. 'Jade is going to spew when she finds out.'

Just then the taxi driver – Magda Trevarrow, who was married to my old school friend Rob, from the garage – arrived to whisk Daisy off to school. I kissed my beautiful daughter goodbye and smiled to myself as I heard her chattering to Magda about coming back later to meet Zack Smith. Magda looked bemused and I got the impression that she'd never heard of him. I also got the impression that by the time she dropped Daisy off she'd know all there was to know about him.

I cleared away Daisy's plate and looked up as I heard voices. Three crew members were chatting over mugs of tea.

'I told you, this shoot is cursed,' said one. He was wearing a baseball cap and a worried expression. The other two laughed but he shook his head angrily. 'I mean it! I set up those three tungstens yesterday for the kitchen scene and left them there overnight, and when I went to test them this morning every single one had blown.'

'Bulbs blow all the time,' said one of his companions dismissively, a heavy-set man with a pockmarked face, the legacy of a teenage acne problem. Baseball Cap shook his head.

'Not overnight when they're not even turned on,' he said. 'They were all new bulbs. Apart from about twenty minutes yesterday when I was setting up, they were unused. All shattered.'

'That's the problem with tungstens,' said Pockmarks, knowledgeably. 'They're good if you're going for natural light but they get too hot and BANG! You're left in the dark and your cast is covered in glass. Happened on the *Live and Let Spy* shoot. Right in the middle of a torture scene, the bulb blows and there's Tom Hardy jumping out of his skin and nearly hitting his head on the ceiling. Power surge.' His companion nodded wisely, but Baseball Cap shook his head again.

'No, you're not listening.' He sounded exasperated, probably by his colleague's blatant name-dropping, I thought. 'They didn't blow when I turned them on. I didn't *need* to turn them on to know they weren't working. I walked in and I immediately saw glass all over the floor where the bulbs had shattered. They'd all exploded.'

Curiouser and curiouser, I thought. It sounded like the saboteur had struck again… I cleared the tables and took the dishes back to the food truck to wash up.

'Got any more ketchup?' The crew member with the pockmarked face was helping himself to a sausage and bacon bap. I smiled and handed him the bottle, then peered round him as I spotted David Morgan engaged in a heated debate with Lucy. So *that* was who he'd been looking out for. The first AD held her hands out in a placatory gesture to calm him down, but he still looked annoyed. So of course I had to go over and find out what was going on. I lurked nearby, pretending to clear a table.

'It was agreed,' he was saying to Lucy. 'No one is to enter the kitchen garden. It's my private space. I know you're filming in the old kitchen, but there's really no need for anyone to go in the garden.'

'I'll ask around and find out who it was,' she said. 'I'm terribly sorry. Do let me know if it happens again.' And she rushed off. I wandered over to the tea urn before returning to the angry house-owner.

'You look like you need a cup of tea,' I said, holding out a mug. He turned around in surprise.

'Thank you,' he said, taking it from me. He took a sip and sighed.

'Better?' I asked, and he gave a small smile. 'It must be hard, having a film crew traipsing all over your lovely house.'

'It is,' he said, with feeling.

'Especially when they go places they shouldn't…' I thought for a moment, and then smiled at him and stuck my hand out. 'I'm Jodie, by the way. We briefly met on casting day.'

'Oh yes, I remember. The lady who'd been here in my predecessor's day.' He looked at my jeans and pinny. 'You're the one who's taken over from the poor man in the food truck?'

'Yes. Between you and me, I'm relieved.' He looked slightly horrified so I quickly clarified what I meant. 'Not about Gino, the poor bloke. I just meant I'm actually a chef by trade, and I'm much happier cooking than acting. I heard you mention your kitchen garden? How lovely. I'd love to have a proper kitchen garden. You can't beat using really fresh produce.'

The poor man didn't have a chance. I turned my charm on full blast, and before he knew it he was giving me a tour of his passion project. To be fair, I *would* love a kitchen garden at home, but as I believe I've already mentioned, I have the opposite of green fingers. I am the Angel of Death when it comes to house plants. Grapes wither and die upon the vine, potatoes get weevils, and courgettes succumb to mildew when I gaze upon them. And don't even get me started on carrots.

But I was with the home-owner, so luckily the shadow of death was averted by the bright light of his horticultural knowledge, which was gentle and soothing after the somewhat self-important busyness of everyone else connected with the shoot. David proudly showed me his perfectly straight rows of pumpkins, which were almost ready to be harvested, and his herb borders. He was very informative, and very, *very* thorough as I had made the mistake of saying I needed a few pointers. I was relieved when his mobile phone rang. He apologised and took the call, then apologised again as he hung up, saying duty called and he had to pop into Penstowan but that he trusted me enough to leave me to look round (which was exactly what I'd been hoping for).

'Also, my wife and I are thinking about using the

house as a wedding venue,' he said carefully, 'and if we do go down that route, we'll be looking for a reliable caterer. Have a think and let me know if you're interested.' And with that he left. I almost shouted, *Of course I'm bloomin' interested!* after him, but decided to use a little decorum and email him later.

I wandered through the garden towards the house, trying to work out where the old kitchen was. It wasn't hard to spot; I could see large movie lights – the tungstens – set up through the window, which was quite high up from the ground. I approached carefully; I didn't think they'd started filming yet, but if they had I didn't want the top of my ugly mug appearing in shot. There was no noise from within, though, so I grabbed the window ledge and pulled myself up, just enough to peer into the room. It was set up as a Regency-style kitchen – very authentic, but pretty useless for actually cooking in. I let go as my arm muscles began to scream at me.

I looked down at the soft earth beneath my feet. There was a confusion of footprints in the soil, and a couple of rows of sad, trodden-down seedlings, although I had no idea what they were. There were a lot of footprints, but it looked to me like they'd all been made by the same pair of feet. The footprints led from the edge of the building, under the window, and out onto the path, meaning—

'They jumped out of the window…' I said to myself.

But why? I planted my feet in the spot that seemed to be the most likely landing place, and looked up at the window. No one had mentioned the window being open, so if someone *had* climbed through, they must have reached up and closed it behind them. Maybe they'd been in the kitchen, tampering with the lights, and had heard someone coming down the corridor towards them. If there was no way out of the room without the person approaching seeing them – and from my previous visit all those years ago, I vaguely remembered that it led out onto a narrow corridor – then the window was the only possible exit.

So that meant that the person tampering with the lights should not have been there in the first place; they couldn't allow themselves to be seen, or they could have styled it out and said they'd found the lights in that state. I reached up to the window, as if to grasp the frame. It also meant that the person who had stood in this spot had been considerably taller than me, because the window, which was an old wooden sash, would have to have been open a fair way for a body to climb through, and I certainly would not have been able to reach up and pull it down again.

That narrows it down, all five foot four of me, I thought sardonically. Zack was probably the shortest male member of the cast I'd seen so far, and he was at least six foot. But of course, it could be a crew member. It could be anyone…

I stepped back and frowned as there was a crunching sound under my trainers. I looked down. There at my feet, twinkling in the autumn sunlight, was a small patch of broken, very thin glass. The sort of glass you make lightbulbs out of.

I strolled thoughtfully back to the food truck. So the shoot saboteur had made their way into the old kitchen, smashed the bulbs to make it look like they'd blown – again, it was a bit of a pointless act, an annoying prank designed to hold things up temporarily, except it hadn't because the lighting guy had gone in and checked before they started shooting – and then climbed out of the window to escape detection, obviously with a few shards of glass on their clothing, which had then ended up in the flowerbed.

But why? Apart from Gino breaking his arm, all these pranks (or whatever they were) were trivial, minor inconveniences. They'd held up shooting, but not for any significant length of time. No major damage or harm had been done (again, apart from poor Gino). It was almost like they'd just been designed to annoy everyone.

Or freak them out… The crew member I'd heard

today had mentioned the shoot being cursed, and Tony had said that Faith considered him her 'lucky charm'. Everyone knew how superstitious actors were, but the crew were in danger of succumbing to it as well. People were on edge. Was that what the saboteur was trying to achieve? Which brought me back to where I'd started: *but why?*

Chapter Nine

I couldn't carry on wondering why, though, because while I'd been in the kitchen garden, the area around the food truck had become a hive of activity. The actors, who I realised must have been there all along, had finished in Hair and Make-Up and were heading over for breakfast. Gino had reluctantly accepted that he wasn't likely to be back for a while yet, so had emailed Lucy a long list of instructions for me; I found them on the truck's counter weighted down with the ketchup bottle to stop them blowing away.

Zack liked to start the day with a protein shake and a banana. At about 10 a.m. he'd be ready for a low-carb, high-protein muesli bar, to keep him going until lunch. He was happy to eat carbs at lunch, as long as they came with a lot of protein, so pasta with a meaty sauce and lots of vegetables was a good option, and that sort of dish was also popular with the crew.

Kimi was a vegetarian, but she would occasionally eat fish, so it was a good idea to keep some in the fridge in case she sprang it on you. She was lactose intolerant and only drank almond milk, but Gino had seen her polish off a massive bowl of ice-cream and chocolate sauce when she was stressed (which was a regular occurrence, apparently), and the dairy hadn't affected her then, so... She also had a mild rice allergy, which meant she could only eat brown rice. For breakfast she enjoyed a smoothie made from almond milk, kale, fresh mango (because of course that was in season in Cornwall in October), apple juice, and carrot. Maybe 'enjoyed' was the wrong word for that sort of smoothie.

Faith was on a special diet for ladies of a certain age. Breakfast was porridge made with soya milk, dried cranberries, fresh blueberries, and a sprinkling of flax and sunflower seeds. For lunch, a nice piece of salmon or chicken, with salad and avocado. The occasional bowl of pasta, if it was going to be a long day.

Jeremy liked bacon, curry, and chips. Possibly all on the same plate. He would eat whatever you put in front of him. You know how pious health freaks always tell you their body is a temple? Well, Jeremy's body really *was* a temple, but it was one of those ancient abandoned ones in India, surrounded by jungle and full of wild monkeys, screeching and swinging from the ruins. I decided I rather liked Jeremy after all.

I made Zack's protein shake and Kimi's smoothie and stuck them in the fridge, so I could serve them the minute they reached the canteen (or their trailer, in Kimi's case; her sister, Aiko, would come and pick up her breakfast so she could eat/drink it in solitary splendour. What Aiko would eat, nobody had bothered to find out). I measured out Faith's porridge oats and left them soaking in the soya milk; they would only take a minute in the microwave. I cooked a load more bacon and put it on the hot buffet, along with buttered rolls and ketchup; Jeremy could help himself, along with the bit-part actors and extras.

'You look busy.'

I looked up and smiled at Nathan, who was standing at the counter. 'Never too busy for local law enforcement,' I said. 'Are you here to check up on our saboteur, or to see me?'

Nathan gave me that smile of his, the one that started out small and ended up taking over most of his face. I always liked being on the business end of one of those smiles.

'A bit of both,' he said. He sniffed and I laughed.

'You had breakfast?'

'I was going to have some at the station,' he said, eyeing the big tray of bacon I'd just set out. I picked up a roll and piled several rashers into it.

'Sauce?' I asked, raising my eyebrows.

'I won't say no if it's you offering,' he said, grinning, and I felt my cheeks get hot. I gave the plastic ketchup bottle a squeeze and it made a horrible farty noise. There went the atmosphere, again.

'Better out than in…' I shook the bottle and got some out this time, then handed him the roll in a serviette. 'Sit down. I'll come and join you.'

We sat at one of the picnic tables and I watched as Nathan nibbled far more delicately at the roll than I would have done. He seemed a bit awkward, anxious or something. I wondered what the matter was, and why he had really come to see me.

'So…' I said, but right at that moment he was having trouble with a stringy bit of bacon fat and couldn't speak. 'So, the mysterious phantom shoot saboteur has struck again, I reckon.'

He swallowed. 'Really?'

I told him about the tungsten lights, the footprints in

the flowerbed, and the shards of glass. He nodded thoughtfully.

'Did you talk to the locksmith?' I asked, and he nodded again.

'Just briefly,' he said. 'Remember, this isn't really an investigation, is it? So far, it's just your copper's instinct niggling at you. No one's made a complaint. But I did pop in to ask about getting some keys cut, and I had a chat with him then.' He dabbed at a spot of bacon grease on his sleeve. 'Bugger… Anyway, I told him I'd heard about what happened, and I asked him if that sort of thing was a regular occurrence, as I was thinking of buying a caravan and wondered if there was anything I should be looking out for.' He grinned. 'Your mum was right.'

'What? Really? It was superglue?'

He nodded. 'He said it looked to him like someone had squirted something into the lock and it had set hard. He had to replace the whole thing – unscrew all the housing and take the entire unit off. He said he was about to go off and get a jigsaw so he could cut it out, when Tony climbed in and kicked the door open.'

'So whoever the saboteur is, they did a proper job…' I said thoughtfully. He nodded.

'Yup. So do you have any ideas who it could be? You must have your ear to the ground here. Everyone must come and see you at some point.'

I shook my head. 'Not really. I've been stuck in the truck most of the morning so far, apart from looking round the kitchen garden. Once the breakfast rush is over I'll go walkabout, stick my nose into a few people's business…'

He laughed. 'That sounds like you. But be careful, okay? So far this person has been pretty harmless, but they might not stay that way, especially if they realise you're sniffing around.'

'I am always the soul of discretion,' I said, and he laughed again.

'But of course you are.' He stood up. 'I'd better go…'

'Wait!' I shot to my feet too. 'You didn't really come here to talk about the prankster, did you? What is it? Has something happened to your dad?'

'No, no, nothing like that,' he said, and he really did look awkward now. I felt a horrible lurch in my tummy. Good news was never delivered by a face wearing that expression. 'It's nothing to worry about. It's just—' He swallowed hard and I could see that he was making himself say it. 'I've been offered a job back in Liverpool.'

It took a minute for his words to sink in, and then when they did, I didn't quite believe I'd heard him right. *No, no!* I thought. He couldn't go back to Liverpool, he just couldn't.

'What sort of job?' I asked, stupidly. He rolled his eyes.

'Hairdressing.' Well, he *did* have good hair. 'My old superintendent contacted me and told me about this new unit he's heading up for Merseyside Police. Drugs and organised crime. He wants me to apply for a DCI position with him. He's more or less said that if I want it, it's mine.'

'Oh … right,' I said, my mind whirling. All I could think was *no, no, no!* But of course I didn't say that. 'Sounds like a good job.'

'Yeah, it is.'

'More room for career progression than sleepy Penstowan,' I said.

'Yeah.'

'Near your parents,' I said. *Stop listing all the reasons why he should take it,* I told myself in exasperation.

'Yeah.'

Near your ex, I thought. *Don't say it… Don't say it…* 'Does your ex still live there?' *Damn, I said it.*

'I don't know,' said Nathan, but I could tell he was lying. To his credit he realised it, and shrugged. 'I assume she does. I haven't heard that she's moved or anything. But I'm not in touch with her, so I wouldn't necessarily know if she had.'

'So when do they want you to start?' I asked, even though I didn't want to think about him leaving. He gave a short laugh.

'I haven't even applied yet!' he said. 'Are you in a hurry to get rid of me or something?'

No, I don't want you to go at all, I thought. But of course I didn't say that either. I opened my mouth to say something – anything – but then his phone rang. As he reached into his pocket to answer it, I looked up and saw Faith and Jeremy approaching. I finally spoke up as Nathan looked at his phone in irritation and declined the call.

'I have to get back to work,' I said. It wasn't what I really wanted to say, but I *did* need to make the stars' breakfasts.

'Oh, yes, so do I…' He tucked his phone back in his pocket and looked around. There were more cast members heading over now, having finished in Hair and Make-Up and taking the opportunity to grab a quick cuppa or some breakfast before filming began. I turned towards the truck but he reached over and touched my arm, stopping me. 'Can we talk later?'

'Of course,' I said, horrified to hear my voice sounding so hoarse. I swallowed hard. 'But really, what's to talk about? It's a fantastic opportunity and it's near your parents.' *And your ex…*

He stared at me. 'So you think I should apply?'

No, no, I don't! 'Don't you?'

He looked at me as if he was disappointed with my

reply, then took his hand off my arm. 'I've got to go. See you later,' he said flatly, then turned and walked away.

'Hellooo?' Behind me, Faith called out to me in a cheerful, friendly tone of voice that for some completely irrational reason made me want to pour that bowl of cold porridge oats over her head. But I showed remarkable restraint and just smiled at her before returning to the food truck.

Chapter Ten

I heated up Faith's porridge and helped Jeremy get a bacon roll together. I had the horrible feeling that he only wanted me to lean across the counter with a couple of baps in my hands so that he could get a quick look down my top – it was boiling inside the truck with the hot plate on, and I'd stripped down to my T-shirt, which was clingier and had a lower V-neck than I'd realised – but I was still too stunned by Nathan's revelation to care about a has-been actor's sexist BS. Zack came over for his protein shake and banana; he smiled charmingly at me, despite being deep in conversation with someone on his phone, but even that didn't make much of a dent in my mood. Aiko came and picked up Kimi's breakfast and looked astounded when I asked her what *she'd* like for breakfast; I got the impression not too many people even noticed her when her sister was around. I gave her one of Zack's low-carb muesli bars and a banana (I guessed she and her sister hadn't managed to maintain figures like theirs by eating bacon sandwiches) and told her to let me know if there was anything special I could make her for her lunch.

'For me? Not for Kimi?' She couldn't seem to get her head around the concept. I smiled encouragingly at her.

'Of course! It's your birthday today as well, isn't it? You should be celebrating, not fetching and carrying for your sister. Let me know, yeah?'

'I will… Thank you…' And she wandered away, still looking slightly bemused. I shook my head, equally bemused; movie people were weird.

I turned off the hot plate and began to clear down, making room for the lunchtime prep. There were probably still a few breakfast stragglers, but there was plenty of bacon in the heated buffet dishes and a pile of buttered rolls, so they could help themselves. There was also a random box of Coco Pops in the cupboard, so anyone who didn't want bacon could have a bowl of that.

I cleaned the workbench on auto-pilot, my mind going over and over Nathan's words. All the times we'd flirted over the last few months… Had it been in the back of his mind then, that one day he'd be going back to Liverpool? Was that why he'd never made a move?

And why did he need to talk about it? It was a no-brainer, surely. If he stayed here he'd more than likely be a DCI for ever. Don't get me wrong, the rank of detective chief inspector is certainly nothing to turn your nose up at (it was higher than I'd got, but then I'd been happy pounding the beat, and being a mum as well already gave me enough to juggle), but Nathan was only thirty-five, and he struck me as being ambitious. But then, he had moved down here in the first place, so maybe career wasn't as important to him as I thought. But he was worried about his parents, and if he moved back he'd be much nearer them – and his ex, whom he'd never really talked about but who had clearly broken his heart. But, but, but… Round and round my mind went, until—

'Oww!' I lent across the hot plate to wipe off a smear of grease, and gasped as my bare forearm touched it. I'd turned if off but those things stayed hot for ages. I dropped my cleaning cloth and clutched ineffectually at my arm.

'Jodie! You all right?' Tony stood at the counter, watching me in alarm.

'Yeah, I just burnt my arm on the bloody hot plate…' I was in pain, but more than that I was furious at myself for being miles away, and furious at Nathan for distracting me even though he wasn't here. I inspected my arm, and when I looked up again Tony was right next to me, inside the truck. He gently took my arm and led me over to the sink.

'Run it under cold water,' he ordered, turning on the tap (the truck was hooked up to a garden hose in the courtyard outside). He held my arm under the flow of water, taking the heat out of the burn.

I blinked madly, wanting nothing more than to burst into tears, but if I did he'd be really sympathetic and lovely, and I'd cry even more, and he'd ask me what the matter was, and then I'd tell him about Nathan and I'd be forced to admit things (to myself as much as to him) that I'd been ignoring relatively successfully for a while now, and that's just not how I do stuff. I don't go around admitting to having feelings, for God's sake. I am a world-class bottle-upperer. Usually.

'Is that helping?' asked Tony. It was so nice to have someone talking to me with such concern in their voice. He was very close, and he had that frilly shirt on again. I shut my eyes and then had to wrench them open quickly as an image of Tony ascending, Mr Darcy-like, from the depths of the ornamental lake floated across my mind. Only this time there was no small dog or pondweed spoiling the picture, his shirt was fully unbuttoned, and the six-pack underneath was so well defined it was practically a twelve-pack. And there was definitely a bit of chest hair lurking there, in my subconscious…

'Are you all right?' he asked, and I forced myself to

smile at him, although by now I wasn't sure how I was feeling, or who I was feeling it about. *Pull yourself together, you daft tart,* I told myself sternly.

'Yeah, I'm just annoyed with myself,' I said, truthfully enough. 'I knew that hot plate would still be warm, and I still leant over it like an idiot.'

He carefully turned my arm around so he could look at the dull but angry red skin on my forearm. He pursed his lips as he inspected it, then looked up and smiled.

'I think we might have to amputate it,' he said. 'Probably from just below the chin.'

'If it gets me out of washing up, I'm game,' I said. He laughed and let go of me, stepping back slightly as he did so. I felt a twinge of disappointment mixed with relief.

'You'll live, Nosey. Us Penstowians are made of sterner stuff than that.'

'It's just a flesh wound,' I said. 'Tough as old boots, me.'

'Not quite as smelly though.'

'Not *quite*?'

'Well, it is proper hot in here, innit? You're sw— I'm sweating like a pig.'

'Nice save,' I said. 'Anyway... I've got to finish cleaning up the breakfast stuff before I can start lunch prep.'

'You mean, *get out my way, Tony*?'

'Something like that. You filming this morning, or do you just enjoy dressing like Long John Silver's camp younger brother?' I pretended to look him up and down with disdain, but actually those tight trousers and the shirt were surprisingly alluring…

Tony laughed. 'Faith says I looked just like Mr Darcy when I rescued the dog yesterday,' he said. My heart leapt.

'Did she?' I sniffed. 'I didn't know there was a dog rescue in *Pride and Prejudice.* Is that the version where he's an RSPCA inspector?'

'You know, you're not as funny as you think are,' said Tony.

'I'm still hilarious, though.'

He laughed. 'Yes, dear, you're hilarious.' He looked out across the counter as, from outside the truck, came sounds of movement. 'Uh-oh, it sounds like Lucy's on the warpath. I'd better go. She wants everyone on their best behaviour today, because Mike Mancuso's going to be here.'

'And Mike Mancuso is…?'

'The producer. One of these old-school Hollywood types, by the sounds of it.'

'A poor man's Charlton Heston with a big mouth?'

'Haha! Yes, going by the way Faith was talking about him.' He looked out again, and then turned back to me. I re-arranged my face – I'd been thinking *you and*

Faith seem VERY cosy – just in time. 'Are you all right now?'

'Yes, I'm fine,' I said. 'Thank you. Now off you go before you get into trouble!' I opened the back door of the truck and held it for him. 'Mind the stairs. Oh, and what we talked about before – the Scooby Doo scenario – be careful, yeah? I think they've struck again. Busted some lights this time.'

Tony raised his eyebrows. 'Really? I'll keep me eyes peeled for anyone suspicious. But with Mike Mancuso around, hopefully they'll be too scared to strike.'

I shoved all thoughts of Nathan's new job and Tony's (possibly hairy) chest to the back of my mind and finished clearing up, then started peeling and chopping veg ready for lunch. I thanked the absent Gino for his menu plans; I wasn't following them exactly, but it was good to have some ideas to work from. A pasta dish, a vegetarian option, salads, and either a curry or some kind of meat and two veg dish. And chips, always chips.

I love cooking, always have, always will. But I had to admit that this hadn't been the type of cooking I'd had in mind when I'd retrained as a chef. I hadn't exactly imagined myself working in a Michelin-starred restaurant; the hours aren't conducive to maintaining a healthy family life, plus there aren't many (any) establishments quite on that level in Penstowan. But I supposed that a part of me *had* wanted that; I *had* wanted the opportunity to experiment with new ingredients and complicated recipes, and I'd wanted to cook the sort of food that would blow people's socks off (in a good way) when they tasted it. But everyone's hosiery was safe from my tuna pasta bake, and you don't get an OBE for Services to the Culinary Industry by serving chips with everything (even if they are golden and crispy).

I sighed as I scraped all the peelings into a plastic bin (they were going to a local farm as food for the pigs). I shouldn't complain; it was less messy than rounding up drunks on a Friday night in Clapham, and it was certainly safer, hot plates notwithstanding. And the cast and crew seemed to appreciate the food that I dished up for them.

'Hello?'

I jumped as the voice disturbed my thoughts, and looked up. A round-faced man with spectacles and a big smile peered across the counter at me. 'Delivery for Gino Rossi?'

'That's me,' I said. The delivery man raised his eyebrows, as I clearly didn't look like a Gino Rossi, but didn't say anything. 'What've you got for me?'

'Just the one.' The delivery man lifted a big insulated polystyrene box up onto the counter. 'Sign here, please.' I scrawled my name on the delivery sheet, and then began tearing at the sealing tape.

Inside, packed in ice, were two fish of a type I didn't think I'd seen before; I certainly hadn't cooked them. I looked at Gino's menu list, but other than a couple of salmon fillets put aside for Faith and a few nondescript white fish portions in the freezer in case Kimi wanted them, there was nothing on the list about seafood.

'All right?' Zack stood at the counter, looking hot and sweaty.

'Blimey, what've you been up to? You look all—'

He laughed. 'You were gonna say 'red in the face', weren't you? I'm black; we don't go red. We just sorta glow. Sexily.' He winked at me and I laughed too.

'Yes, I was, and yes, you do.'

'We just did this big fight scene,' he said, pouring himself a glass of water from the jug on the counter. 'Well, it'll *look* like a big fight scene, but we'll shoot most of it in the studio in front of a green screen later. You know what that means?'

'They superimpose the background and that afterwards?'

He nodded. 'Yeah, that's right. All we shot was the end bit, with the house in the background so they can copy it into the CGI. I just beat this dark knight bloke in a sword fight and I'm standing there with my foot on his body and my blade drawn…' He drew his sword –

which was ornately carved and set with a red jewel in the handle – and brandished it, clearly enjoying himself. 'And I'm like, yeah, I'm the man, and in the background on the horizon this massive dragon monster appears.'

'Cool.'

'Yeah.' He put his sword back in its sheath, sighing in exasperation as the jewel fell out of its setting. He bent down and picked it up. 'Bloody thing keeps falling off. Plastic tat. Sam made me run around for half an hour like a nutter, to get me looking like I'd just beaten the crap out of the evil horde. I'm knackered now.' He nodded to the insulated box. 'That my fish? I got a text from Gino saying he got a text from the delivery company…'

'This is yours?' It made sense now. 'Of course, for tonight. What is it? I don't think I've cooked it before.'

'Don't worry, I'll be preparing it. It's fugu.'

'Fugu?'

'Pufferfish.'

I stared at him in amazement. 'Pufferfish? But that's poisonous, isn't it? Unless you know what you're doing.'

'I *do* know what I'm doing.'

'But…' I shook my head. 'We had a talk from a sushi chef on my course, and he said that chefs have to study for like two years before they're allowed to prepare it. Restaurants won't take on a fugu chef unless they've got this specific qualification.'

'I know, and I've got it,' he said. 'I lived in Japan for

nearly a year when I was filming *The Black Samurai*, and while I was there I learnt how to do it. I trained under a fugu master.' He did a mock kung fu pose. 'Seriously, I'm a black belt in fugu.'

'Really?' I was sceptical. *Well, I ain't eating it,* I thought, but then I wasn't going to anyway, was I? The star of the movie, Kimi, was. A massive *THIS IS A BAD IDEA!!!* klaxon went off in my head. 'Um, you do realise this shoot is cursed, don't you?'

He laughed. 'Ah, come on, I thought you had more sense. I know the others think that, but I'm not superstitious. I grew up in South London, I had enough real stuff to be afraid of without jumping at shadows.'

'I know, and no, I don't really believe in curses. But you can't deny that weird stuff keeps happening. Faith getting locked in, Kimi's dog, Gino's accident…'

Zack looked uncomfortable. 'Yeah, I know… But I wanted to do something really nice for Kimi and Aiko. Now Kimi's famous they spend most of their time in America, and I know Aiko misses Japan.' He didn't meet my eyes and, despite what he'd said about not going red, I could tell he was blushing. So it was *Aiko* he'd been trying to impress with his dog-sitting skills, not Kimi. Bless him. He shook his head. 'Anyway, if it *is* cursed it's already gone wrong, because it was just supposed to be the three of us, and then Kimi invited Faith and Jeremy along too, because she said she goes to bed early and she thought I'd be bored if I got left alone with Aiko.' Poor Zack. Getting left alone with Aiko had obviously been his plan, but now he'd been roped in to cook for all of his co-stars. I smiled at him.

'We'll make it a really nice night for Aiko and Kimi,' I said, deliberately putting Aiko first. He blushed again. Aww, sweet. 'I'll help out and do some Japanese rice and veggie dishes or whatever you want me to do, and you concentrate on the fugu. But if I have any doubts over the safety of what you're serving, I'm putting a stop to it, okay? I'm the qualified chef here, and it won't look good on me if something happens.'

He looked like he was going to protest for a moment, then stopped. 'Okay.' He looked around at the sound of someone calling his name. 'Gotta go. Monsters to kill and all that. Laters.'

Chapter Eleven

I was still unconvinced that serving potentially poisonous pufferfish was a good idea, but I could see why Zack wanted to do it; he was desperate to impress Aiko. Well, I'd make sure he impressed her with a proper Japanese banquet, so if I managed to convince him not to serve the fugu it wouldn't be obvious that a major part of the meal was missing. I put a cauliflower pasta bake (a cauliflower cheese/mac 'n' cheese crossover, made with vegetarian cheddar) in the oven and left a chicken casserole simmering on the stove, then grabbed my phone and went down a Google rabbit hole, looking for Japanese recipes. There were a lot of them…

I briefly surfaced in time to serve up lunch – Tony popping by for a plate of the yummy cheesy pasta and to check I hadn't tried to set fire to myself again – and then I was left to my own devices. Sam, the director, had apparently been cracking the whip today in a bid to get filming back on schedule, and instead of the leisurely, drawn-out lunches of the last couple of days, with cast and crew wandering in and out of the canteen area as they were free, it was a case of fill up with carbs and get back on the horse – in some cases literally.

I rifled through the cupboards in the food truck and was relieved to see that Gino had already bought in some Japanese ingredients; he'd obviously had the same thoughts as me. I was pleased to see jars of *umeboshi* (pickled Japanese ume plums) and *fukujinzuke* (or 'lucky god' pickles, containing seven types of vegetables to represent the seven gods of fortune), as, according to Google, pickled veg was a must at a Japanese feast, and all of the recipes I could find for it took at least two days to prepare. I only had a few hours. There were several packets of soba noodles and some miso paste, so I earmarked them too, and a small bottle of *sake*; the rice wine, when mixed with soy sauce, garlic, ginger, and lots of black pepper, would make a great marinade for fried *karaage* chicken, and I could do something similar with tofu for Kimi, leaving out the sake because of her rice allergy. And I could make a tempura batter and fry up lots of different vegetables in it, to serve with the noodles.

I was so intent on my research that I didn't see who

left the box on the food truck counter. I didn't even know it was there until I turned round to make myself a cup of tea. It was a plain white cardboard cake-box, no decoration, no card. I looked round but there was no one about, so I carefully lifted the lid. Inside were ten cupcakes in shiny gold paper cases, all topped with a swirl of snow-white frosting. Each was beautifully decorated with the palest pink hand-crafted, sugar-paste cherry blossoms, sprinkles of red, pink, and black picking out the colours of the flowers. Sugar jewels studded the centre of each bloom, and a fine, powdery red glitter dusted the ridges of frosting. Each one was slightly different, all equally stunning and delicate but unique works of edible art.

'Whoa…' I said out loud, in awe of whoever had made these amazing and no doubt delicious treats. There was no card or message inside the box, but the Japanese cherry-blossom theme made it obvious who these cakes were intended for. I just wished I knew who they were from.

'Wow, those are amazing!' Daisy was as impressed as I was.

'What are you doing here?' I asked in surprise. 'Did you finish early? The taxi—'

She rolled her eyes. 'It's half past three. What are you like?' I looked at my phone (not that I doubted her), and was amazed to realise that I'd spent the last two hours planning Zack's Japanese feast. I'd only really done it to keep myself busy and avoid thinking about Nathan, and it had worked, only now I *was* thinking about him. Goddammit. Every time I thought about him leaving it made my tummy feel funny, like I'd eaten a live eel and it was slithering around inside me. It's bizarre when you think about it, the way they (whoever 'they' are) always talk about the heart when it comes to love, because as far as I can tell the stomach is the true seat of the emotions. When I'm happy I celebrate by eating cake or ice-cream or chocolate (or all three); when I'm unhappy, I smother it with, well, more cake and ice-cream and chocolate. And when I'm in love, it feels like it's full of butterflies. Or eels… Not that I was in *love* with Nathan or anything daft like that. Ha! As if. Hmm…

Daisy was looking hungrily at the cakes. I sighed.

'Sorry, sweetheart,' I said, 'but I assume they're for the dinner party tonight. Someone dropped them off.' I put an arm round her shoulder. 'But I know where there are some chocolate biscuits, *and* I know where one Zack Smith is filming.'

'Really?' That made up for not being able to eat a cupcake.

'Yup. Dump your school bag in the truck and let's go and watch.'

We wandered around to the other side of the house, munching chocolate biscuits (I had to quieten that eel down somehow) and chatting about our days. Daisy's best friend Jade had mentioned going to the pictures, something I normally wouldn't allow on a school night, but I was going to be busy with Zack's party and I wasn't sure when I'd be finished. Mum was planning to stay the night at mine so she could babysit Daisy (not that I was allowed to use the word 'babysit' anymore, not when she was going to be a teenager in a week or so), but I was prepared to admit that an evening with her nana watching *The Chase* and playing Scrabble probably wasn't that enticing a prospect. Jade was going to ask her mum Nancy, and *if* she agreed to take them, and *if* it was an early enough showing, I was happy to allow it.

We reached the edge of the shoot and stood watching from a distance. They were filming outside this afternoon, as Zack had said earlier, and there was a huge number of cast and crew milling around. The film's time period was somewhat confusing. Half the time they looked like something out of Jane Austen (that image of Tony dressed like Mr Darcy flashed across my mind again and I dismissed it in disgust, but not before dwelling for a few seconds on that six-pack…). It seemed to be a cross between Jane Austen and the Regency period, and King Arthur and his knights. In this scene there were soldiers on horseback, and they were wearing a weird mix of nineteenth-century dress and armour. *That's what they mean by a 'fantasy period drama'*, I thought. *They bought a mixed job-lot of costumes off eBay and wanted to use them all…*

We watched as a group of noblemen (including Tony, which made us both giggle) waited at the door of the house. Zack stood in front of them, his sword drawn, looking bored, as Sam Pritchard spoke to a group of actors on horseback a few metres away.

We took advantage of the momentary break in filming and moved closer to the action. I caught Tony's eye and gave him a thumbs-up, but Zack saw me and thought I was looking at him, and he gave me a big cheesy grin and a wave. Daisy looked at me in amazement; her old mum was cooler than she'd thought. Tony, however, who had seen both my initial gesture and Zack's response, was not quite as impressed, and actually looked quite put out. *Oh my God, is Tony jealous?* I thought. I wasn't sure why that idea seemed surprising to me; after all, *I* had been just a *teeny* little bit jealous of Faith's fawning all over Tony after he'd kicked her door down. Hadn't I?

I was saved from these rather uncomfortable thoughts by the director striding decisively away from the horses and Lucy herding the two-legged actors into place. Daisy and I crept closer until we were right behind the camera.

The atmosphere had changed. It had gone from a

group of slightly bored people standing around in daft costumes, tired of waiting, to the collective human equivalent of a coiled spring; everyone was suddenly alert and ready to go.

Lucy looked around. 'Quiet on set!' she called. I had a horrible premonition of my phone ringing and mucking up the shot, so I took it out and turned the ringer off, gesturing to Daisy to do the same. Lucy saw us and looked annoyed, but didn't tell us to leave. 'Roll sound!'

'Speed!' called a crew member in headphones, who I assumed was the sound guy. He nodded to another crew member holding a microphone on a long pole – the boom, I remembered hearing someone call it. The boom operator gave Lucy a thumbs-up.

'Turnover!' called Lucy.

'Speed,' said the camera operator. *Ooh, this is exciting,* I thought. The magic of the movies!

'Mark it.' Lucy nodded to a young girl holding a clapperboard. She stood in front of the camera.

'Scene eight, take six, mark,' she said, snapping the clapperboard shut and scuttling out of the way.

There was a pregnant pause, and then—

'Action!' called Sam. It was so cool it made me quiver a bit. Although I had absolutely no acting pretensions or desire to see myself on the big screen (unlike Tony and Debbie), I had, like so many others of my generation, grown up going to the pictures every week with my mates – no Netflix or streaming services for us. Seeing stuff on the big screen rather than the telly really did make it feel like there was some kind of magic at work, a magic that could transport you to faraway places, to past times or an imagined future, or into the life of a princess, or a gladiator, into a hero or a villain, or even a ghostbuster. The kind of magic that—

'Cut!' called Sam. What? Was it over already? The actors had barely moved! The director strode back over to the group on horseback, who had trotted forward a grand total of about three metres, waved his arms about a bit until they turned around and got back into position, and then headed back to his spot behind the camera operator. I could see that he was watching the action (such as it was) on a monitor, so he could see exactly what it would look like on screen.

Lucy went through the rigamarole with the sound, camera, and clapperboard girl one more time, we all held our breath again, and then—

'Action!'

I made sure to pay attention this time, in case it was over in seconds again, but this time Sam was obviously happy as the actors on horseback made it all the way to the house before parting to reveal Jeremy on a white stallion. His perpetual air of blokey leather-jacket-and-jeans-ness had disappeared, to be replaced with an upright, regal bearing, and a cold, aloof expression. The riders halted and Zack stepped forward to greet him.

'Your Maj—'

'You!' snarled Jeremy. He drew the sword from the scabbard at his side and held it out straight, the tip coming to rest millimetres from Zack's throat. I couldn't see Zack's face from this angle – they would have to film the whole thing again, I realised, with the camera pointing towards Zack rather than the riders – but he didn't flinch, just stood his ground.

'You dare come to my house?' demanded Jeremy. His voice was disdainful, imperious – the voice of a king, not Jezza the Liverpudlian scally who was only interested in women, football, and beer. 'You, peasant!' He addressed one of the extras, not taking his eyes off Zack for even a second. A scruffily attired, skinny boy stepped forwards, and I recognised him as being a trolley collector from the Co-op, which slightly spoilt the effect, but not for long because King Jeremy on horseback was mesmerising in his emotionless menace. 'Prepare the stables. And tell my queen I am here.'

The peasant scuttled off and Jeremy remained staring coldly at Zack, the sword in his hand firmly pointed at his target and never wavering. *Oh my God, chills!* I thought.

'Cut!' said Sam, and immediately His Royal Highness disappeared and Jeremy the cheeky scouser came back to life. He lowered his sword and rubbed at his arm, then lent over to slap Zack on the back.

Daisy and I both let out a long breath.

'Wowsers, who is *that*?' she said, Zack almost forgotten.

'Someone I clearly underestimated,' I said.

Chapter Twelve

As interesting as it had been to watch the filming to start with (and as amazing a revelation as Jeremy Mayhew's performance had been), the constant stopping and starting soon began to get a bit tedious. I once again thanked my lucky stars (and silently apologised to Gino) that events had conspired to get me out of being an extra and back to doing what I loved most. No, not eating or confusing myself over what passed (just about) as a love life, but cooking. I could honestly say that I would not have swapped places with anyone on that film shoot; they could keep their fame – although I wouldn't have minded a bit of their fortune – if their working day consisted of standing around in uncomfortable clothing, and being forced to repeat the same lines, the same scenes, over and over and *over* again. An actor's life was not for me.

We watched as Sam and the camera operator (or 'director of photography', as I heard someone refer to him) discussed where to put the camera next; they were going to re-shoot what we'd just seen them do (five times) from another angle, and then they'd shoot it *again*, from another angle, to get Zack's reactions. Some of the actors dismounted and stretched, but Jeremy stayed on his horse, leaning forward to pat it and fuss with its mane. I saw the horse's ears twitching as he talked to it; they'd obviously made friends.

Daisy was quite taken with the horses (and Zack, of course, although he hadn't had the chance to do much other than stand around and look hunky while Jeremy acted the bejesus out of himself), but even she had to admit that she was getting bored, cold, and hungry, so we turned and headed back towards the warmth of the food truck. I'd found a couple of fold-up chairs tucked away, which Gino obviously used when he wanted to hide in the truck away from demanding customers, and thought we could sit in there and warm up until it was time for me to drop Daisy home.

We hadn't got very far when there was a loud BANG! and a commotion behind us. We turned back just in time to see Jeremy and his mount charging straight at us. The horse's nostrils were flaring and it looked alarmed, but Jeremy was clearly a good horseman; he didn't panic and just hauled back on the reins, all the while still talking to the frightened beast. I grabbed Daisy and threw her out of the way, then instinctively reached out to grab the bridle. I was lucky that the horse had begun to slow down, otherwise it probably would have dragged me along, but the combination of Jeremy's surprisingly calm voice and my brute strength (I was pleased to see that I hadn't gone completely soft) managed to bring the poor thing to a halt.

'Oh my *God*, Mum!' cried Daisy, rushing over to us. I preened for a moment, thinking she was going to tell me how brave I was, but— 'That was so stupid! You could have been trampled!' I deflated a bit, but at least it meant my daughter loved me.

'Your ma's a hero!' protested Jeremy. I tried not to notice that he had a similar accent to Nathan. He slid down off the horse and held it firmly by the bridle, so I let go.

Lucy and Sam arrived at a run.

'Are you okay?' asked Sam. 'What happened?'

'Didn't you hear that bang?' Jeremy demanded angrily. 'What the bloody hell was it?'

'I don't know,' said Lucy. 'Are you all right?'

'I'm fine,' said Jeremy, calming down. 'Just tell me it didn't get caught on camera. I don't want it on YouTube, me being rescued by the caterer.' He looked at me. 'No offence, love.'

'None taken,' I said, although there was a *little* bit taken.

'Wow, you'd better make my movie that exciting!' We all turned to look at the owner of the booming American voice behind us. I am rubbish with US accents, but I could place this one: pure New York, or 'Noo Yoik' as he no doubt would have said. He turned to me. 'You sure got some balls on you, ma'am.'

I shrugged modestly. 'It was nothing…'

'Was it? Okay then.'

Daisy looked massively affronted but I shook my head: ignore it. Movie people.

'Mike! When did you get here?' said Sam. So this was the famous producer, Mike Mancuso, was it? I had to restrain myself from saying, *'Hey, Mikey!'* like something out of *Goodfellas;* he looked and sounded like an extra from an early De Niro movie, but I wasn't sure how he'd take it.

'Got here just in time to catch the excitement,' he said. 'I hope this ain't gonna hold up shooting.'

'Of course not,' said Sam, testily, and I got the feeling there had been words between them – probably about the hold-ups the saboteur had been causing. Had this been another act of sabotage? I wondered. It seemed unlikely to be a coincidence, but at the same time, there could have been no way of knowing that Jeremy's horse would take fright; none of the other horses had bolted.

My question was soon answered as a technician rushed over to talk to Lucy and Sam.

'The generator's packed up,' he puffed. Lucy groaned and Sam looked exasperated.

'What? How did that happen?' he asked, irritated.

'I don't know,' said the technician. 'All the fuses blew and it tripped the power breaker, so we need to reset the whole thing—'

'That's what went bang?' I asked, and he gave me a 'who-the-hell-are-you?' look before nodding.

'Well, what blew the fuses? Did you overload it or something?' Sam was furious but the technician stood his ground.

'No, we didn't. In fact, I went and checked it myself this morning and made sure the bare minimum was plugged in, just in case ... well, you know, what with this...'

'This what?' Mike looked puzzled.

'This curse thing.' The technician looked at him defiantly but withered under the man's steady, no-nonsense New York stare. 'I don't believe in it or anything, but everyone's saying—'

'Oh, for God's sake!' muttered Lucy under her breath. He bristled.

'Yeah, I know it sounds daft but look at all the weird

stuff that's been happening! And now the generator. There's absolutely no reason for the power breaker to trip; it should have been easily able to cope with what we had plugged in. If it's not a curse, what's causing it all?'

Wrong question, I thought. *The real question is, WHO'S causing it all?*

'Is there really a curse?' whispered Daisy. I shook my head.

'Of course not. Let's leave this lot to it.' I took her arm and steered her away from the group, who had barely noticed us while we were standing right next to them, and sure as hell didn't notice us leave.

I got a text from Jade's mum, Nancy, agreeing to the cinema plan, and half an hour later the two of them came to pick up Daisy. I'd offered to pop out and drop her at their house, but Jade was very keen that her mum should come along to the shoot 'to help me out'; I was certain it was nothing to do with the fact that Daisy had been texting her about seeing Zack Smith in the flesh, and that Jade had absolutely no interest in meeting him herself... I made Nancy a coffee and we sat at a picnic table, wrapped in our coats, while Daisy took Jade over to where they were filming, both giggling.

'And so it begins...' Nancy said, ominously. 'They've

discovered that not all boys are annoying little brothers who were only put on this earth to hide your Sylvanian Families and eat all the crisps.'

I laughed. 'Life would be so much easier if they were.'

We had just finished our coffee and were about to go and round up our errant daughters when they came back anyway; filming had apparently 'wrapped' for the day by the time they'd got there, but they had spent the last twenty minutes talking to Zack and making a fuss of the horses. Both of them were flushed and giggling even harder than before. Nancy rolled her eyes at me and herded them into her car.

Again, I'd left food on the hot buffet for anyone who needed it, but the extras were heading home and the stars, who would normally have headed back to their hotel for an evening meal, were getting changed in their trailers, ready for Zack's dinner party.

'You done for the day?' Tony made me jump. He stood at the counter, peering in as I cleaned down all the surfaces.

'No, I'm helping Zack with his dinner party.'

Tony nodded. 'Oh yeah, I'd forgotten. You and Zack…'

I snorted. 'Don't say it like that! Like there *is* a 'me and Zack'. He's at least fifteen years younger than me. It'd be like, like…'

'Like me fancying Faith?' he said, grinning. I felt

uncomfortable. Was he saying he *did* fancy her? Or was he trying to wind me up because he knew I'd felt a bit … not jealous, not really, just sort of…

'Well, she's still a good-looking woman,' I said carefully.

'Yes, she is. She's also old enough to be my mum,' he said. I laughed.

'Only just. Can you imagine her at the OAPs' coffee morning?'

'Now that sounds like a blast.' Zack stood behind Tony, grinning. I saw Tony's face tighten for a moment; oh yeah, he was jealous, all right. Was I pleased about that? Did a little thrill run through me at the thought of it? Now that Nathan was leaving (the emotional tummy-eel started up again), maybe I needed to look elsewhere…

Tony or no Tony, I still didn't want to think about Nathan's departure.

'You ready to get your pinny on?' I said to Zack. He nodded and clapped Tony on the back.

'Thanks for lending me your girlfriend for the night,' he said, and I nearly died on the spot. Tony's face turned bright red.

'She's not— We're just mates,' said Tony stiffly. 'And even if she was, it wouldn't be down to me to 'lend' her to anyone.' He turned back to me. 'I'll see you tomorrow,' he said, and walked away.

'Oh dear,' said Zack. 'I think I upset your boyfriend…' He grinned at me mischievously and I rolled my eyes.

'He really isn't my boyfriend,' I said, 'but don't worry about it. Today seems to be the day for over-sensitive male friends. Now get in here and sort your bloody poisonous poisson out before you annoy anyone else.'

Chapter Thirteen

Zack turned out to be a surprisingly good cook. He methodically selected his chopping boards, lined up the knives he would be using (he had brought his own set, a very high-quality, expensive-looking set as well, better than mine), and got everything ready to hand before he started. He had disposable gloves and plastic bags ready to dump the fish waste in, so as not to contaminate anything. I was impressed.

I had turned on the radio, concerned that it might be a bit awkward being alone with a bloke I didn't really know in such close proximity, but he was also surprisingly good company: chatty, but not *too* chatty, because we were both busy. And pretty soon we were both tapping our feet as we worked, then humming along to the music, and then eventually singing along at the tops of our lungs. *This* was my happy place, not standing around in front of a camera. Exciting food, good music, and friendly company. If Zack ever had enough of the movie business, I would offer him a job as my sous-chef.

He gave me a hand with peeling and chopping veg, not wanting to prepare the fish too early; *fugu sashimi,* being raw, needs to be freshly prepared and served quickly, so he didn't want it sitting around on a plate for too long.

First I prepared the seasoning for spicy *karaage* chicken. Zack grated garlic and ginger for me, which I mixed together with some of the sake rice wine and soy sauce, then plenty of freshly ground black pepper to give it a really good kick. I cut some boneless chicken thigh into bite-sized chunks, then tossed it in the marinade and left it to chill in the fridge for an hour; it wouldn't take long to fry, so again we wanted to leave the cooking of it until Zack's guests were assembled and ready to eat. I mixed up some more of the marinade for Kimi, this time leaving out the sake, and tossed in some chunks of tofu.

I peeled and chopped carrots into thin matchsticks, then did the same with a large purple sweet potato I found lurking in the cupboard. I sliced an aubergine and cut a head of broccoli into florets, then chopped the stalk (which is surprisingly flavoursome, but which everyone chucks out) into thin strips, like the carrot. I set them aside for frying in tempura batter.

I mixed the miso paste with sesame oil, then added more of the grated ginger, some runny honey, and a good squeeze of lime juice. I tossed a handful of cherry tomatoes into the dressing, then roasted them in the oven, using the leftover dressing to marinade some more tofu. As I shut the fridge door I sent up a prayer of thanks to the gods of YouTube, who had taught me everything I know about Japanese cooking. Of course, they hadn't taught me everything *they* knew about Japanese cooking, so I was hoping I'd learnt enough.

Zack and I worked well together in the small space, and after the emotional ups and downs of Nathan (*don't say it*) leaving (*dammit!*) and my sudden interest in Tony's chest, it was something of a respite to be in close proximity to a handsome young man whom I had absolutely no interest in (sexually or emotionally) and who I knew felt exactly the same about me. I kind of wished I hadn't witnessed Tony's tight trousers or his Mr Darcy-esque dog rescue; it was confusing me. He was my friend, for God's sake. Nathan— But there was no point thinking about Nathan, was there? Liverpool was too far away, and I wasn't into long-distance relationships; they always petered out eventually…

'Hello, Zack.' Aiko had the same distinctive Japanese-American accent as her sister, but it was far less strident and demanding; it felt more Japanese, somehow, while her sister seemed firmly American. Zack looked up and smiled at her through the flap in the side of the food truck. I'd left it open, as the truck tended to get stuffy when cooking, plus we needed to see when the guests were ready.

'All right, Aiko?' he said, and bless him, he stuttered a little bit; he had it bad. 'Is it that time already? I was going to set some lights up out there and everything.'

She smiled and shook her head. 'I'm a little early. But I don't think we can eat out here. It's cold, and it's just started to rain. Kimi doesn't like the cold.'

'Kimi can stay at home, then,' he said gruffly, and she laughed.

'But it's her party.'

'Not only hers.'

I had shuffled discreetly away from them, as far as I could, but the truck was too small. I didn't want to listen to them but I could hardly help it. I cleared my throat.

'Why don't you eat in your trailer?' I said. 'We can carry all the food over. It'll be more intimate…'

Zack blushed a little bit, making Aiko smile. *Aww she likes him too!* I thought, feeling all maternal for my sous-chef. My love life might be in tatters but it didn't mean I didn't want Zack to be happy.

'Go on,' I said. 'Go and set everything up, then come back and do the fish when you're ready. All this stuff needs cooking kind of at the last minute, so I'll just get it ready and wait for you.'

'Are you sure?' said Zack, looking at me gratefully. I smiled.

'Of course. This might be my kitchen – for the moment – but it's your party. Go on.' I gave him a little shove.

'All right, all right, I'm going! Jeez…' He grinned and slipped the apron off over his head. 'I've got everything in my trailer anyway, so I won't be long.'

'Don't forget your cakes!' I nodded towards the cake box. He looked surprised.

'What cakes?'

'You mean you didn't order them?' I lifted the lid and he peered in.

'Oh, wow, they are *sick*…' From the expression on his face I assumed that meant 'amazing', although I wouldn't have chosen that word to describe something I was about to eat. 'One of the others must've ordered them. Niiice.'

He turned away from the counter so Aiko couldn't see him, and tugged at his T-shirt, smartening himself up.

'You look lovely,' I said, and he smiled ruefully.

'Is it obvious?'

'That you fancy the pants off Aiko? Er yeah, just a bit. Go get her, Tiger!'

He laughed. 'Thanks, Mum. I won't be long.'

Left alone, I turned the radio down and the truck's heater up; I was standing inside what was basically a big, poorly insulated tin can, and it was starting to get chilly, especially without the warmth of another body nearby. I cleared the serving counter and pulled it up, closing off the truck from the outside world. I turned on some more lights; it was dark outside now, and even during the day, with the counter flap shut, the one small window at the end of the room didn't let in much natural light.

Outside, the rain was starting to get heavier. It beat against the roof of the truck. I turned the heater up full and put the kettle on to boil as I cleared away all the prep stuff and got everything ready to cook. I looked at my watch; I'd told Zack to take however long he needed because I liked him and I wanted to give him some time alone with Aiko, but I was beginning to regret my generosity. I was beginning to think longingly of my nice warm house, and my nice warm dog, and my slippers… Oh God, I was becoming middle-aged. It wasn't even late; it was only 7 p.m.

There was a rumble of thunder and the lights flickered…

Luckily, I am a hardened ex-copper and I am

perpetually wearing my big-girl pants, so I wasn't freaked out. The weather was bad. Of course it was; it was autumn, almost winter. And of course the lights were flickering; I was in a caravan, hooked up to a generator that had already packed up once today. There wasn't some ridiculous curse, locking women in caravans, exploding lightbulbs or tripping power breakers—

The door of the food truck rattled and a small, involuntary shriek escaped from me. I casually picked up Zack's filleting knife that was lying on the chopping board closest to me, and flexed my arm. *Bring it on,* I thought.

'Whew, it's getting wild out there!' Zack stepped cheerfully inside the truck, giving himself a little shake like a soggy dog. He saw me holding the knife and gave me a curious look.

'Just admiring your set of knives,' I said, turning the blade over in my hand and looking at it appreciatively. 'Very nice. Professional.' I put it down again, feeling a bit daft. 'Let's get cooking, shall we?'

I mixed together plain flour, potato starch, and ice water to make the tempura batter then popped it into the fridge. I took the black-pepper-and-sake-marinated *karaage* chicken and tofu chunks, dusted them with more of the potato starch to make them nice and crispy, and turned on Gino's deep-fat fryer to heat.

Zack, meanwhile, had started on the pufferfish. I watched him cut around the mouth of the fish and pull off the skin; there were no scales, and it really was unlike every other fish I'd ever seen. There was a layer of jelly underneath which he carefully washed off with a paper towel before removing the eyes. He dumped skin, eyes, and paper towel in a plastic bag, then took the sharp filleting knife I'd, ahem, admired earlier and very, very carefully gutted the fish. He slowly, gently removed the ovaries and the liver – these were the organs that contained most of the toxin, and if they were punctured it would contaminate the whole fish. His face was a picture of pure concentration; his hand was steady – far steadier than mine would have been under the circumstances.

He finished gutting the fish and let his breath out slowly, then placed the fish waste in the plastic bag, discarding the gloves with it. I picked up a tea towel and reached over to mop his brow.

'Well done, doctor,' I said, and he laughed.

'Yeah, reckon I could do open-heart surgery now,' he said. 'One down…'

The fryer had reached the right temperature, so I turned my attention to the *karaage* chicken and tofu. The tofu went in first, and it only took a couple of minutes to turn it into something hot, crispy, and hopefully tasty. I left it to drain on kitchen paper and started on the chicken, cooking it in batches. It smelt wonderful; I tried a small piece, and it tasted great too.

I piled the food into bowls, watching as Zack arranged the fugu on a serving dish. I flash-fried the miso-dressed tofu with some spring onions in a wok, and tossed it through the drained soba noodles, along with the roasted cherry tomatoes. Finally, I sprinkled the chopped vegetables with seasoned flour and dipped them in the tempura batter, then fried them up until they were hot, crisp, and golden. Everything went in the lidded serving trays Gino used on the hot buffet; they were very handy as although the rain had eased somewhat it hadn't stopped.

The door of the food truck rattled again as Aiko stuck her head round it.

'Kimi says she's getting hungry,' she said. I admired her restraint; I'd have been rolling my eyes or telling Kimi to cook her own blasted food if she was that hungry. But I didn't say anything. Zack just smiled at his beloved (aww!).

'Your timing is perfect,' he said (*like the rest of you,* I thought). 'We just finished. You can help me carry everything over.' He suddenly slapped his forehead. 'What are we going to drink? I hadn't even thought about it. I didn't think I should get any beer, not with Jeremy coming.'

Aiko smiled. 'That's very considerate of you. But

Mike's bringing some sake anyway.' Her tone of voice made it clear what she thought about Mike and his sake. Zack and I exchanged looks and laughed.

'Oh dear. What's wrong with it?' I asked.

'It's *nigori* sake,' she said, distastefully. Which didn't make it any clearer for me.

Zack nodded. 'Right… That's the cloudy white sake, isn't it? The unfiltered stuff?'

'Well, it is still filtered, but not in the same way, and the taste is less … subtle. It's very American,' she explained.

'Big and brash?' I suggested, and she smiled.

'Exactly. It *is* Japanese, but it's far more popular in the States than at home. The flavours are very strong, which the Americans seem to like, but in Japan we prefer something that doesn't overwhelm the food. I wouldn't even think of serving it at a dinner party, but Mike was so pleased with himself for finding some that it would be rude not to drink it.'

'Well, our cooking might not be completely authentic, but hopefully you'll want to eat it because it tastes good and not just to be polite,' I said. She sniffed at the bowl of *karaage* chicken and smiled.

'It smells delicious. And it looks like the real thing, too!' she said.

I offered to help carry everything to the trailer, but Zack was adamant that the two of them could manage, so out they went in a good-natured bustle of stainless-steel dishes and romantic hopes (on one side, at least). I shut the door after them and sat on one of the folding chairs, suddenly feeling very old and very, very alone.

A fresh burst of rain spattered against the window at the end of the truck, and there was a flash of lightning. The lights flickered again. I decided I wouldn't hang around waiting for the generator to conk out; I'd clean down and get everything shipshape for tomorrow. Zack could wash up what was left on his own; I wasn't going to sit here and wait for his party to finish.

I tied the handles of the plastic rubbish bag full of fish waste together and put it by the door, then did the same with the bag of vegetable peelings and other junk; they could go in the big plastic wheelie bin in the courtyard when I left. I carefully washed down the chopping board and knives that Zack had used, first with hot, soapy water and then with bleach; I didn't want to take any chances with possible contamination from the pufferfish guts.

I had just filled the sink with more hot soapy water and plunged my hands in when the lights went out. *Oh, wonderful,* I thought. There are few less convenient places to find yourself during a blackout than with your hands in a sink full of soapy water (although I can think of a couple, both of which involve having your pants down), particularly when that sink is situated in a cramped caravan full of sharp utensils, parked in the grounds of a remote country manor house. During a thunderstorm. On a cursed film set.

Stop it, stop it, stop it! I told myself. Stop thinking about stupid curses. There was an ominous rumble of thunder – but then let's face it, *all* rumbles of thunder are ominous – as I fumbled along the counter for a tea towel. There was a crash as I knocked something on the floor. So *that* wasn't the tea towel.

'Bugger,' I muttered, and it felt weird, talking to myself in the silent food truck. Silent, apart from the meteorological Armageddon that suddenly seemed to be taking place outside.

The door rattled. I froze. Was it just the wind that had picked up and was clearly thinking about howling around the trailers? Was Zack coming back for more noodles? Was it the Phantom Shoot Saboteur, coming to … what? Hide all the tea towels? I laughed (almost) to myself; if he (or she) turned up now, I'd have to ask them what on earth they were trying to achieve, because so far they'd just been bloody irritating…

The door opened with a bang and I shrieked.

'Jodie?'

The lights came on and there stood Nathan on the steps, soaking wet, peering anxiously inside. I almost collapsed with relief.

'Oh sweet holy mother of— Come in, you berk!' I

said, reaching out to haul him in out of the rain by his coat lapels. He tripped over the doorstep and put out a hand to stop himself falling over, and ended up clutching at me, his arm half around my waist. He pulled himself upright but didn't let go, and stared into my eyes. I felt my knees turn to jelly, not from being within swooning distance of him, I told myself, but as a delayed reaction to the shock. Yeah, I didn't believe it either.

'I'm sorry. I didn't mean to scare you,' he said, looking slightly alarmed himself. I forced my knees to behave and straightened myself up.

'I wasn't scared!' I said. *Methinks the lady doth protest too much,* whispered the little voice in my head.

'Yeah, right.' Nathan grinned. 'It's a good job you weren't, because I was terrified.'

I laughed, noticing that neither of us was in a hurry to move apart. Even though he was bundled up in a thick coat, I could smell his aftershave, or deodorant, or whatever it was; he always smelt so nice and clean…

'So what brings you out on a night like this?' I asked him, gazing up at him in what I hoped was a coquettish fashion, rather than looking like I'd lost one of my contact lenses. He took a deep breath.

'Jodie,' he began. He seemed nervous. My tummy-eel decided to do a quick lap of my lower intestine. Did he (Nathan, not my tummy-eel, which was just as likely to be female as it was male) … did he have some news about his new job? Did I want to hear it? Would it be bad? Should I stop asking stupid hypothetical questions and babbling about imaginary aquatic creatures living in my abdomen and just listen to him? Did I—?

We were both completely thrown by the loud, hysterical scream that echoed across the courtyard, and the cries for help that followed.

Chapter Fourteen

We dashed outside and looked around. On the other side of the courtyard, the door of Zack's trailer had been flung open. Zack stood in the doorway for a second, looking around wildly, then ran down the steps towards us. We met him in the middle of the yard, Nathan pulling his coat up over his head and attempting to shelter me with it too. I noticed and thought it was sweet, even amidst the panic.

'What's happened?' asked Nathan. Zack shook his head.

'Aww man, it's bad, it's so bad—'

'Calm down!' I ordered. 'What is it? What's the matter?'

'He's dead!' cried Kimi dramatically. She stood in the doorway of the trailer, cradling her dog in her arms.

'What? Who? The dog?' Nathan and I exchanged looks – it would be typical of a bunch of actors to overreact – but then the dog wriggled and barked, and we realised she wasn't talking about her fur baby. Nathan shook his head impatiently and made for the trailer. He bounded up the steps but I was right behind him.

Inside, Faith sat on the other side of the trailer, eyes wide in horror at the scene before her. There had been seven for dinner, and they'd all crammed into the small space around the table, four on the built-in seating and the rest on fold-up chairs. It can't have been that comfortable, but it should have been intimate and fun. Except the fun had stopped and the chairs had been tipped over, as Sam and Mike knelt down next to the body on the floor.

Aiko stood by the sink, drinking a glass of water with trembling hands and looking down at Jeremy, who was sprawled out on the floor. A puddle of vomit lay next to him.

'Oh my God…' I said, horrified. Nathan carefully stepped around the body, then looked up at Zack, who had followed us back in.

'Has anyone called an ambulance?' he asked. Zack didn't speak, still too shocked to do anything except stare at his late co-star.

'Zack,' I said. 'Zack! Pull yourself together!'

'He's dead,' said Sam. 'I can't find a pulse.'

'We still need an ambulance,' said Nathan firmly. He handed me his phone. 'Call it in for me. Ring Matt Turner.'

I found the number of DS Turner and spoke to him, explaining the situation as Nathan gently but firmly ushered the other guests out of the trailer, making sure they didn't touch anything. Kimi's was next door, so he herded them in there and shut the door on them, then joined me back in Zack's trailer.

'Holy crap,' I said, as I finished the call. Nathan nodded.

'What the hell has gone on here?' he said, squatting down next to Jeremy. I joined him, gingerly; I've seen quite a few bodies in my time but it's never pleasant, and there was something about the tortured expression on Jeremy's face and in his contorted, claw-like hands. Something that had begun to ring a very loud bell.

'Oh my God...' I said, horrified, as I realised what his twisted body reminded me of. Nathan reached out to check for a pulse in his neck and I snatched his hand out of the way. 'Don't touch him!' I cried out. Nathan looked surprised. 'There might be a possibility of contamination.'

'What...?'

'He's quite clearly dead. But look at him. Look at the

way his hands are clenched.' I swallowed. 'I've seen that before. Haven't you?'

Nathan looked at me keenly. 'What is it? What are you thinking?'

I stood up and moved to the other side of the trailer, where I couldn't see Jeremy's vacant staring eyes; they were freaking me out slightly. To my immense relief, Nathan stood up and joined me.

'You remember the Salisbury poisonings?' I asked. Nathan nodded.

'Of course I do. The Russian guy and his daughter, and the poor local lady who died. Novichok poisoning.' He raised an eyebrow sardonically. 'You're not telling me Jeremy was poisoned by Russian spies?'

'No, of course not. But one of the Salisbury coppers got sick from touching something at the scene, so the Met taught us how to recognise the signs in case there were other attacks. There are a lot of Russians in London, you know…' I gave a hollow laugh. 'Daisy was already keen for me to leave the force, but that, and then the nutter with the van, they were the final straw.' I'd left the Met after a terrorist had driven a van at a crowd of people I'd been helping to evacuate from a tube station following a hoax bomb threat. 'Anyway, I'm no expert, but this looks like a nerve agent.' I swallowed hard. 'A neurotoxin. Like the toxic substance in pufferfish.'

The police came, and the ambulance, but as we already knew, it was too late for Jeremy. Scene of Crime had come along as a matter of course; they always attended, wherever possible, when an unexpected or unusual death had occurred. Nathan told them of my suspicions, and as pufferfish poisoning wasn't exactly a common cause of death in the UK, let alone in sleepy Cornwall, every precaution was taken; I wasn't the only one who'd had training after the Salisbury incident in 2018. The trailer was cordoned off, and officers in disposable gloves, masks, and overalls went in to examine the body. *The body*. It hadn't taken long for him to go from being Jeremy to 'the body'. It always felt wrong to me, somehow, to stop using the victim's name so quickly. It was like you were reducing someone to the lowest common denominator: alive or dead. The deceased.

I sighed. I always get philosophical when I'm tired.

'I know nothing about pufferfish,' began Nathan.

'You surprise me.'

He smiled. 'Good, I do try. I know nothing about pufferfish, but is there any reason why Jeremy would have a reaction to it but not the others?'

I stared at him. There was a horrible feeling in my gut that had nothing to do with that over-emotional eel I'd had problems with earlier. 'Oh God, I hadn't even thought about that. It's nothing to do with having an allergic reaction or anything. It's mega toxic. If they all ate it, they'll all get sick.'

'So assuming all or at least some of them did eat it, why is there only one dead body on the carpet?' asked Nathan.

'Has anyone checked Kimi's caravan to make sure they're all still alive in there?' I asked. We looked at each other, then hightailed it up the steps to the leading lady's trailer. We nodded to PC Trelawney – or Old Davey, as he was known, despite not being that old (that's a famous Penstowan long story) – who was stationed on the door, and went inside, half expecting to see the rest of them laid out on the floor.

Thankfully, they weren't. Everyone was sitting quietly, wrapped up in their own thoughts. Zack and Aiko sat together, holding hands, which made me feel glad for a moment, although quite how she would react when we told them what we suspected the cause of death to be, I didn't know. I *did* know, however, that by the look of abject misery and guilt on Zack's face, he already knew.

'Thank you for waiting,' said Nathan. Mike Mancuso snorted.

'Like we got a choice.'

Faith looked annoyed. 'A *good* man died tonight. Have some respect,' she spat. I noticed the slight emphasis on *good,* and it struck me as being a little odd, but then maybe she just didn't like Mancuso. He was loud, brash, and a touch abrasive, and he perhaps wasn't the best company to be cooped up with in a caravan, certainly not after losing a friend and colleague in such horrible circumstances.

'Can you tell us exactly what happened to Mr Mayhew?' asked Nathan. Everyone immediately opened their mouths and began talking, so Nathan held up his hand and turned to Sam. 'You, please. Mr…?'

'Pritchard. Sam Pritchard. Well, we were all sitting around the table eating, everything was great, and then Jeremy started acting kinda weird, like he was drunk—'

'Was that weird for him?' I asked. 'I understand he had a drink problem.'

'He was fighting it,' said Faith. 'He was on the wagon, until tonight.'

'Yeah,' said Sam. 'And he'd only drunk a little, which was what made me notice it. And then he just kinda went rigid, like he couldn't move. He couldn't even open his mouth, because he was trying to say something…'

Aiko shuddered, and I saw Zack reach over with his free hand to squeeze hers.

'And then he started moaning and had a seizure, and ended up on the floor, vomiting, and then he just … stopped. Dead.'

I shivered. What a horrible way to die. Nathan wrote everything down in his notebook, then looked up.

'It's too early for us to say for definite what caused Mr Mayhew's death, but at this stage it appears to be misadventure rather than a deliberate act, so—'

Zack looked up at me, then at Nathan, and said quietly, 'It was the pufferfish, wasn't it?'

'Until we get lab results back…' said Nathan calmly, but Zack shook his head and stared straight at me, a hint of pleading in his eyes; he just wanted to know the truth.

'It was, wasn't it?'

I couldn't say yes for certain, but the poor young man was in an agony of not knowing and I wanted to relieve him of it if I could; although, of course, that would lead to the even worse agony of *knowing*, knowing that he'd been responsible (albeit unintentionally) for someone's death.

'We really don't know for certain, Zack, but that's what it looks like,' I said. Kimi looked at him in fury.

'What do you mean, it was the pufferfish? The *fugu*? You told me you knew what you were doing!' she hissed at him. She shot to her feet, clutching Princess the Pekinese to her chest as if she were going to flounce out of the trailer. Except it was her trailer, and she didn't have anywhere else to flounce off to at the moment.

'I *do* know what I'm doing!' he protested, then subsided. 'At least, I thought I did. I trained in Japan—'

'Well you obviously didn't train hard enough!' spat Kimi. She rounded on me. 'You. You were supposed to be keeping an eye on him. What kind of goddamn chef are you?'

I felt my cheeks flush. Because yes, I *was* the chef, and maybe the buck should have stopped with me. But I'd watched him and I had been so pleasantly surprised, impressed, and in actual awe of his filleting skills that it hadn't even crossed my mind to stop him serving it. I wasn't sure what to say, but by now Kimi had turned on someone else: Sam.

'And you! How could you ever let him think this was a good idea? This has put the whole movie into jeopardy, hasn't it? You totally should have put your foot down and told him he couldn't serve it.'

'I told him it was fine,' said Mancuso. Faith looked up sharply and glared at him. 'What? It's eating raw fish, for Chrissakes, it ain't diving with sharks.'

'Except it killed Jeremy,' said Zack, his words heavy with enough guilt and grief to silence everyone else. 'I killed him.'

Aiko wrapped her arms around him as he buried his head in her shoulder. Kimi, who was still standing, watched her sister, her lip curled with disgust and her foot tapping angrily.

'When you've *quite* finished,' she said, 'perhaps you'd like to tell me what's going to happen to everyone else who's eaten this killer fish. Hmm? Has no one else thought of that?'

I looked at Nathan; we'd needed to warn them that they might feel some ill effects too, but Kimi was going to make them hysterical and convinced they were all going to die if we weren't careful. And to be fair, what I knew about pufferfish you could probably write on the back of a postage stamp, so who knew? Maybe they *would* all die. But I didn't think so.

The others were starting to look alarmed. We had to nip this in the bud. I looked at Nathan with a question on my face: *may I?*

'Knock yourself out,' he murmured.

'Okay, I'm not an expert, but the speed with which Mr Mayhew took ill and then died suggests to me that he either had more of the fish, and therefore more of the toxin, than the rest of you; or, that the toxin wasn't distributed evenly throughout the fish, and he was unfortunate enough to get a piece that was more heavily contaminated than the rest, meaning that you may have got lucky and been given a portion that was less toxic, or even not toxic at all. Or the final possibility is that he had some underlying health condition that may have made him more susceptible.' I looked around at the assembled guests. 'Basically, the fact that he's dead and the rest of you are all still standing suggests to me that none of you are about to join him.'

Aiko swallowed hard. 'I feel nauseous,' she said. Sam nodded.

'I do, too,' he said.

Nathan and I exchanged looks that said, *oh crap.*

'Okay,' he said. 'There are cars outside. Maybe we should get you all checked out at the hospital—'

'But there's no antidote, is there?' said Zack. *Shut up!* I thought. 'We'll just have to ride it out.'

'What do you mean, 'ride it out'?' demanded Kimi, angrily.

'He means you're just gonna have to get sick, and if you're lucky you won't die,' said Mancuso. It was a rather more brutal way of saying what Nathan and I had been thinking, but at least it shut them up.

Chapter Fifteen

The diners got themselves together as Nathan arranged cars to take them all to the nearest hospital, in Barnstaple. Although there were already a couple of police cars on the scene, we decided it would be prudent (and less conspicuous) to use unmarked ones. The last thing Mike and Sam wanted was word getting out about Jeremy, at least not until they'd spoken to the movie's investors, and the last thing Nathan wanted was swarms of press in Penstowan, crawling over the town, pestering him, and getting in the way of the investigation. The slightest whiff of fame was enough to set some of them off, and the scent of a celebrity death, probably caused by *another* celebrity, would be sure to cause a stampede to our little part of the world.

Aiko was naturally very pale, but she was starting to

look even paler. She really did not look well. Zack saw me watching her as she went to get into a car, and gave me a wan smile.

'Well, this ain't quite the end of the night I was hoping for,' he said. 'But I caused this, and I feel fine, so I'm going to stay with her in the hospital and look after her.'

I patted him on the back. 'Don't beat yourself up over this,' I said. 'It was an accident.'

'I won't,' he said, but I could see by the look in his eyes that he would never forgive himself, even if everybody else did.

The first two cars departed, leaving Nathan to drive Faith and Kimi. Kimi had looked massively put out when Aiko had got in the car with Zack, and Faith hadn't looked too keen on sharing with Kimi and her dog, but that was tough.

Nathan was on the phone. He ended the call and turned to me. 'That was Dr Hawkins at the hospital. They've managed to find beds for everyone, and she's on standby in case they need her. Not that there's anything much she can do except try and be reassuring.'

I watched Kimi fussing over her dog inside the car. 'It must be scary, knowing you've eaten something that could kill you. Did she say how long it could take for it to affect someone?'

Nathan shook his head. 'She really doesn't know. But

her educated guess is that if it's going to do anything, it'll do it tonight. Hopefully the worst that will happen is a headache and vomiting until it's out of their system.' He looked at me, a wry smile on his face. 'Why is it that every time I try to have a serious conversation with you, a dead body turns up?'

I smiled. 'Maybe fate is trying to tell you something.'

'I hope not.' He looked into my eyes. 'Jodie—'

In the front passenger seat of Nathan's car, Faith had obviously got sick of waiting because she leaned across and pressed the car horn, making us both jump.

'Keep your hair on,' muttered Nathan.

'To be fair, she might be feeling poorly herself,' I said.

'Yeah.' He looked at me, suddenly serious. 'Do you feel all right? You were there with Zack when he was preparing the food. Did you try any of it? Or touch anything?'

'No, no, I'm fine. I still can't believe that he did anything wrong, to be honest. I was really impressed with his knife skills. Anyway, I cleaned down with soapy water and bleach, so if there was any toxin on my hands it'll be long gone. And you? You didn't touch anything at the scene?'

'No.' We became aware of Faith who had turned around in her seat and was glaring at us. He shook himself. 'I'd better take them.' He reached out to touch my arm. 'Take care, okay? I'll see you tomorrow.'

'Okay. See you tomorrow,' I said. It felt completely inadequate.

I got home around 9.45 p.m. Daisy was already in bed, Germaine with her, but the dog padded softly down the stairs to greet me as I shut the front door. I could hear the theme tune to *Mile End Days* from the living room; Mum must be watching it on catch-up. I wasn't sure I could watch it anymore, not now I'd met landlady Clara Brown in real life. Faith had not lived up to her public image – not as far as I was concerned anyway – and I didn't think it was just because she'd tried to monopolise Tony.

I made a fuss of Germaine and tiptoed up the stairs, hoping Daisy would still be awake because I really needed a cuddle; but when I stood in the doorway of her room I could hear her steady breathing, and I knew she was in the Land of Nod. I toyed with the idea of accidentally-on-purpose making a noise and waking her up, but soon dismissed it. I'd done that once when she was a baby and had regretted it immediately – and for the next three hours during which she'd cried solidly.

'Night-night, sweetheart,' I whispered, and went back downstairs, Germaine following quietly. At least I could cuddle the dog.

'I thought I heard you come in.' Mum looked up as I

entered the living room and flopped on the sofa. Germaine jumped up next to me and put her head on my lap, gazing up at me adoringly. When she'd first come to us I'd had such good intentions about not letting her get up on the furniture, and they'd lasted all of about five minutes. 'Did Nathan find you?'

'What?' I was surprised. 'Did he come here?'

Mum nodded. 'Yes, didn't he find you?'

'Yeah, he did. He didn't say he'd come here first…'

'He said he really needed to talk to you,' said Mum. 'Poor Nathan, he must have a lot on his plate, what with his dad being ill and so far away. Did you have a talk?'

'Not really. We got distracted.' Mum grinned at me and I rolled my eyes. 'Not like *that*,' I said, aware of a note of disappointment in my voice. 'Stuff happened, that's all.'

'What stuff?'

I groaned. I knew she'd pester me until I told her, but she was about as good at keeping secrets as ducks are at basketball. I fixed her with a stern glare.

'If I tell you, you cannot say anything,' I said.

'When have I ever gossiped?' she asked, all innocence. I guffawed loudly. 'Okay, I might be one for spreading the local news, but that's not the same as gossiping, is it?'

'Erm, yes, yes, it is. I mean it, Mum, you can't tell

anyone. It'll be all over the news soon enough and then you can say you already knew, but not before then.'

She looked at me with wide eyes. 'Blimey, what happened? Tell me!'

I sighed. 'Jeremy Mayhew died at the dinner party tonight.'

She gasped – a genuine gasp of surprise. 'Not that bloke from *Bagnall*? Daisy was just saying earlier how good he was.'

I nodded. 'Him.'

'Oh no! What a waste. Proper 'andsum in his younger days, he was. I wouldn't have said no to him even now, to be honest.'

'Mum! The poor bugger's dead. Have some respect.'

'How's it disrespectful to say he was a looker? He was a proper bad boy when he was younger, always in the papers... So what happened?'

I hesitated. It was looking ninety-nine per cent certain that the pufferfish had done for him, and that it was therefore Zack's fault, but I so wanted it *not* to be his fault that I didn't want to blame him until we knew, absolutely, definitely, one hundred per cent what the cause of death was. So I just said, 'We're not sure. We think it was something he ate.' Which was true.

'Oh, that's terrible! Not something you cooked?'

I flushed. 'No, not something I cooked! It was ... an

allergy or something. We don't know yet. It happened very quickly.'

'Poor man. Nasty way to go.' She was right. It must have been very nasty.

Mum went to bed not long after. I changed into my pjs and made myself a hot chocolate, then went to read in bed, but I couldn't concentrate. My eyes went back over the same words, over and over again, without taking anything in. Eventually I gave up and just let myself think. Maybe it *had* been an allergy? Maybe that was why none of the others had been affected. Aiko and Sam had both complained of nausea, but the upset of the evening was enough to make anyone feel ill; it could just have been shock. Lots of people seemed to have allergies these days. Look at Kimi, with her long list of dietary requirements – although I wasn't sure whether they were genuine or just her being faddy.

I reached into my bedside drawer and rifled around in it until I was forced to concede there was no paper in there, then went downstairs, found a writing pad and pen, and went back to bed. I propped myself up comfortably on the pillows, made room for Germaine (who had gone back to her usual spot by Daisy's feet, but had come in to see what all the commotion was about and decided my bed was comfier), and started writing.

I was woken the next morning by the ping of a text message reaching my phone, which I'd left on top of my chest of drawers. My first thought was that it was Nathan, telling me someone else had died, but when I dragged myself across the room and read it, bleary-eyed, I saw that it was a group message from the film production office, telling all extras that filming had been temporarily suspended. *That's going to put the cat amongst the pigeons,* I thought, and sure enough about ten minutes later I got a text from Tony, making sure I'd got the message and asking me if I knew what was going on … to which I replied that yes, I had seen it, but I didn't answer his question. And then five minutes later Debbie rang me.

'What's the goss?' she asked, the minute I answered.

'Good morning to you too,' I said, stifling a yawn.

'Yeah, yeah, whatever,' she said. 'Come on, spill. Callum saw Tony last night and he said you were still at the shoot, doing some dinner party. And then the next day everything grinds to a halt. What did you do? Slip some arsenic in Faith's pudding to stop her flirting with Tony?'

'No, I didn't bloody poison anyone! And why would I care about her flirting with Tony?' I said, although of course I sort of *did* care.

'So why has shooting stopped?'

'What makes you think I'd know?'

She snorted. 'Because you're so bloomin' nosey.'

I sighed. It was a fair cop. I opened my mouth, not knowing what I was going to say, but was saved by a beep as another call came in: Nathan.

'Sorry, Nathan's calling me,' I said, 'and quite frankly he's better looking than you, so...'

She laughed. 'I ain't one to stand in the way of true love,' she said, because of course she had no idea that Nathan was leaving. I blinked hard, refusing to accept the sudden tears that threatened my eyes. 'Off you go. Say hi to him from me.'

She hung up, and I answered Nathan's call.

'Morning,' I said, with forced cheeriness.

'Morning. How are you? No sickness or anything?' he asked.

'No, I'm fine. What about the other diners? Anyone else popped their clogs?'

'I don't know. I haven't rung the hospital yet,' he said. 'I wanted to check on you first.' I felt my heart swell; I'd been the first person he'd thought of. It was lucky I was already sitting on my bed or I might've swooned. 'And of course they'd have rung me if anyone had died.' Well yes, there was that, of course…

'So anyway, I've been thinking…' I said, and he groaned.

'Here we go,' he said, but it was good-natured.

'How long until we get the lab results back about cause of death?' I asked. He laughed.

'You mean how long 'til *I* get the results back. *I'm* the police, remember?'

'Sorry, Detective Chief Inspector, I know my place.'

He laughed again at that. He had a nice laugh. 'Yeah, right. I think a pig just flew over my head… It helps that the lab knows what they're looking for, so with any luck we'll hear back by the end of the day if there was tetrodotoxin – pufferfish toxin – in the victim's bloodstream. They'll do a full screening, but that'll probably take longer.'

'Okay, so until then we shouldn't assume anything, should we? We shouldn't rule out other causes.'

He sighed. 'Here we really do go again. Are you telling me you don't think Zack did it? Because you were the one who mentioned pufferfish in the first place.'

'I know, and I still think that was the cause of death.'

'But…?'

'Oh, I don't know…' I lay back on the bed, momentarily wishing Nathan and I were having this conversation in person, right there on my duvet. Or preferably under it. 'I hate the thought of Zack being responsible. He's a nice bloke and the guilt will do his head in.'

'I didn't speak to him much last night, but yeah, he seems like a nice fella. It was an accident, though.'

'Yeah,' I said, but for some reason that made me feel uneasy. I shook my head. 'Anyway, all I was really going to say is, I've made a list of everything that was in the meal last night, every single ingredient we used, and I think we should get everyone who was there to make their own list of everything they ate. Just to see what correlation there is between who was sick, if any of them were, and exactly what they ate. I mean, I've never seen pufferfish poisoning before – I've never seen *any* neurotoxin at work, apart from on my training course – so I could be totally wrong.'

'Hmm…' Nathan sounded thoughtful. 'Fair enough. Even if it was the fish, it's still weird that Jeremy Mayhew died so quickly, while the rest of them were fine. They were, last I heard, anyway. I should probably go and check…'

We made arrangements to meet at Polvarrow House later on; Nathan had to go back to the death scene and I needed to check on the food truck – I'd left it in a bit of a hurry the night before and I was very aware of the fact that it wasn't mine.

I could hear Daisy getting up, and then Mum moving

around in the spare room (which was really her bedroom, but we still called it the spare room to maintain the illusion that she was a strong, independent woman with her own home and she was only staying over as a favour to me). It was a school morning, and the madness was about to begin.

I flopped back onto my pillow, trying to ignore the fact that I needed to get up and be a responsible adult. I shut my eyes and hoped with all my heart that this wouldn't be the last case I got to investigate with Nathan.

Chapter Sixteen

I managed to get Daisy to school without telling her too much about the night before. She wanted to hear all about Zack, and I'd half-forgotten she was signed up as an extra too so she'd also got a text message about the shoot being cancelled. I told her it was probably just some technical hold-up and that she hadn't lost her chance at stardom, then Germaine and I dropped her off at the gates and were about to drive away when Debbie leapt in front of the car.

'Oh no you don't, missus!' she said, blocking my way. 'There is so much you're not telling me…' I had to admit defeat and go for a coffee with her.

We sat in Rowe's – where the scent of freshly baked pasties and sausage rolls was enough to make a true Cornishman (or woman) weep with longing and

Germaine, who had tucked herself under the table, salivate all over my trainers – waiting for the waitress to bring our drinks over.

'Thank you.' I smiled up at the woman who, like at least three-quarters of this town's inhabitants I vaguely recognised (possibly from school, although it was just as likely to be from coming into the bakery all the bloomin' time), and stirred my cappuccino as I waited for Debbie to start grilling me.

She took a deep breath (oh, this was going to be one heck of a grilling, I could feel it) and opened her mouth. But before she could speak, the thing that had really been on my mind since I'd learnt about it yesterday – even more than Jeremy's death – burst out of my mouth before I could stop it.

'Nathan's leaving,' I blurted. She stopped mid-mouth-opening with such a look of surprise on her face that I almost laughed. But then I remembered what I'd just said and didn't feel like laughing after all.

'What?' she said, looking stunned. 'When? Why? What are you talking about?'

'His old boss back in Liverpool has offered him a job. And his parents are getting on and his dad's ill, and his ex still lives there and—'

'Bloody hell!' she said, still looking gobsmacked. 'I can't believe it. When's he going?'

'I don't know,' I said. I felt sick. I fiddled with a sachet of sugar, my fingers turning it over and over, just as my thoughts were turning over and over in my mind.

'Well, he's a dark horse, ain't he? Has he told his ex?'

'No, no, he said he's not in touch with her anymore. I believe him. But it's a really good job, and it'll be near his parents.'

Debbie leaned back in her chair, shaking her head. 'Still, I really can't believe it. I thought … you and him… Tony'll be pleased, though.'

I looked down at the table. Tony wasn't the one I wanted, was he? There were good reasons why Tony would be the perfect man for me. Daisy loved him (but then she'd given Nathan the seal of approval after he'd eaten with us the other night), Mum loved him, Germaine loved him… And there was the small matter of that six-pack and his sudden, completely unexpected Darcy-esque hotness. Germaine gave a little whine and lay her head on my feet.

As if she knew what I was thinking, Debbie said, 'One thing's for certain, Tony'll never leave Penstowan.'

No, I thought. That was probably the main reason we'd only ever been friends, apart from those two weeks in 1994.

'Anyway,' I said, 'I don't really want to talk about it. And that's not what you ambushed me for, is it? You want the skinny on the shoot.'

'Yeah,' said Debbie, although she seemed less

interested about it now. She clearly wanted to keep discussing Nathan and Tony but I made it equally clear that I didn't. 'So what's going on?'

'You have to keep this to yourself for the moment. It will get out, but you are sworn to absolute secrecy for now.' She laughed and went to speak but I stopped her with a serious look. 'No, I mean it.'

'Okay, I promise. I won't say anything.'

I told her what had happened. She let out a loud 'WHAT?', but then shut her mouth and listened intently.

'So what'll happen to the movie now?' she asked. I shrugged.

'No idea. I suppose it depends on how many of Jeremy's scenes they've already shot. If it's only a few, they could just recast the part and shoot them again.'

'Yeah...' she said. 'Or they might be able to use a stand-in and CGI. They CGI'd Carrie Fisher into a scene in one of the newer *Star Wars* films, didn't they? They might be able to do that.'

'Maybe. But the one thing they probably can't do is just stop. They must've already poured a lot of money into it, and they won't get that back unless they finish shooting and get the film out there.'

We finished our coffees and said our goodbyes, Debbie pulling me in for a hug that took me by surprise and made me feel a bit weepy. Then Germaine and I made our way to Polvarrow House.

I was horrified to discover that I'd left the food truck in a much worse mess than I remembered. The lights had gone out while I'd been in the middle of washing up, and then Nathan had turned up, somewhat drenched and windswept and looking a little bit Heathcliff, if truth be told (although, as book boyfriends go, Heathcliff didn't really do it for me; he was a bit of a bully); it had taken all my strength to not trot out some cheesy line about 'getting out of those wet things'. And then we'd heard a scream (Kimi), and the night had descended into chaos…

I apologised to Germaine as I tethered her to the caravan steps, leaving her a long enough leash that she could have a sniff around. I left the door open so she could see I was still there, but she was too busy nosing around in the grass, following all the exciting scent trails as far as she could before being restrained by the lead.

'Sorry, sweetheart,' I said. 'I will take you for a good long W. A. L. K. later, I promise.'

I pulled the plug on the sink full of cold water and refilled it with hot soapy bubbles, putting away the bottles of cooking oil, soy sauce, and so on while I waited for it to fill. Thank God I'd remembered to turn the deep-fat fryer off the night before, otherwise there might not have been a food truck to come back to. Germaine gave a little yap and I knew someone was there before they spoke.

'All right?' I looked up to see Zack standing hesitantly in the doorway. He looked awful. I smiled sympathetically at him and motioned him inside.

'How are you this morning?' I asked. 'Were you ill last night?'

He nodded. 'Yeah, a little bit. Threw up once and felt better. Not like Aiko.' He grimaced. 'She was up nearly all night being sick, and she had a splitting headache.'

'Oh no! Is she all right now?'

'She's fine now, just really wiped out,' he said. 'They discharged her and she's back at the hotel now, resting.' He smiled, but it was a sad, almost tearful smile. 'It was pretty scary, if I'm honest. I thought I might have killed her too…'

'Oh Zack…' I gave him a big hug and we stood like that for a few seconds, while I patted him on the back and he got himself together. I stood back and looked at him seriously. 'Don't be so hard on yourself…'

He snorted. 'Who else is there to blame?'

'I know, I know, but it was an accident, wasn't it?' *Like all the other 'accidents' that have been happening,* I thought, but what else could it be? We might not have had the test results back yet, but it had definitely been something Jeremy had eaten, and one of the things he'd eaten had been the notoriously poisonous pufferfish. It *had* to be that. And yet…

And yet it niggled at me. *Something* had niggled at me when I'd spoken to Nathan earlier, but I hadn't known what it was; it had felt like a vague uneasiness, or a faint itch inside my brain. No matter how hard I tried to ignore it, it was still there, whispering to me. *Just another accident? Or something else?*

I pulled myself together. It wouldn't help Zack if I mentioned my misgivings, and they turned out to be wrong.

'What are you doing here, anyway?' I asked. 'You don't need to be on set, surely?'

'I left my knives and everything here,' he said. 'Although I don't think I'll be using them again any time soon.'

'Now that would be a waste,' I said. 'I was impressed with your knife skills last night. They're better than mine, and I went to catering college.'

He smiled and pulled himself up with a bit of mock-swagger. 'I grew up in South London, didn't I? I'm well used to knives.'

I laughed. 'Yeah, yeah, whatever. I lived in South London for the best part of twenty years, it ain't that bad.'

'Did you? Whereabouts?'

I thought about making something up, but dammit, I

was a good copper and I wasn't going to lie about it. 'I was a police officer in the Met. Based at Stockwell.'

If Zack was horrified, he managed to hide it. 'Were you? Wow. I'm from Deptford.' He leant in towards me. 'Don't tell anyone because it's bad for the image, but I never had any real run-ins with the police. I had mates that were always in trouble, but I was more likely to be at drama club than running wild.' His smile faded. 'That's all gonna change now though, ain't it?'

'Don't be daft; it was an accident. The coroner will rule it as death by misadventure. You didn't intentionally contaminate the fish, and you didn't force it down Jeremy's throat.'

He sighed. 'I still don't see how I contaminated it. I didn't puncture any of the organs, or let the skin touch the flesh, and those are the bits that contain the poison. I just don't understand it.'

I patted him on the back. 'Well, let's wait for the lab results and make sure that *is* what killed him, before you start writing off your cooking skills.'

He stared at me, a look of faint hope on his face. 'Do you think there's a chance it was something else? Like he was allergic or something?'

'Well…' I said, gently. 'Maybe. But of course you and Aiko were sick as well, weren't you? And maybe the others too.'

'Yeah…'

Poor Zack. I had washed up his knives last night, along with the chopping boards he'd used to prepare the fish, so I handed them over and sent him on his way.

I finished washing up everything else, then picked up the two bags of rubbish I'd left by the door the night before and carried them outside, making sure not to trip on the broken stair. *Like all the other 'accidents'*, I thought again. Hmm. I carried the bags over to the big rubbish dumpster in the courtyard, threw in the one of vegetable peelings and general kitchen debris, and then stopped. The other bag was full of fish waste – the internal organs and skin of the pufferfish. I turned on my heel and headed to Zack's trailer.

The trailer was cordoned off, although the forensics team had finished their initial investigation and left; as far as anyone else was concerned it was an accident. It was just me who was beginning to think it wasn't, but I had absolutely nothing to base that on.

Davey Trelawney had just come back on shift and was standing guard outside.

'All right, Davey?' I said. He nodded.

'Aye, I'm all right. Looking for the guvnor, are you?' he asked. I wondered if he knew Penstowan would be looking for a new DCI soon. I nodded.

'Is he around?'

'Just talking to the SOCO,' he said, nodding over to where a police squad car and a couple of unmarked ones were parked. Nathan was talking to a Scene of Crime officer I didn't recognise; Penstowan didn't have its own forensics people, and had to use the team based at Barnstaple.

'Thanks,' I said, grasping my bag of rubbish tightly and striding over to them. Nathan looked up as I approached, and a smile spread over his face. He quickly wiped it off and turned back to his companion, ever the professional.

'Hello,' I said. The SOCO nodded at me and went to get in his car. 'Hold on,' I said, stopping him. 'I've got a present for you.' I held up the bag of rubbish. It was starting to smell. 'Fish guts.'

He grimaced. 'You shouldn't have.'

'It didn't look like there was much food left on the plates last night, so I thought you might want to swab this lot and make sure it matches the victim's toxicology report,' I said. The SOCO looked surprised, then nodded appreciatively as he took the bag.

'Good thinking,' he said, then he looked at me. 'You're Eddie Parker's daughter, aren't you? I didn't know him very well – I hadn't been in the force long when he passed away – but he was a good bloke. Very encouraging. I've heard all about you since you've been back.'

I must've looked as alarmed as I felt because Nathan laughed. 'All good, I hope,' I said.

The SOCO grinned. 'Mostly.' He held up the stinky rubbish bag. 'Thanks for this. I'll swab it for tetrodotoxin as soon as I get back to the station and we should have the results by the end of the day, along with the toxicology report on the body.'

We watched him drive away.

'Go on, then,' said Nathan.

'What?'

'Your sixth sense is tingling, isn't it?' He turned to look at me. 'You're going to do it again, aren't you? Turn my nice, neat, cut-and-dried case into a convoluted murder mystery worthy of Sherlock Holmes.'

'I thought I was Magnum PI?' That was what he'd called me in the early days of our relationship, when we'd butted heads over the murder of Tony's ex-wife. Everything had pointed towards Tony being the killer, but I'd been convinced that I knew better and, as it turned out, I had. But when I'd told Nathan he was wrong and that I was going to investigate it myself, he'd thought it was the most hilarious thing he'd ever heard. I'd enjoyed proving him wrong. My tummy rolled over at the thought that I might not get to prove him wrong ever again.

Nathan laughed. 'I didn't know you properly then. Coffee?'

'If I say yes, does that mean we go back to the food truck and I have to make it?'

'Yes. And if you've got any biscuits floating about, I'd be happy to take them off your hands. Didn't have time for breakfast.'

'I think we can do better than that,' I said, an image of me dressed as a Fifties housewife (complete with frilly apron) making breakfast pancakes for him floating across my mind. *In his dreams!* I thought, then felt sad because that obviously wasn't in his dreams if he was leaving. I cleared my throat. 'I mean, I'll make you something if you like.'

We walked back to the truck and I made some coffee. Nathan wouldn't let me make him breakfast, but I found one of Zack's protein bars and gave him that instead. Then we sat at one of the picnic tables, Nathan bundled up in his thick coat opposite me and me wrapped in a blanket that Gino had tucked away. Germaine sniffed around Nathan's feet, hoping for a little piece of whatever he was having, then gave up and whined until I picked her up and sat her on the bench next to me, where she rested her nose in my lap.

I fumbled in my pocket and pulled out a sheet of paper as Nathan blew on his coffee. 'Here. A list of everything I used in last night's meal, just in case.' He reached for it and his fingers touched mine for a second, making them tingle. *Oh my God, get outta here with your Mills-and-Boon stuff,* I thought, but I couldn't help it. Nathan looked at me but didn't say anything, then pulled the list towards him and started to read through it.

'Blimey, Jodie, what is half this stuff? '*Fukujinzuke*'?'

'Japanese pickled veg. I didn't make it; it was in a jar. I should probably have listed what was in it…'

'Yeah, well, maybe if the lab results come back negative for tetrodotoxin. This is everything you served them last night, then?'

'Yes,' I said, but then something occurred to me. 'No, wait, they had cupcakes too, if they got round to eating them before poor Jeremy carked it. I didn't make them, either.'

'Were they from a shop or did someone here make them?'

'I don't know.' I looked at him, my mind working furiously. 'I was busy doing something and then I looked up and there they were, on the counter, in a proper cake box. I didn't see who delivered them, and Zack didn't know anything about them. They looked like they'd come from a shop, but there wasn't any name or anything on the box, so I couldn't say for certain.'

'Hmm…' Nathan looked thoughtful. 'Maybe one of

the others could have ordered them? I'll make a note of it.'

'So did you talk to the hospital? Were the rest of them ill?'

Nathan nodded. 'Yes. Aiko Takahashi seems to have had the worst of it.'

'Zack said she was throwing up most of the night.'

'Yes, the doc said he called her at one point because he was so worried about her. She'll recover, but it's really taken it out of her. She checked on Sam Pritchard around midnight and he'd just been sick. The nurses didn't see much of Mike Mancuso – he managed to wangle himself a private room – but he was apparently talking to the toilet bowl half the night too, and Faith says she felt 'funny' but managed to sleep it off.'

'What about Kimi?'

'Kimi said she was fine and discharged herself after they told her the dog couldn't stay at the hospital, even if she was in a private room.'

'Did she actually eat any of the fish?' I asked. 'She's supposedly vegan, but only when it suits her. She told Zack she'd eat it.'

'I don't know,' said Nathan. 'But it would explain why she wasn't ill.' He looked at me. 'And it would make it even more likely that it really was the pufferfish.'

I sighed. 'I know…'

He copied my sigh. 'But…'

I reached across the table and swatted him. 'I'm not that bad!'

'I know,' he said, then sighed again. 'But…' I reached across the table to playfully slap him again, but he laughed and grabbed my hand. 'I could have you for assaulting a police officer, you know.'

I snorted. 'I'd like to see you try.'

He smiled, but didn't let go of my hand. 'I've noticed something. Every time I try to talk to you lately, we either get interrupted or you run away.'

I felt my face get hot. *Don't talk to me about your new job*, I thought desperately, *I don't want to think about it*. But he clearly was going to talk to me about it.

'Ever since I mentioned that job offer—'

'Are you DCI Withers?'

Nathan held my hand and my gaze for a few seconds longer, then dropped both and turned to the owner of the voice. David Morgan stood behind Nathan, looking thoroughly annoyed.

Nathan gave him a placatory smile. 'What can I do for you, sir?'

'That policeman over there' – he gestured vaguely towards Zack's caravan, where Davey was still on guard – 'he told me you're in charge. Can you please tell me what the devil is going on here? I've just heard some of the crew saying they're pulling the plug on the shoot, and there's all sorts of wild rumours flying around.'

'And who might you be, sir? I don't believe we've met.'

'David Morgan,' he snapped. 'I'm the owner of Polvarrow House.'

'Nice to meet you, Mr Morgan,' said Nathan, holding out his hand to shake. Morgan's irritation subsided, eroded by Nathan's charm. 'Has no one from the production company contacted you?'

'No, I've heard nothing,' said Morgan. 'To be honest, Detective Chief Inspector, I'm starting to wish I'd never agreed to them filming here.'

'It must be difficult, I can imagine,' said Nathan agreeably. 'All I can tell you is that last night, one of the cast members was taken ill after shooting and subsequently died. We're not currently treating it as suspicious, but of course we do have a duty to investigate any unexpected death. Hence there'll be a few of my uniformed colleagues around for a couple of days, and I'll be here as necessary as well. What that means for the shoot I can't tell you, I'm afraid. I assume they're trying to decide how best to proceed. You should probably take it up with Mr Mancuso.'

'Someone died? Who? How?' Morgan looked horrified.

'Jeremy Mayhew,' I said. 'It looks like an allergic reaction to something he ate.' Nathan looked at me sharply, then nodded.

'We're still waiting for the official cause of death, but that's certainly what it looks like,' he said.

'How terrible,' said Morgan, although he looked almost relieved. 'Well, I'll just… Things to do,' he said, lamely. 'Thank you for your help, DCI Withers.'

We watched him leave. Germaine, whose ears had been pricked and alert all through the exchange with Morgan, gave a heavy sigh and settled down again.

'He really doesn't like having them here, does he?' murmured Nathan.

'No,' I said, 'which is a shame, because I met him on casting day and he was really excited about it. They got his back up when they trampled all over his flowerbed, the day the lightbulbs got smashed.'

'Yes…' Nathan looked thoughtful.

I smirked. 'You're doing it now. It's niggling you too, isn't it?'

'Nothing's niggling me,' he said, but he didn't sound convincing and he knew it. 'Oh all right, yes, yes, it is.'

'Too many accidents.'

He nodded. 'It's all just a bit … *convenient*, isn't it? So many accidents, people thinking the shoot's cursed, and then there's a death. So maybe it *is* cursed. Except you and I know these things don't exist, don't we?'

'We do.'

'The only curse that exists is the one between me and you. The one where we get interrupted every time I try and—' Nathan's phone began to ring. He rolled his eyes and looked at me. 'See? Every. Single. Time.' He answered the phone. 'DCI Withers… How are you feeling today, Mr Mancuso?' He raised his eyebrows and looked at me as he talked. 'So no more sickness? That's good… Of course… Well, maybe we should have a little chat first… Oh, are you? That's handy, so am I. We can use Ms Mackenzie's trailer.'

He grinned at me as he disconnected the call. 'So that was Mike Mancuso, wanting a case reference number so he can claim on the shoot's insurance. Fancy coming for a chat?'

Chapter Seventeen

The movie producer was looking surprisingly chipper for someone who had been throwing up all night, and whose movie was presumably dead in the water along with one of its stars.

He stood up as we entered Faith's trailer and strode over to us, then pumped Nathan's hand. 'Thanks for coming, Detective, appreciate it.'

'No problem,' said Nathan. 'There were a few questions I wanted to ask you about last night, so we can kill two birds with one stone.' He smiled and gestured to the built-in seating in the trailer's kitchen area. 'Shall we?'

Mancuso's smile hardened; if he'd thought he was calling all the shots, Nathan had just firmly (but politely) shown him otherwise. But he was no doubt used to being the most powerful person in the room, and it would take more than that to throw him off his stride.

'Of course.' He looked me up and down, then turned back to Nathan as he sat down. 'We really gonna talk in front of the caterer?' He looked down as Germaine gave a little whine, then up at Nathan again. 'And the mutt?'

'Ms Parker's catering business is just a sideline,' said Nathan. 'She's a consultant with the Devon and Cornwall Constabulary, and obviously this particular case is well within her sphere of expertise.' He paused. 'The dog's just along for the ride.'

I knew Nathan was only saying it to stop Mancuso objecting to my presence, but I still preened slightly. *He called me an expert!* I thought.

'Case?' said Mancuso sharply. 'Surely Mayhew's death was an accident, right? The pufferfish toxin—'

'We're still waiting for confirmation of the cause of death,' said Nathan calmly. 'Until then, we can't rule anything out.'

'But you know it *was* an accident, right?' He looked from Nathan to me for confirmation.

'Maybe it was the curse,' I said. He rolled his eyes.

'There ain't no such thing,' he said. 'I know there've been a lot of ... mishaps, but all this talk of a curse... Movie stars are like racehorses; they're highly strung and easily spooked. There ain't no curse. It was an accident, I'm telling ya.'

'You're probably right,' agreed Nathan. 'But we still need to ask you a few questions. I believe you were ill overnight? Tell me about that.'

'I had a headache and vomiting,' said Mancuso. Nathan waited. 'What, you wanna description?'

'We're trying to work out why you were all affected to varying degrees,' said Nathan. 'Why do you think Mr Mayhew was so acutely affected? If it *was* the pufferfish, do you think he had considerably more than anyone else?'

Mancuso shifted around in his seat. 'I don't know. Ain't like I was watching what everyone was eating.'

'Fair enough. Can you tell me what you ate?'

'The pufferfish, of course. I ate everything; it was delicious.'

'Did you have a cupcake?' I asked. Nathan shot me the briefest of glances and I got the impression that was exactly what he'd expected me to ask.

Mancuso nodded. 'Oh yeah, at the end Zack brought out the box of cupcakes and we all had one. They were good.'

'Did everyone eat one?'

He thought. 'I think so… although Kimi made a big thing about not eating sugar, so I guess she didn't. I don't know.'

'And were you in the trailer for the whole meal?' Nathan made notes on his pad, which Mancuso was eyeing uneasily. I wasn't sure if it was a sign of guilt (guilt about what, I didn't know), or if he was just generally a shifty character. He was a New York movie producer, so my money was on the latter.

'Yeah,' he said. 'Oh, except right at the beginning, before we started eating. I got a call from my daughter, so I went outside to take it. She's staying with me during the shoot.'

'Okay…' Nathan wrote that down, then looked up with a smile. 'So what happens now?'

'What do you mean?'

'Are you closing down the shoot? Or can you keep going without Jeremy?'

'You'll lose money if you just shut down,' I said. 'Or are you insured against stuff like this?'

Mancuso looked a bit put out. 'Why do you wanna know?'

'She's an ex-copper,' said Nathan. 'She's nosey, like me. Humour us.'

I held my hands out in defence. 'I'm just interested, that's all. Half the town signed on as extras, so they'll all want to know what's going on.'

He didn't look too keen to go into details and for a moment I thought he was just going to ignore me, but then he obviously decided I wasn't a threat and gave me a big, false smile.

'Of course we're insured; it's standard for all big

shoots. It covers your losses if you're forced to stop filming, whether it's temporarily or for good.'

'So if a member of the cast or crew is accidentally killed during filming—' began Nathan.

'It pays out, yeah.'

'But Jeremy didn't die as a result of an accident during filming, did he?' I said. I could see Nathan looking at me keenly, although I wasn't even sure myself what I was getting at. 'Kimi told Sam he should have stopped Zack serving the fish, but you said you'd okayed it. I'm sure I read something once about movie stars wanting to do risky stuff like, I dunno, motor racing or water-skiing during breaks between filming, and the production company forbade them to do it because it was dangerous and would jeopardise the movie.' I looked at Mancuso thoughtfully. 'But this *was* dangerous, and you okayed it. Why would you do that?'

'Because the caterer – Gino, the *real* caterer – assured me it was safe. He said he would make sure it wasn't dangerous.'

Nathan and I exchanged looks.

'How was he intending to do that?' asked Nathan.

'Jeez, I don't know!' Mancuso sounded exasperated. 'I guess he was going to watch over Zack and make sure he prepared it properly.'

'But then Gino broke his arm,' pressed Nathan. 'You

didn't think maybe you should advise Zack against it, without Gino there to watch him?'

The producer laughed, but it sounded forced. 'Hey, you sure you don't work for the insurance company?'

Nathan laughed as well, and his didn't sound any more genuine. 'If your insurers are anything like mine, they'll give you a much more thorough grilling than that. You should've heard the fuss they made over a simple fender-bender. And me an honest copper, too.'

Mancuso stood up, obviously hoping we would follow suit and leave, but both of us stayed seated.

'Look, okay,' he said. '*Maybe* I should have thought about stopping Zack, but cards on the table, I got a lot on my mind during a shoot and it didn't occur to me there could be a problem. I'm a busy man, so sue me.' He went to the door and opened it. 'Now, like I said, I'm a busy man, so if you don't mind…'

'I don't mind,' said Nathan pleasantly, not moving immediately. 'Oh sorry, did you want us to leave? What am I like? Of course, you've got important things to do. I've just got to find out for certain how one of your main actors died.' He stood up and I followed his lead. Nathan took a business card from his pocket and wrote a number on it. He walked to the door and handed it to Mancuso. 'Here's the case number, if the insurance company asks for it. Thank you for your time.'

He stepped through the door but I knew Nathan, and

I knew he wasn't done yet – and I was right. He stopped and turned back to Mancuso. 'I wouldn't file that claim yet though, if I were you. Bye now.'

Nathan strode down the stairs leaving Mancuso glaring after him. I smiled my most charming smile, said, 'Bye!' and followed, picking up Germaine as her little legs had trouble with the stairs. I knew how she felt.

Nathan was almost back at the food truck before I caught up with him. He turned and grinned at me, a mischievous grin that turned my knees to jelly and (if I'm being honest) loosened my knicker elastic a little.

'That was fun, wasn't it?' he said. I laughed.

'What was that all about?' I asked, and then added, mimicking his accent, ''I wouldn't file that claim yet if I were you.' Oh my God, I nearly died.'

'What can I say? I didn't like the bloke.'

'Really? I couldn't tell…'

Nathan laughed, then stopped and looked at me. 'We make a good team, don't we?'

'You mean, like, 'good cop, bad cop'?'

'I was thinking more, 'wannabe cop, actual cop'…'

'Oi!' I lifted my hand to slap him and he caught it.

'Again with the hitting. Do I need to handcuff you?' He pulled me towards him, and I thought, *Oh my God,*

AT LAST, he's going to kiss me. And then I thought, *and then he'll bugger off back to Liverpool…* Nathan hesitated, and then—

His phone rang. He sighed. 'Every. Single. Time.' He let go of my hand and dug his phone out of his pocket. He looked at the caller ID, then declined the call.

'Who was that?' I asked, thinking, *That's the second time he's declined a call in front of me…*

'My old super,' he said.

'The one back in Liverpool? You should probably talk to him if he's going to be your boss again.'

He shook his head, almost angrily. 'I told you, I—' But he was interrupted by his phone ringing again. 'Oh for God's sake!' He looked at it, but this time he took the call. 'Hi Matt… Already? That was quick. Go on… Right. Have they cross-checked that against the bag of rubbish…? Okay. Well, I'm pretty much done here, so I'll be back in the office in a bit.' He hung up and looked at me. 'The lab results are back. Apparently it really does speed things up if you know what you're looking for.'

'And…?'

'There was tetrodotoxin present in the deceased's body. A lot of it.'

'So it *was* the pufferfish? Damn.'

'Is that, damn because that proves it was Zack's fault, or damn because you were hoping for a more exciting outcome?'

I gave a short laugh. 'Yes. To both.'

We stood smiling at each other, and for a second I thought the words *I really don't want you to leave* were going to burst out of my mouth before I could stop them, but I was saved from making an idiot of myself by his bloody phone ringing AGAIN.

Nathan looked at the caller ID and groaned.

'Is it him again?' I asked, and he nodded. 'Look, just take it or he'll keep calling you. I'll see you later.'

'Okay,' said Nathan, reluctantly. He answered the call. 'Hi, can you hold on just one second?' He turned back to me. 'The lab hasn't had the results back from the fish guts yet, and I'm not going to make the cause of death official until we have them. But if you want to forewarn Zack, be my guest.'

'I think I will,' I said, then Germaine and I left him to his phone call.

Chapter Eighteen

Zack had left Polvarrow and had gone back to keep an eye on Aiko, so I finished off at the food truck, locked up, and drove to Parkview Manor Hotel, where the cast was staying.

As I walked into the foyer I tried not to remember that this was where I'd first met Nathan, but it was impossible not to replay the scene in my head. It had been the day of Tony's ill-fated wedding, and I had been sitting with him in the formal dining room. It had been beautifully decorated and should have been playing host to all his family and friends, not the two of us trying to make sense of his ex-wife's death and his bride-to-be's disappearance. I glanced in through the open door; we'd been sitting at that table there, near the bar, when the extremely handsome, well-dressed, and (I'd thought) arrogant new CID officer had sauntered in and made some sarcastic (but ultimately correct) remark about me being a cook, not a copper. He'd completely dismissed me, banishing me to the kitchen while he questioned Tony. He'd made repeated attempts to get rid of me throughout that investigation, but after a few days of constantly running into me had been forced to admit that I'd given him misgivings and made him feel like maybe, in this case, the most likely explanation wasn't the real one. Eventually he'd taken me into his confidence and told me that he had no one in Penstowan to talk to, no one to brainstorm with or discuss aspects of the case with that he found puzzling. So he'd turned to me. And he'd gone from being someone I dreaded bumping into (because, to start with, every time I bumped into him I was doing something I shouldn't be doing, somewhere I shouldn't be doing it) to someone I missed when he wasn't around…

I gave a big sniff and tried to force the tears that were threatening to spring into my eyes back into my tear ducts, but unfortunately tears don't really work that way. I swiped at them instead with the sleeve of my coat and turned towards the reception desk, intending to ask for Zack.

'Hey! What are you doing here?' Kimi had entered the hotel behind me, Princess in her arms, panting (the dog, not the actress). The hotel was dog-friendly, and was also the place where I'd first met (and fallen in love with) Germaine, who had now seen the Pekinese and given her a welcoming bark.

'Hello! You just been for a walk?' I asked, turning around and reaching out to pat the dog. Kimi yanked her baby away from me.

'Princess needed some quality time with me after last night. Poor baby! So many bad vibes floating around…' She looked about her. 'What happened to the handsome police officer guy who was with you? Is he here?'

Blasted movie stars, I thought. If it wasn't Faith undressing Tony with her eyes, it was Kimi lusting after Nathan. *Hands off my men!* Although neither of them was really mine, were they?

'Nope, just me. I came to see Zack, but actually, can I ask you a couple of questions?'

She looked me up and down. 'I thought you were the chef?'

'I was moonlighting. This is my real job.' I carefully didn't elaborate on what 'this' was. I'd found that if I just turned up and started asking questions, people assumed I was a police officer without me having to lie about it. It was always best not to risk getting arrested for impersonating a police officer.

She looked at me thoughtfully. 'Hmm… Does this mean you know what killed Jeremy?'

I smiled, noncommittally. 'I might do.'

She glanced around, then shrugged and walked into the hotel bar. I followed. She seated herself at a table and looked at me expectantly. I smiled and went to sit down, but her expression changed into something disapproving, so I shot to my feet again.

'Er…'

'I'm kinda thirsty after that walk,' she said. Ah, right. So the dog wasn't the only Princess around here.

'Of course. Can I get you a drink?' I asked, thinking, *I wonder if I can put in an expenses claim for this?* But I was an unpaid consultant, so it seemed unlikely.

'I'll have a glass of Deep Sea,' she said. *Please,* I added silently. I went to the bar and rang the bell – it was the middle of the afternoon and there was no one around – and waited for the bartender to show. His smile faltered somewhat when he saw Kimi sitting at the table, but he was a professional and it was back before I'd even had time to properly register it was gone.

'What can I get you?'

'Could I have a cup of tea, please?' I asked. I hadn't realised it before but I was gasping for one. 'And something called a 'Deep Sea' for Miss Takahashi, whatever that is.'

'Of course,' said the bartender with a smile. 'I'll bring it over. That's £18.50, please.'

£18.50? For two drinks? Kimi must have ordered a champagne cocktail or something. At this time of day, with her being a social media healthy-eating guru as well. 'Charge it to Miss Takahashi's room,' I said brightly, and he winked.

'Right you are.'

I joined Kimi, who was fussing over a speck of imaginary dirt at the corner of Princess's eye. *She needs to have a baby,* I thought sardonically, as Germaine settled herself across my feet with a loud, echoey, and unapologetically pungent fart. Daisy had gone through a phase when she was a toddler of getting into my pot plants – and I mean, *literally* getting into my pot plants – and of rolling around the muddiest reaches of her grandparents' back gardens. I'd soon learnt that 1) dirt washes off, and 2) there's no point washing it off until bedtime, because the little darling will undoubtedly be covered in mud again the next time you turn around. Becoming a parent really gives you a much more relaxed idea of what number of stains on an item of clothing is socially acceptable (clue: it's more than you'd think), and exactly how dirty your child needs to get before you really have to change their outfit.

'She's a lovely dog,' I said, more to get on Kimi's good side than because I actually thought that, because to tell you the truth, the dog had a definite look of drowned rat about her. But it worked because Kimi graced me with a smile and her whole face changed. She really was beautiful. I definitely had to keep her away from Nathan…

'She's a pedigree,' said Kimi. 'She's very sensitive to the emotions and atmosphere around her. She can sense when I'm upset or worried.'

'Yes, that's why dogs make such great companions,' I said, as my own loyal, sensitive companion let rip with another one. Kimi's perfect nose wrinkled. I ignored both the noise and the smell. 'Anyway, I just wanted to see how everyone is today. I heard about your sister being quite sick in the night.'

'Uh-huh,' said Kimi, although she didn't look or sound terribly sympathetic. 'At least she had Zack to take care of her.' Her disapproving expression told me everything I needed to know about her feelings on that relationship.

'Yes, it's quite sweet really,' I said. 'He obviously really likes her.'

She sniffed. 'Does he? I don't know. Too many times, men have used my sister to get to me.'

I think you're deluded, love, I thought, but I just smiled. 'I'm sure that's been true in the past, but Zack strikes me as completely sincere. Anyway, that's not what I wanted to talk to you about. I really wanted to know if you were taken ill at any point last night?'

She shook her head firmly. 'No, I wasn't. I have a very strong constitution. I don't know if you follow me on

Instagram…' I diplomatically didn't say anything, because of course I didn't flipping follow her on Instagram. 'I've talked extensively about the importance of clean, healthy eating. I follow a plant-based diet. I just can't eat anything that has a face.'

Bacon doesn't have a face, I thought stubbornly. *Nor do sausages. Or cheeseburgers.*

'A vegetarian or vegan diet is definitely healthier than eating a lot of red meat,' I agreed. 'But there are some things I couldn't give up. Like fish. Gino said you do occasionally allow yourself a piece of fish—'

'If it's sustainably sourced, yes,' she interrupted. 'Wild rather than farmed, line-caught, dolphin-friendly…'

The bartender came over with a tray. He placed a pretty china tea pot, milk jug, and cup in front of me, and a glass of water in front of Kimi.

'Your tea, madam, and your Deep Sea, miss.'

'Hold on, what's that?' I asked the bartender, but Kimi waved him away. I turned to her. 'No, I think he's made a mistake. He's given you a glass of water.'

'Yes, Deep Sea water.'

'But he charged me eighteen quid for this round!' I said, staggered – though of course I hadn't actually paid for it; the movie company would. 'What the heck is Deep Sea water?'

She looked at me like I was mad. 'It's deep sea water.

The name, like, *literally* tells you what it is. It's sourced from three thousand feet below the surface, from a remote archipelago off the coast of Hawaii. It's full of minerals and electrolytes. I asked the hotel to ship it over from the States specially for me. It's the only water I drink.'

'But that glass must have cost about fifteen quid…' I said weakly.

'What price sustainability and the natural goodness of the sea?' she said piously, but of course it was easy for her to say that when the production company would be footing the bill. Not to mention paying for it to be flown in a terribly environmentally unfriendly fashion all the way across the Atlantic to Cornwall.

'But sea water… Isn't it salty?'

She looked at me like not only was I mad, but I was also wearing a straightjacket and dribbling onto my chin. 'Of course it isn't. It's been desalinated. It's the cleanest, smoothest, crispest-tasting water in the world.'

'Oh right… Can I have a sip?'

'No.'

Germaine lifted her tail and gave us her opinion on the world's cleanest, smoothest, most ridiculously expensive water, and I had to admit I agreed with her, despite being slightly concerned about what she'd been eating to become that flatulent. I poured myself a cup of tea, by now feeling like an absolute peasant with a farty mongrel for a pet.

'Anyway…' I had to get this conversation back on track after the unexpected derailing. 'So you were telling me about the fish…?'

'Uh-huh. Zack gave everyone a piece and I *said* I'd eat it, because he'd done it especially for my birthday…' *For your sister's birthday, you mean,* I thought, but I restrained myself from saying it out loud.

'So you did eat it?'

'No.' She smiled at me, one of those aren't-I-terrible-but-everyone-still-loves-me kind of smiles. 'I felt kinda bad about it, but I just couldn't bring myself to eat it.'

'What happened to it? Did you give it to Jeremy?'

'No, I didn't want Zack to see me get rid of it, so I gave it to my beautiful baby.' She picked up the dog and held her to her face, snuggling into her and making baby noises. I gaped at her in disbelief and she got defensive, obviously thinking I was judging her pet-care skills, but I really wasn't. 'Princess loves fish,' she pouted. 'The oils are totally good for her hair.'

'Yeah, yeah, I know,' I said. 'That was why you were so annoyed at Zack, wasn't it? When he mentioned the pufferfish, you were terrified that you'd inadvertently poisoned Princess.'

She nodded. 'Yes, I was. I was *so* scared, like you would not believe. I sat up with her all night, waiting for her to get ill. The guilt! How could I have lived with myself if she died, because of something I'd fed her?'

'She looks perky enough now, though,' I said.

'Of course she is. She didn't get sick,' said Kimi. 'So what was it that killed Jeremy?'

What indeed. Because if the pufferfish really had been contaminated enough to kill a fully grown man, whose insides must have been pickled and preserved in alcohol after years of drinking, how come it hadn't knocked over the small dog currently sitting in her owner's arms, sniffing delicately at the air and trying to get her tongue into a glass of the World's Most Ridiculously Expensive Water™?

Chapter Nineteen

'That's interesting…' said Nathan. I'd been worried that he might decline my call after I'd forced him to talk to his old detective superintendent, but he'd answered on the second ring.

'That's what I thought,' I said. 'Kimi said that Zack dished up the fish and gave everyone roughly the same amount, so Princess ate just as much as Jeremy. So why wasn't she ill? How come a small dog could eat the same amount of supposedly contaminated fish and not die?'

'How come Jeremy died at all, when everyone else was just sick?' mused Nathan.

'Because it wasn't the fish,' I said. I heard Nathan groan. 'Don't be like that! You were having niggles as well. I bet you, when the lab get back to you about the fish guts, it'll be negative.'

'That's not why I was groaning,' he said, and I could hear amusement in his voice. 'I'm groaning because I have the horrible feeling you might be right. Which means…'

'Which means it was murder.' I felt a thrill run through me, and thought, *Oh my God, am I a terrible person or what?* But I couldn't help it. I felt like Sherlock Holmes. *The game is afoot!*

'Well…' Nathan sounded a cautious note. 'We can't say that for sure. Maybe the toxin naturally occurred in something else?'

I rolled my eyes, which was completely pointless as he was on the other end of the phone and couldn't see. 'Oh come on—'

'You're rolling your eyes, aren't you? I can tell, you know.'

What is this witchcraft? I thought.

'No,' I lied. 'But tell me this: how would tetra-whatever-it-is – pufferfish toxin – how would that come to be in any other food? Unless someone put it there?'

Nathan was quiet for a moment and I swear I could hear him thinking. 'Okay,' he said eventually. 'So what food was it in? What did Jeremy and the others who were sick eat, but Kimi didn't?'

'Kimi gave me a lecture on the evils of sugar,' I said. 'She said she hadn't eaten it since 2017.'

'What?'

'I know, right? And get this. She's not diabetic or anything; she gave it up *voluntarily*. She voluntarily gave up biscuits.'

'And chocolate?'

'And cake. I mean, are you really even alive if you don't eat cake?'

Nathan laughed. 'So you won't be following her advice, then?'

'Not any time soon, no. So anyway, I'm assuming from that that she didn't eat any of the cupcakes.'

'And we still don't know where they came from?'

'Nope. I'm still at the hotel though, so I can ask around the cast.'

'Okay,' said Nathan. 'Just don't upset anyone…'

'Who, me? I will be the soul of discretion.'

Nathan laughed. 'Yeah, I bet you will be…'

I grinned at the phone, but again, it was completely pointless because he couldn't see me. But hopefully he knew what I was doing. We did seem to be very much in sync… And that thought made me feel sad, because it would be impossible to be in sync with him if he was in Liverpool while I was in Penstowan.

There was a slightly awkward silence and I knew we were both thinking about it. I cleared my throat.

'So did you talk to your old superintendent?' I asked. My voice sounded husky and I cleared my throat again.

'Yes,' said Nathan. He sounded reluctant. 'He's pushing me for an answer.'

'An answer? To what?'

'To the job offer, of course. I haven't said I'll take it yet.'

My heart leapt. It wasn't a done deal. Maybe he wouldn't go after all. Maybe I could say something to make him stay?

And if I *did* get him to stay, what then? What would he be expecting of me? I enjoyed his company and was hugely attracted to him, but… Was I ready for a serious relationship? My ex-husband, Richard, had cheated on his first wife with me, and then cheated on me with someone else – and for all I knew, he was cheating on her now too; being taken in by a man like that had not done much for my self-confidence. What if Nathan was the same? No, I knew he wasn't. But what if it was me? What if we got together and I screwed everything up and drove him away? I couldn't face getting my heart broken again, and of course it wasn't just me now; it was Daisy too. What if he regretted not going for that job? It had much better prospects, and had to be more exciting than sleepy Penstowan. What if he resented me for keeping him here?

Oh my God, I wasn't ready for this.

'But it's a great job,' I said. 'You'd have to have a really good reason to turn it down…'

'Yes,' he said, and I got the impression he was waiting for me to say something else. But I couldn't. He sighed. 'Okay, I've got to go. Talk to you later.' And he put the phone down.

I gulped as I stared at my now-silent phone. He'd sounded ... upset? Annoyed? I didn't know. So much for us being in sync.

Germaine gave a little whine. I recognised what that whine meant; it meant we had to go outside pretty sharply and I'd better have a poop bag handy, or things could get messy. Not as messy as my love life, though.

It had started to rain. But of course it had. Germaine was about ready to burst but I dragged her around the side of the building, as even a doggy-friendly hotel has its limits and would not be impressed with her pooping on their doorstep. Most of the staff knew me by now – my investigations always seemed to lead me here, at some point – and the manager, Mr Bloom, turned a blind eye to me hanging around and harassing – I mean, *chatting to* – his VIP guests, but I didn't want to push my luck.

On this side of the building, though, stood the white painted gazebo, covered with climbing roses which were now well past their best. A few months ago, when they'd been in full bloom, Nathan had led me there firmly by the arm and sat me down to have a go at me. He'd caught me trying to get into a hotel room to prove Tony's innocence, and had been losing patience with me. But what had begun as an attempt to warn me off had turned into him confessing that I might actually be right. He'd given me a lift home afterwards, but not before taking me along with him to question a potential suspect. It had been the tentative start to our partnership, which, unlike the roses, had carried on blooming. Until now.

It was pouring with rain by now, but I couldn't bring myself to step up onto the gazebo and get myself undercover, so I stood there feeling utterly miserable while Germaine did her business. At least with it raining so hard no one would be able to tell if I was crying or not.

'Jodie?' I turned round to see Tony standing there, looking at me quizzically. 'What are you doing out here? You're getting soaking wet, you muppet.'

I gestured vaguely to Germaine, trying to resist the urge to run over and sob all over my old friend. *He'd* never bugger off to Liverpool (or anywhere else, for that matter) just for a job. *He'd* never leave me or let me down; he never had so far.

He squinted at me through the rain and shook his head.

'Come on, you idiot, you'll get pneumonia.' He took my hand and led me up the stairs into the gazebo. Germaine had done what she needed to do, so he took the lead from my hand and tied it to one of the wooden posts. 'Poo bag?' He held out his hand and I gave him the bag, and he went out in the pouring rain to dispose of Germaine's unmentionables.

I sat down – not on the same bench I'd sat on with Nathan; that would be too weird – and watched Tony make a fuss of Germaine before joining me.

'So what's going on?' he asked.

'I'm fine. I just didn't realise it was raining and I left my coat inside,' I said. He laughed.

'I know you're all right; you always are,' he said, and I felt a little pang. *Even my oldest friend doesn't understand me,* I thought in a moment of self-pity. 'I meant the shoot. You're Nosey Parker; you always know what's going on.'

I forced myself to laugh. 'I thought we'd stopped using our childhood nicknames, Snot Face.'

'Yeah, yeah, I know how to blow my nose now but you still can't keep yours out of anything interesting. Is it true about Jeremy?'

'Why, what have you heard?'

'He's dead. It *is* true, innit? You can't hide stuff from me. You know that...'

I obviously can, I thought. 'Who told you?'

'Faith did.' He had the decency to look a little bit embarrassed.

'Oh yeah? You two are very chummy.' A thought occurred to me. 'Are you here to see her?'

He went all the way through 'embarrassed' and made it to 'defensive' in about three seconds flat.

'Yeah, well, like you said the other day, she's still a good-looking woman, and we're both single, and it's been a while since ... since I lost Cheryl, and I'm a grown man; I've got needs, just like everyone else, you know.' He stopped and then muttered under his breath, 'And nobody else is bloody catering for them.'

I looked at him for a moment, stunned, and then laughed.

''I've got needs too',' I mimicked. He laughed.

'Oi! Cheeky mare.'

'I'm sorry, I just can't... I mean, Faith? *Faith?* She's not... You can't really fancy her, surely?'

'Are you jealous?' He looked very amused.

'Of course I ain't bloody jealous!' But I kind of was... I stood up so I wouldn't have to look at him, in this spot that reminded me so much of Nathan. I tried not to imagine the six-pack lurking under his puffer jacket. Oh God, I was so confused and over-emotional; I really should just stick to dogs and murder cases...

Tony stood up and put out his hand to stop me untying Germaine and escaping. 'Now you know how I felt when you were seeing Duncan.'

I gaped at him. I'd had a short-lived, ill-advised, and, as it turned out, pretty chaste fling with the artist Duncan Stovall when he'd visited Penstowan as part of the town's arts festival. I knew Tony hadn't exactly approved of the relationship, but jealous?

'But … I…' I started, but I had no idea where the sentence was going. We looked at each other, the atmosphere charged with … something, and before I knew what was happening, Tony lunged at me, sweeping me into his arms and pressing his lips against mine. I wasn't wholly against the idea, and he wasn't a bad kisser; his breath was fresh, and he was gentle and tender and did all the things that make a good kiss. And yet…

He pulled away and looked at me, with a slightly puzzled look on his face. Neither of us spoke for a moment, and then he took a deep breath. *Oh God,* I thought, although I wasn't sure why. My mind was spinning like a disoriented hamster on a wheel.

'Okay,' he said. 'First off, sorry for just grabbing you like that—'

'No, no, it's fine,' I protested. 'I wanted you to. I think.'

'Oh, good.' He looked at me awkwardly. 'I ain't normally a grabber…'

'No, I know you're not. It's fine.'

'Good.' We stood and stared at each other again, not entirely sure what was going on here.

I have to get the hell out of here, I thought to myself, tearing my eyes away from his. *I have to get Germaine and escape before he insists on discussing what just happened because—*

He took another deep breath.

Oh crap, too late…

'All right, I'm going to say it if you won't,' he said, and then stopped. I waited, because I sure as hell wasn't going to say anything. Say *what,* exactly? He sighed. 'I must've played that scene over and over in my head hundreds of times over the years, and it was never quite… I mean, you know I'm daft; I was expecting fireworks, violins—'

'Choirs of angels,' I added. He nodded.

'Choirs of angels, yeah. I weren't expecting—'

'Weirdness.' I hadn't known that was what I was feeling until I said it. His face cleared.

'Oh, thank Christ for that. Yes, weirdness. It felt like—'

'—kissing your sister.'

He nodded. 'Yeah. It just felt … odd.' He forced on a smile, trying to lighten the mood. 'I mean, don't get me wrong, I'd still happily have sex with you. I mean, I *am* a bloke—'

'Yeah, well, the idea doesn't *entirely* repulse me either,' I said.

'Oh, well, that's good then.'

We stood and stared at each other again for a

moment, and then he laughed. And then I did too, and it was still awkward but we knew we'd get past it.

'I'm not suggesting that we *should* sleep together, mind you,' he said, suddenly alarmed. I shook my head vehemently.

'Oh no, definitely not!' I said. 'Sorry, that came out more forcefully than it was meant to. It's not that you're not attractive, it's just…'

'You love me like a brother.' He smiled ruefully. 'I know. I was certain this was what I wanted an' all. I am proper flummoxed.'

'Bamboozled.'

'Flabbergasted.'

'Discombobulated.'

'Is that a real word?'

We looked at each other and laughed softly again. I sighed and reached out to take his hands.

'You know that I'm not given to talking about my feelings,' I said, and he nodded. 'I'm only going to say this once, so you'd better pay attention.' I took a deep breath. I could feel myself getting emotional, and I gave myself a stern talking to before continuing. 'I love you, Tony Penhaligon. I really do. My life is all the better for having you in it. You're a brilliant male role model for Daisy – so much better than her flipping useless father – and my mum loves you; even the dog loves you. And I think maybe we had to do this, just to see what it was like.'

'But…?'

'I think we had our moment, and we missed it.'

He looked so sad at that, that I nearly relented and shouted, *'Kidding!'* and flung myself into his arms again, but it wouldn't be right. And more to the point, Tony knew it wasn't right too.

'I should have kissed you twenty years ago,' he said, and I nodded.

'Maybe you should have. But back then, I was determined to leave Penstowan, and you've never wanted to live anywhere else.'

'I might have moved, for you,' he said, and I had to blink back sudden tears.

'You would have hated London, and you'd have ended up hating me for dragging you there,' I said. *And Nathan might hate me if I make him stay here,* I thought.

'I could never hate you, Jodie.'

'Well, this way we'll never have to find that out, will we? Because if you and I stay best friends, we'll be in each other's lives for ever.' A tear escaped my stupid, stupid eyes and I swiped it away. Because it was true. We might have made a go of it years ago, but we'd been friends for too long. There was no way I wanted to risk losing that, and neither did he.

'You're right,' he said. 'When you told me on that

New Year's Eve a few years ago that you'd split up with Richard, I thought, *finally* you'll come back and I can tell you how I feel. That were my New Year's resolution. But you didn't come back straightaway, and I met Cheryl, and… I think I've just been really lonely since the wedding that never was. And you are my best mate. And I thought…'

I burst into tears, which was daft because this was all completely mutual and everything, but in the back of my mind there'd been that reassuring thought that if all else failed, there was always Tony. And now there wasn't. Not like that. And it would never have been fair on him, anyway.

He pulled me in for a hug and we stood there for a long time while I cried like a complete idiot (I think he may have cried a little bit too, but he'd mastered the art of doing it discreetly). And I knew that I wasn't just crying for him, but for Nathan too, because it was only now he was on the verge of leaving that I dared admit to myself that he was the one I wanted to be with.

Chapter Twenty

I finally pulled myself together and headed back into the hotel. Tony had reassured me that my eyes weren't red or puffy, but I didn't entirely believe him. Luckily, having been soaked through, I looked so uniformly awful now (especially compared to these glamorous actorly types) that I guessed the rest of my appearance would draw attention away from my freshly wrung-out eyes.

'I'll see you later,' said Tony, as I ran my fingers through my straggly wet hair.

'Aren't you coming in?' I asked, surprised. 'What about Faith?'

He smiled ruefully. 'I changed me mind. I don't want to be just somebody's booty call after all.' He laughed.

'Amazing, innit? I'd have loved being that when I was younger, but nobody was interested then.'

'You've matured nicely,' I said, smiling, wishing that I fancied him after all. But I didn't, despite the six-pack, and despite the fact that he was actually far more attractive at forty than he had been at twenty. We looked at each other and both of us sighed, then went our separate ways.

The lady at the reception desk – Karen, according to her name badge – looked at me curiously as I entered.

'It's pouring out there and I left my coat in the bar,' I said, unnecessarily. She smiled.

'Who are you here to see?' she asked, but before I could answer Faith came swanning into the foyer from the guest spa, clad in a snow-white fluffy bathrobe. Her hair was pinned up carelessly, with blonde tendrils spilling down her neck in an effortless but casually elegant way that had probably taken ages to achieve. I pin or tie my hair back when I'm cooking but it never looks like that; it has a tendency to escape from the hairband, so I have to pull it back so tightly that I look like I've had a facelift. *She probably HAS had a facelift*, I thought, but then told myself off. I should be celebrating the fact that an older woman was still successful and sexy. Even if it killed me to admit it.

She wafted over in a cloud of Chanel No. 5, the

slightly smug smile on her face disappearing as she saw me.

'Oh, it's you,' she said, clearly disappointed. Why was no one ever pleased to see me?

I nearly said, *Expecting someone else?* But again, I told myself off. She wasn't a rival, I wasn't jealous (not really), and there was no need for nastiness. I *knew* she was expecting someone else, and I also knew he wasn't coming.

'Afternoon, Ms Mackenzie,' I said, smiling pleasantly. 'How are you? I hope you're over any sickness?'

She smiled benevolently. 'I wasn't terribly ill. Nothing a session in the spa won't cure.'

Yeah, I know EXACTLY what sort of 'session' you were hoping for, I thought, before I could stop myself, but at least I managed not to say it out loud.

Faith looked around, then spoke to the receptionist. 'Karen, sweetheart, I'm expecting a visitor. Can you let him know I'm in the spa? I wouldn't want to miss him.'

'Sorry,' I said, interrupting them. I hadn't been planning to say anything; Tony had told me he was going to ring her, but he was a bit of a coward when it came to stuff like that and he obviously hadn't done it yet. And although part of me *was* still stupidly jealous, I needed to rise above it. I'd been stood up in the past and it wasn't nice. Better to let her know than to let her carry on waiting. 'Sorry, I couldn't help overhearing. If you're waiting for Tony, I just spoke to him and he's had to cancel. He said he was going to call you.'

She stared at me for a moment. Behind her, Karen discreetly looked down at some work (real or imaginary) on the desk in front of her. Faith narrowed her eyes then laughed, sounding just like her cockney matriarch soap character.

'Okay, message received loud and clear,' she said. 'He did say you and him weren't, you know…' I could feel my cheeks start to get warm.

'We're not, but would it have stopped you if we were?' I asked, and she laughed again.

'Not necessarily. But if I were you I'd be getting my hands on that dishy detective from last night.'

'Ah, now *him* you really do have to keep your mitts off,' I said, although I had to admit I'd so far managed to keep my own off him, and it was looking less likely every day that I'd get a chance to change that. She smiled.

'All's fair in love and war, or sex and movies,' she said, 'but I do try not to step on other women's toes.' She sighed. 'So that's my plans for the afternoon out the window.' She looked me up and down. 'You look like you could do with a facial.'

So that was how I ended up lying next to the woman I'd spent the last few days being jealous of, clad only in a towel. I'd decided I didn't like her because of the way she'd tried to monopolise Tony, but I had to admit she was a laugh. And I had no right to be jealous, because I had no intention of getting together with Tony. I should have realised all along that, if we were meant to be an item, it would have happened years ago. It didn't stop me feeling a pang when I thought of him with other women, though, and I knew that any future partner of his would have to be very special indeed for me to accept them. I pitied them already.

Germaine enjoyed (or endured) a pampering in the hotel's doggy daycare centre, while I and my new bestie Faith had facials – an organic revitalising bio-active cleanse and tone, no less (I still had no idea what that actually was, even after having it done), followed by an Ayurvedic Vishuddha detoxifying massage, which may or may not have detoxified me but which certainly pummelled me into submission. We sat by the spa's private plunge pool, wrapped up in fluffy white towels and sipping at freshly squeezed fruit juice, and I marvelled at how all the stress I'd been feeling without even really being aware of it had just faded away… And of course the minute I realised the stress had gone, it started creeping back. I banished it to the back of my mind. I'd had an emotional morning and I was now being thoroughly spoilt – and I was going to make the most of it.

But I *was* here for a reason, and although the ex-copper part of me was feeling bio-actively cleansed and Ayurvedically detoxified, it was still on duty. Kind of.

I sipped at my mango and pineapple smoothie and gave a little moan of satisfaction, then turned to Faith. She was lying back with her eyes closed and for a moment I thought she'd fallen asleep. But she hadn't, because without even opening her eyes she said, 'What?'

'Last night ... you really weren't ill?'

She opened her eyes and sat up to take a sip of her drink. 'No, I wasn't. I did feel a bit funny but I think now it was more psychological, more because I was *expecting* to feel ill. Was it the pufferfish? Does your hunky copper know something?'

I shook my head, hoping I looked innocent. 'The lab results aren't back yet, but he's pretty certain it was. It's mad, innit? You all ate it, but only Jeremy died. And you didn't even get sick.'

She looked at me suspiciously. 'Do I need my lawyer?'

I laughed. 'No! Not unless you've got something to confess...'

She sighed. 'All right, I have. I didn't eat the fish.'

I looked at her in surprise. 'You didn't? But you were clearly angry about it last night; you looked like you were ready to take a pop at Mike Mancuso for letting Zack serve it.'

'I know. I did try a tiny, tiny piece, just to be polite,' she admitted. 'Raw fish is not my thing, but I didn't want to upset Zack. And Jeremy… It was horrible, the way he died…' She shuddered, and looked genuinely upset. 'We'd just watched a big, strong man die so quickly, and it was really disturbing…' She fixed me with a frank expression. 'Jeremy and I had a past. We had a fling years ago, when we were both married to other people, and, well, let's just say it didn't end well. We'd worked together since, and he seemed fine, but I always felt a bit awkward with him. I didn't wish him dead, though.'

I reached out and patted her hand. 'I'm sure you didn't.'

'Anyway, I forced myself to eat some of the fish because I didn't want to hurt Zack's feelings. I already get the feeling he doesn't like me, for some reason. No idea why. But I really didn't like it, so when no one was looking I gave it to Kimi's dog.'

So Princess had had TWO portions of the fish, and wasn't even sick? I thought. *Then it definitely wasn't in the fish…*

'When I realised what had poisoned Jeremy, I felt terrible. I was scared for myself, of course – I don't know how much pufferfish you'd have to eat for it to kill you – but I was also worried about the dog. Have you seen how Kimi talks to it? Like it's her baby.' She shook her head. 'I know you've got a dog, but I'm really not a doggy person. More of a cat lady.'

'And our friendship started off so well…' I said. She snorted.

'No, it didn't. You helped rescue me from my trailer and I tried to snare your boyfriend in return.' I opened my mouth and she spoke again quickly. 'I know, I know, he's not your boyfriend. There's *something* there though, isn't there?'

'We're best friends,' I said. 'The best you can get without it being more than friendship. And as it turns out, we're both happy with that.'

She nodded. 'I see… I decided a long time ago that life is less complicated when you're single. But it does get lonely, especially when you're filming somewhere away from home … and Tony does have a nice smile, doesn't he?' I nodded, because he really did, even if it didn't have the same effect on me as one of Nathan's. 'So yes, I felt terrible about the dog, but it doesn't seem to have suffered any ill-effects.' She frowned. 'So maybe it *wasn't* the fish. Is that why you're here?' She looked at me more closely. 'I can't work out if you're just the caterer or some kind of cop. Although you are sitting here in a towel, so you're obviously not on duty…'

I laughed. 'Busted. I'm a private investigator-cum-consultant. *And* a chef. We genuinely don't know for certain yet if it was the fish, but it *was* a similar kind of neurotoxin that killed Jeremy, so…' I wasn't going to share my suspicions with her, even if she had just shouted me an afternoon in a swanky spa getting my blackheads done.

'If it wasn't the fish, there has to be something else everyone who got sick ate,' said Faith thoughtfully. 'Kimi says she wasn't ill, and I can't imagine she ate everything on offer, so it'll be something she turned her nose up at. I'm not saying she's fussy, but—'

'But she has very high standards when it comes to what she puts in her body,' I said, diplomatically. Faith laughed.

'That's a very good way of putting it. It's all part of her brand, isn't it? I don't go in for social media but I hear she's all over the Instagram with this 'clean-eating' stuff.'

'I much prefer messy eating,' I said, and Faith sighed.

'You have no idea how much I miss fish and chips,' she said. 'I do like eating healthily and looking after myself, but sometimes all I want is a big bowl of sticky toffee pudding and custard.' She sighed again, lying back and closing her eyes as if imagining the calorific but delicious dessert in front of her. 'But I'm a woman over fifty, and in this industry that means I'm already practically invisible. If I put weight on…'

'Bugger that,' I said, with feeling.

'It's not fair, is it? Look at Jeremy. He was a bloody

good actor, but he smoked and drank, and he ate like a pig. *He* was allowed to get a paunch on him; *he* was allowed to age without the roles drying up.' She shook her head. 'It's hard enough as it is to find decent parts as an older woman, let alone if, God forbid, you actually look your age.'

'You *don't* look your age,' I said, and she smiled.

'Bless you, that's very kind. But it's not fair that I'm not allowed to.' She looked at me closely. 'You must be, what, fifteen, twenty years younger than me? But I bet you've still been discriminated against over the years, just for being female.'

I nodded, thinking of all the times during my police career – in the early days, anyway – when I'd put up with sexist remarks from senior officers, or been the one sent to the canteen to get the teas in, or been the person expected to take notes during a meeting, like I was the flipping secretary. 'Of course.'

'I started in the film business nearly forty years ago,' she said. 'It was soul-destroying. It was all 'stand there and smile and look pretty'. Let the men get all the good lines and all the good plots. Want a part? Then go to dinner with the producer, let him leer at you, make him think he has a chance with you, and if you *really* want it that bad, well… I had to work twice as hard as the blokes in the room to get half the respect. It was only a few years back, when I was going through the menopause, and it really made me re-evaluate what it means to be a woman; it made me think back to those days and I decided I wasn't going to take it anymore. I don't want younger generations having to go through the same thing I did.'

'But you're still watching your figure.'

She laughed, with only a small trace of bitterness.

'I'm only one woman, and I do still want a career. But at least I have some respect now, and a little bit of power.'

'So what did you eat last night? If we can find something that neither you nor Kimi ate, then I can get DCI Withers to look into it.'

'I ate everything, I think.' Faith pursed her lips as she thought. 'I loved the fried chicken and the tempura. I did have some of the noodle dish but I have to admit I picked out the tofu. I've never enjoyed the texture.' She looked at me. 'Did you cook all of that? It was really tasty.'

I smiled. 'Yes, I did. I'm glad you enjoyed it. Anything else? How about the cupcakes, did you have one of them?'

'No,' said Faith. 'They looked lovely, but that's just one more thing I have to limit my intake of. I allow myself a small bar of chocolate on a Friday; that's my weekly treat. I wasn't going to forgo that for a cupcake.'

'I see…' I said, trying to keep the excitement, or

victory, or whatever it was out of my voice. I was right; I had to be!

It wasn't Zack and his pufferfish that had killed Jeremy and made the others sick. It was the cupcakes. The cupcakes had been spiked on purpose with the neurotoxin, and whoever had done it had made sure that there was a little bit in all of them so that it looked like food poisoning from the *fugu* rather than deliberate, targeted murder. All I needed to do now was find out who had sent the cakes. Another thought occurred to me: how had the murderer known that Jeremy would eat the right cake and consume enough toxin to kill him?

Chapter Twenty-One

I rescued Germaine from the hotel's doggy daycare; someone had taken it upon themselves to give her a good brushing and tie a ribbon around her neck. The ribbon came straight off but I had to admit, she scrubbed up well. I felt guilty that I didn't brush her as regularly as I probably should, but I was self-aware enough to know that the guilt would soon wear off and wouldn't make me do it any more often.

It was almost 3 o'clock, so I drove from the hotel straight to Daisy's school. She walked home with Jade most days, but if I was passing I'd swing by and collect them both. The girls jumped in, still chattering about meeting Zack the day before, and I realised with *another* guilty pang that I hadn't seen him at the hotel, despite that being my main reason for going there, and that he was still under the impression that his pufferfish had killed Jeremy. I didn't have his phone number, but I could ring the hotel and speak to him, or leave a message for him to call me; I didn't want him to feel guilty any longer than necessary. It briefly flashed across my mind that I should call Nathan and tell him what I'd discovered first, but after he'd basically put the phone down on me in a huff (and after I'd kissed Tony), I was feeling a bit of an emotional wreck.

We dropped Jade off, then pulled into our own driveway a few doors further up the road. Daisy bounced up the stairs to change out of her uniform while I put the kettle on.

'Wondered where you were,' said Mum, appearing in the back doorway. I jumped and nearly knocked a mug off the counter. 'Ooh, you're proper nervy today, ain't you? I was just putting some food out for the birds. Those blasted squirrels have been at the feeder again…'

I let Mum chatter on, not really listening to her, as I got teabags and milk out.

'You all right, sweetheart?' Mum had crept up on me, whether intentionally or because she was just naturally stealthy I didn't know. She did have the air of a geriatric ninja about her sometimes.

'Not really.' Did I want to tell her about today? I decided I did, even if I got a lecture out of it, because sometimes you just need to talk to your mum, don't you? 'Tony and I kissed today.'

'Oh, right…' She looked at me closely. I couldn't tell if she was pleased or disappointed by the idea, but she didn't look that surprised. 'So how was it?'

'You mean how was the kiss, or how was it afterwards?' I asked, but I knew what she meant. 'Because honestly, I'm not sure on either count.'

'How was it left? Are you boyfriend and girlfriend, or…?'

'Or. Definitely or.'

Mum nodded. 'I see. Brenda will be disappointed. She's been convinced for years that you two would get together. She's probably already chosen her hat for the wedding.'

'What about you?' I asked. 'I know how much you like him, and he's so good with Daisy…'

'None of that matters, if you don't feel the same.'

'Neither of us do. Which was a bit of a surprise to both of us.'

'Are you upset?'

'Sort of… I don't know. I did have a massive cry all over him, so I suppose I must be a bit.'

Mum pulled me in for a hug and kissed me on the cheek, then led me over to the kitchen table. She pulled out a chair.

'Sit there and I'll make you a Mum special,' she said,

and I smiled. A 'Mum special' was just a cup of tea and a plate of something sweet, but it had always worked when I was a teenager and it still worked now. I sat there feeling a bit sorry for myself as the kettle boiled and she opened a packet of Jaffa cakes, then joined me.

'You love each other,' she said, 'but you're not *in* love with each other.'

I nodded. 'Yeah, I suppose so…'

'Being *in* love is basically being a bit daft about each other,' she said. 'It's when you can't stop thinking about each other, and you get butterflies in your stomach – all that nonsense.' I opened my mouth to protest about her use of the word 'nonsense' – it seemed a bit harsh to me – but she stopped me. 'I know, I know. It's daft, but it's nice. Eventually it wears off, and if you're lucky you find out that you're best friends and you can still stand sharing the same bed every night. Companionship is far more important than passion, in the long term.'

'So by that measure, you think I should go out with Tony, even though it felt weird kissing him?' I shook my head, almost angry at her, because she was supposed to be giving me the benefit of her wisdom. But she laughed.

'Oh my Lord, no. That's not what I mean at all. You need that daft phase, so that during the times when you want to kill each other you can look back and think, 'He might be fat and bald now, and so annoying that I want to brain him with the iron, but we'll always have Paris…' or some other romantic malarkey. You and Tony have bypassed the passion and gone straight to companionship.'

'Riiight…' I said, doubtfully. 'So, Tony and I *shouldn't* be together? Which is just as well, because we're not.'

'Tony's like a pair of comfy slippers,' Mum said. 'Nothing wrong with that. You know what you're getting with him, and he'd always treat you well. But you're not ready for a pair of slippers.'

'I dunno, sometimes I feel like I am…'

Mum shook her head firmly. 'No, you're not. You need someone who can be a whole shoe shop for you. You need someone who takes you out dancing, like a pair of sexy kitten heels, and who goes on adventures with you, like a pair of hiking boots—'

'You must really be regretting using the shoe shop analogy about now,' I said. She ignored me.

'You need someone who's like a pair of ballet shoes.'

I looked at her for a moment and then shook my head. 'Nope, not getting that one.'

'They keep you on your toes,' she said. 'To be honest, that's what Tony needs too.'

'What, ballet shoes? You mean I'm *Tony's* comfy slippers?'

'Is everything all right?' I looked up and saw Daisy

standing in the doorway. I smiled and patted the chair next to me, which, to be fair, she was already eyeing up as she'd spotted the Jaffa cakes.

'Everything's fine,' I said. 'I'm just getting relationship advice from Dr Scholl.'

'Uh-oh,' she said, plopping herself down next to me and reaching for a Jaffa cake. 'Do I want to know?'

'Probably not.' We nibbled in silence for a few minutes, letting the chocolatey, orangey, cakey goodness seep into our bones…

'So how was your day?' I asked her finally. 'Did you have that maths test?'

'Bugger the maths test—'

'Um, language please! You're not thirteen yet.'

'Oh, can I swear when I'm thirteen then? Can I at least say shi—'

'No you blood— Blooming can't. There's not a sliding scale of cuss words, depending on your age, you know. I don't swear.' Mum raised her eyebrows. 'I don't! Not really. I made myself stop when I was a copper. Dad told me that if you swear at a suspect you've lost, because they'll see that you're stressed or angry, and *they're* the ones who should be stressed out, not you.'

'I remember that,' said Mum. 'He used to use all sorts of daft words instead of swearing.'

'Anyway, forget the maths test—' Daisy started again.

'Fudging heck!' cried Mum. We both looked at her,

alarmed. She smiled, lost in a haze of nostalgia. 'That's what your father used to say when he got angry.' Daisy and I looked at each other, then carried on.

'Anyway,' said Daisy, patiently. 'The maths test was fine. But I've spent the whole day dodging questions about the shoot. Everyone expects me to know what's going on.'

'Why should you?'

'Because their parents all went to school with you, and they all reckon you're really nosey.' She snorted. 'I can't think why…' She and Mum giggled.

'Yeah, yeah, all right…' I'd sworn not to tell anyone, but the news must already be getting out. Even if Debbie had kept her mouth shut (and I rather thought that my bombshell about Nathan leaving had knocked her more than the death of Jeremy Mayhew), Kimi had probably already posted about it on Instagram, and I got the feeling Faith liked a good gossip too, if she was bored. 'Okay, but none of this leaves this house, not for the moment, okay?'

They sat open-mouthed as I told them about the dinner party, and Jeremy Mayhew's untimely demise from tetrodotoxin. And because I was still working through the events of the day (the non-romantic ones, anyway), I told them about the suspicious cupcakes.

'So it wasn't Zack's fault after all?' asked Daisy. She

had been quite upset at the idea that he'd (inadvertently) killed someone. 'That's a relief.'

'Well, yes, it is for Zack, but if I'm right then it now means we're looking for someone who deliberately spiked something else – probably the cupcakes – with a neurotoxin to make it look like accidental food poisoning, when all along it was murder.'

'Who would want to murder Jeremy Mayhew?' asked Mum. 'He was a bit of a hellraiser, by all accounts, so he probably wouldn't have lived to a ripe old age anyway. All they had to do was wait a few years.'

'No idea,' I said. 'Faith admitted that they'd had an affair years back and that he wasn't exactly her favourite person, but there was no reason for her to want him dead.'

'It's so sad,' said Daisy. 'I'd never heard of him before yesterday, but when we watched that scene they were filming he was sick.'

'He was sick?' Mum looked puzzled. 'So maybe that's why—'

'That's sick as in 'really good',' I explained. 'Zack uses that expression too…' Daisy blushed but looked pleased.

'So we need to find out who could have had a grudge against Jeremy,' I said.

'Or Zack,' said Daisy. I looked at her sharply. 'I mean, why else use pufferfish toxin? Can you just go and buy it in Tesco's?'

'No. No, you can't…' I said thoughtfully. Why hadn't that occurred to me? My daughter was beautiful *and* clever. 'So the murderer made a point of using it to implicate Zack… The poor bloke's wracked with guilt. I don't know, but it could even end his career…' I looked at Daisy. 'That's very insightful, you know. I hadn't thought of that.'

She smiled. 'So would now be a good time to admit that the maths test was actually really rubbish?'

I laughed. 'Who needs maths anyway? I want to phone Zack and tell him he's off the hook, but this is all still speculation at this point. Until we get the lab results back on the fish guts, anyway. And I should probably talk to Nathan first…'

Mum looked at me. 'Is there a reason why you don't want to?' There was, bless her, but she was probably thinking it was to do with Tony, and I didn't want to tell her the real reason in front of Daisy because she might be upset and I couldn't handle that.

I was saved from answering because my phone rang. I immediately thought, with a sick feeling in my tummy, *That'll be Nathan,* but when I looked it was a number I didn't recognise.

'Hello?'

'Is that Jodie? What the crikey hell is going on? I leave my food truck for a few days and someone dies—' The

Italian was getting overexcited. Any minute now he'd cry *mamma mia!* and I would lose it.

'Gino, Gino, calm down! The police—'

'They contacted me, this DCI Winters—'

'Withers. His name's Withers.' *And it really is a TERRIBLE surname,* I thought. Jodie Withers did not sound great. It didn't have a nice ring to it. Honestly.

'DCI Whatever, he told me that Zack had poisoned someone with his *fugu sashimi* and I told him, that's impossible! But I don't think he believed me.'

'Why is it impossible? I think you're right. I don't think it was the fish, but—'

'Of course it wasn't the fish! You think I let him have poisonous fish?' Gino sounded exasperated, and he was making me feel the same way.

'Look, just calm down and tell me. Why couldn't it have been the fish?'

'Because it was *Takifugu Oblongus* – the North American pufferfish. I got it from a supplier up in Scotland, a fish farm. It's the only type they sell to the general public.'

'Let's assume I don't understand the significance of that, shall we?' I said patiently. 'Why couldn't it have been this North American pufferfish?'

Gino sighed, clearly disgusted at my lack of knowledge around the genus *Tetraodontidae,* because *of course* there was a lot of call for pufferfish in Cornwall, generally speaking… 'Because it's not toxic.'

I recovered from my shock long enough to calm Gino down and get the name of the seafood supplier from him. I promised him that the food truck was still in safe hands, death by poisoning notwithstanding, and that I would keep him informed of further developments.

Mum and Daisy were looking at me, having only heard my side of the conversation. Knowing that it was terribly unprofessional, but reminding myself that as I wasn't a professional anymore I didn't have to worry about stuff like that, I filled them in on Gino's bombshell.

'Wow!' said Daisy.

'Fudging heck!' said Mum.

'Innit?' I said. 'I didn't even know there was such a thing as non-toxic pufferfish. And Zack obviously didn't, either.' I thought back to what Mike Mancuso had said earlier – that he'd allowed Zack to go ahead and serve the *fugu* because Gino had told him he would make sure it was safe. But he hadn't told him *how* he'd do that.

'I'd better tell Nathan,' I said, frowning. I caught Mum looking at me curiously again, but there was no way I was going to tell her about him leaving when I didn't want to even think about it, let alone discuss it with someone who wouldn't let me pretend I didn't have any feelings for him… I have tackled drunken hooligans waving broken bottles at me, and disarmed a knife-wielding maniac more than once, and yet at that moment I would rather have faced one of them than Nathan. Physical risks I'm okay with; emotional ones, not so much.

'I need another cup of tea,' I said, and wandered over to the kettle with my phone. While I waited for it to boil, I typed a text message to Nathan. Yes, I am a coward. I've never pretended I wasn't.

Just spoke to Gino and he says the fish was a NON-TOXIC variety. So was definitely NOT the fish!

I hesitated for a moment, then put:

J x

Then hesitated again and added:

xx

And hit send before I wussed out and deleted them. And then of course I wished I hadn't put three x's at the end, because, you know, *one* could be a kiss from a friend, like the way you kiss someone hello on the cheek, *two* could possibly be construed as being European (one on each cheek), but *three* ... three kisses was definite I'm-thinking-about-snogging-you territory.

Maybe I was overthinking it...

My phone pinged almost immediately with a reply. Nathan.

So THAT'S what he was going on about lol. He was a bit overexcited when he rang me and he put the phone down on me before I could work out what he was saying. He's like an Italian Gordon Ramsey lol.

(I'd never seen so many 'lol's in one of his messages before, and I imagined him giving a nervous laugh as he typed each one in).

Can you talk?

Yes, and I rarely stop, I thought, but I didn't type it. *No, no, no,* I also thought, but I didn't type that either. *You are SUCH a coward, Parker,* I berated myself, but fair's fair, it had been a very emotional day one way or another, and I needed to be in control of myself before I spoke to him again.

Not really. Got a terrible headache and about to go to bed.

I hit send and got a reply almost immediately.

Sorry, I hope you feel better after a good sleep. Talk tomorrow? xxx

I wanted to cry. But instead I just typed:

Definitely xxx

And made some more tea.

Chapter Twenty-Two

I spent the evening watching TV and playing Scrabble with Mum and Daisy, studiously avoiding any thoughts of Nathan, Tony, or the case. But mostly Nathan.

It was almost impossible, though. After a very healthy dinner of salmon (brushed with sweet-chilli sauce and baked in the oven), served with brown rice and stir-fried veg, which I thought might almost get the Kimi seal of approval, I made mini microwave chocolate lava mug cakes, which definitely wouldn't. Daisy had requested them specially, as she enjoyed making them with me almost as much as she enjoyed eating them.

I watched as she measured the ingredients out into the mugs: a quarter of a cup of flour, a teaspoon of baking powder, two tablespoons each of sugar and cocoa powder, and a pinch of salt, mixed with two tablespoons each of vegetable oil and milk. She repeated the same amounts for each mug and then mixed everything to a paste, adding a touch more milk here and there to loosen the mixture.

As she did that, I grated the zest of an orange and added that to each mug, along with a squeeze of juice. Then the final ingredient: a big wedge of chocolate orange, tucked into the middle of each cake.

'Oh my God, they smell amazing…' Daisy inhaled deeply and I laughed.

'Yeah, Nathan really liked it when I made him one the other night…' I said, my laughter trailing off before I knew it was happening. Luckily Daisy was too intent on popping a mug into the microwave to notice my sudden downer. And fifty seconds later, I had a hot chocolate cake with an oozy, orangey, chocolatey centre to console myself with.

It almost worked.

I took Germaine for her nocturnal walk around the block, but Nathan had joined me on that walk several times, so it was difficult not to think of him. I remembered the night he'd come for dinner and then walked with me, when his phone had rung and he'd said to his mum, 'Yeah, her.' I'd read so much into those two words; they meant he'd told his mum about me, which surely he wouldn't do if I was just a friend? But if I was more than a friend, then he wouldn't still be debating whether or not to take this job offer, would he?

I sighed, and at my feet Germaine cocked her leg and sighed too, before unleashing a torrent on a poor, unsuspecting weed.

I went to bed early that night, not long after Daisy and Mum – not because I was tired, but because I was bored and restless. Nothing on TV interested me, and I couldn't get into the book I was reading even though I'd been enjoying it the night before. I lay back on my pillow and stretched out across the bed, but instead of enjoying the freedom of having the whole thing to myself, I wished that there was a body next to me, someone to snuggle up to or warm my cold feet on.

As if she'd read my mind, Germaine trotted in through the bedroom door. I always left it open slightly; it was a hangover from Daisy's younger days, when she'd often wake in the night after a bad dream, but nowadays it was just as likely to be Mum I was listening out for. Germaine leapt up on the bed and made herself comfortable in the crook of my knees.

'Aren't you meant to be on Daisy's bed?' I whispered, stroking her snout, but she just snuffled my hand and settled down even more. If they ever made 'getting comfy' into a sporting event, that dog would win Olympic gold. I smiled and reached out my other hand to turn out the light.

I woke the next morning feeling surprisingly refreshed. Surprising, as I'd tossed and turned all night and had the most ridiculous dream. I'd been back at Parkview Manor Hotel, which was decorated once more for Tony's wedding. No, *mine* and Tony's wedding. I was in my hotel room, getting into my wedding dress – an over-the-top, meringue-like confection of pure white silk and lace, the sort of dress I wouldn't even wear to my funeral, let alone my wedding – and I was struggling to do the zip up on my own, and it was getting closer and closer to the ceremony, and I wasn't ready, and every time I tried to ring someone for help my stupid fingers kept dialling the wrong number and not getting through. I gave up and found myself in my jeans, in the hotel kitchen, which for some reason was full of guests (none of whom I recognised). Sergeant Adams, the desk sergeant at Penstowan police station and one of my late father's few remaining recruits, was officiating. At the altar (which looked somewhat out of place, being next to the big walk-in fridge) Tony turned and smiled at me, only now it wasn't Tony, it was Jeremy Mayhew, and he was looking a bit peaky. Well, dead.

I was relieved when I woke up. I had the horrible feeling that when Sergeant Adams got to the bit about anyone objecting, Nathan would pipe up from somewhere near the oven and say it should be him, and then he and Tony/Jeremy would ride off into the sunset together. It would have made about as much sense as the rest of the dream.

The dog had deserted me in the night, and I heard Daisy talking to her in her bedroom. I looked at the clock, then relaxed as I remembered that it was Saturday: no school run, and with the shoot suspended, no work either. It was nice to have a lie-in, but not so nice when I thought about the money I was missing out on. I probably had enough now to buy Daisy's birthday present, but I had to admit that the Gimpmobile, the elderly van I'd bought for Banquets and Bakes, was probably not going to get replaced. It would have to limp on for a while longer...

I crept out of bed and made myself a cup of tea, not wanting the rest of the house to hear me and think it was time to get up, then took it back upstairs and sat in bed, drinking and trying hard not to think about anything in particular. I'd turned my phone off early the night before, not wanting to talk to anybody, but had felt absurdly guilty about it; what if someone needed to contact me? *Who?* I'd asked myself. *Everyone you're responsible for is right here, under this roof.* I'm not a slave to my phone, but I did feel slightly uncomfortable with it sitting on my bedside table, dead, so I turned it on and immediately got a ton of text messages (well, four).

The oldest one was from Debbie.

Oh my God, Tony just told Callum and he told me! Hope you're ok. Call me if you want to talk.

I toyed with the idea of ignoring her, because I *was* okay and I didn't want to talk, but I knew that she had a good heart and would be worried if she didn't hear from me and, more to the point, she'd be on the phone demanding to know the details if I didn't reply soon. I sent her a quick message telling her I was fine and I'd call her later. Much later…

The next one was from Tony himself, sent just before bed, just two words:

We good?

My reply was almost as brief:

Yep, we're good.

The third message had come in about an hour ago, and it took me by surprise: a group text to all background talent telling us the shoot was back on. So much for my day off, but at least it meant maybe my old van was getting replaced after all.

And the last message had come in around the time I'd woken up, from Nathan.

Morning, I hope you're feeling better now x

I sipped at my tea, trying to come up with a reply that would convey the rush of emotions that swept over me every time I saw him, that had swept over me now just at the sight of his *name,* for heaven's sake, without scaring the bejesus out of him and making him run for the hills (or, more to the point, Liverpool), but had to settle for:

Much better, thank you. Think I was just tired. You heard the shoot is back on? Will be at the food truck in an hour or so.

Nathan couldn't possibly have been waiting in anticipation for a reply, but he must have had the phone close by because within twenty seconds of me hitting send:

Heard about the shoot. There are a few things I want to look at so see you there. Glad you're better xxx

The three kisses at the end made me feel better and worse all at the same time. I typed back:

Later, alligator xxx

Ping! That was quick.

In a while, crocodile x

I showered and dressed quickly but with care, which I can neither confirm nor deny had anything to do with wanting to look nice for Nathan later. Daisy gave a yelp of excitement from the bedroom as I was making toast downstairs, and flew into the kitchen waving her phone; she'd got a text message too, and today was the day she'd be making her big screen debut. I hoped for all our sakes she wasn't going to be a peasant like me, especially as her bestie Jade was in it as well. Jade's mum Nancy was Cornish, born and bred, but her dad was Spanish, and both Jade and her little brother had ended up with a beautiful combination of blonde hair and an all-year-round Mediterranean tan skin tone. I could just imagine her being cast as some kind of ethereal pixie, while my beautiful but very Anglo-Saxon-looking daughter would be reduced to wearing a smaller version of the flipping itchy potato sack I'd had to contend with during my very brief acting career.

But for now, anything was possible, even being noticed by the director and given a few lines, and *then* being signed up on the spot by an agent, and *then* being cast in this generation's version of *Harry Potter* or *The Hunger Games* or whatever. So Daisy fussed over her hair and put her favourite jeans on even though they were technically due for a wash (because of course they were the only thing that would come close to bridging the gap between her and stardom, so she couldn't possibly wear her other pair), forced herself to eat some breakfast, and then danced about on her toes waiting for me to get a move on.

Would you believe it, Mum also had her big break today. I had to forcibly restrain her from getting a taxi back to her house to get her best outfit (the light-blue skirt suit she'd worn to my cousin Kevin's wedding five years ago; it made her look like a cross between Mrs Doubtfire and the Queen Mum), and it was only when I told her about the chaotic communal dressing room where she'd have to leave her precious outfit during filming that she acquiesced and put her normal clothes on.

That meant there was no one to dog-sit Germaine today, so the whole family piled into the car and headed off to Polvarrow House.

The shoot was a hive of activity. The crew bustled around, hurriedly setting stuff up that had just as hurriedly been dismantled for safe storage the day before when it had looked like the shoot was over. If anyone was upset or even bothered about the death of Jeremy

Mayhew, they were doing a bloody good job of hiding it. It felt a little bit tasteless to me, a little bit … *unseemly*, for want of a less Jane Austen-esque word. I knew the old saying that the show must go on, but really, must it? And so soon?

I delivered Daisy and Mum to the Wardrobe trailer and headed to the food truck. When I saw Mike Mancuso and Sam Pritchard in heated debate nearby, I went the long way round in an attempt to hear what they were talking about, but by the time I got close enough Pritchard had already stalked away. Mancuso saw me, so I gave him a businesslike nod, which he completely ignored. Fair enough.

I opened up the food truck, tethering Germaine to the steps on a long leash, and thought back over the conversation Nathan and I had had with the producer the day before. He'd been keen to get the case number so that he could claim on the production's accident insurance, and I'd laughed at Nathan's veiled warning about not claiming just yet; but despite the fact he'd only said that to wind Mancuso up, Nathan had turned out to be right. Mayhew's death was looking like a deliberate act, not an accident or even misadventure, and knowing how hard most insurance companies will fight not to cough up any money on even the most genuine claim, I couldn't believe they would pay out on a possible murder. Maybe that was why the shoot had started again? A production of this size must cost … well, I had no idea how much it cost to make a film, but you hear about Hollywood movies with budgets the size of a small country's GDP, and with a cast and crew of this size, and with the hire of Polvarrow House, and all the equipment – even things like the horses and Gino's food truck (and me) – they probably couldn't afford to keep paying all those people for just sitting around and doing nothing.

I fired up the big catering urns so the cast and crew could at least have tea and coffee, then got some bacon cooking. Film crews *love* bacon baps, Gino had told me, and he was right. Once that was done I would take Germaine for a walk around the set to stop her getting bored and into mischief.

'You're back, then,' said Lucy, the first AD. She was standing by the counter, waiting for the urns to heat up. 'I thought maybe it was Gino. Sam seemed to think you were actually a copper, not a chef.'

'Bit of both,' I said, smiling. 'I have to say I'm surprised to be back. I thought the shoot would be shut down for longer.'

Lucy smiled tightly. 'Yeah, me too. It seems there's little room for sentiment in filmmaking…'

'A shoot like this must cost a lot to run,' I said. 'And these people still want paying, even when they're not able to work.'

'Yes,' she said. 'I was under the impression that's what we have insurance for, but obviously not.'

'No…' So maybe it wasn't common knowledge yet that it had been murder? Or maybe it just hadn't occurred to her that an insurance policy was unlikely to cover that eventuality. She made herself a cup of tea and nodded to me before wandering off.

I turned around to flip bacon, but it wasn't long before I was interrupted again.

'All right?' Zack's voice didn't have that usual note of cheerful swagger about it; he must still be wracked with guilt. I was surprised that Nathan hadn't told him he was off the hook yet.

'How're you doing?' I asked, in a sympathetic tone of voice. He shrugged.

'Been better.'

'And Aiko? Has she recovered?'

'She's on the mend, still a bit weak though.' He smiled sadly. 'Not the best start to a relationship, is it?'

'You really like her, don't you?' I asked. He gave me a slow, shy smile. *Aww, sweetheart!* I thought. I reached over the counter and patted his hand. 'I'm sure it'll be fine. If it's meant to be, it will be.' I thought of Tony as I said that, and I sincerely hoped for Zack's sake that *his* relationship *was* meant to be. 'Look, about the fish—'

'I know, I know, I should never have served it,' he

said. He shook his head. 'I still can't believe I cocked it up.'

I looked around, but there was no one else about. I had to tell him and put his mind at rest. 'I don't think you did. This can't go any further, okay?' I (metaphorically) rolled my eyes at myself; I'd been saying that a lot over the last couple of days, and I really hoped that all the people I'd sworn to secrecy really could keep quiet.

Zack looked mystified. 'Of course! Go on.'

'It wasn't the fish.'

'But – I heard they found the neurotoxin…'

'They did. But the fish Gino got you, it's non-toxic. That's why he was happy to order it for you. I just wish he'd told me about it before.'

Zack sagged suddenly and I thought for a moment he was going to pass out.

'Oh my God…' he said.

'Go and sit down,' I told him. 'I'll bring you a cuppa.'

I turned off the stove (the bacon would have to wait a few more minutes) and joined Zack at a picnic bench, untying Germaine so she could come and be sociable. I pushed a mug of hot tea over to him as she snuffled at his feet and put her paws sympathetically on his lap. He smiled and patted her, then looked up to see me watching him closely.

'Don't tell me, I've gone all pale,' he said, and I laughed.

'Well, you have gone a bit beige…' He gave one of his big belly laughs, and I knew he was feeling better.

'Keep what I just told you to yourself for the moment,' I said. 'The police haven't made it official yet, and we don't want to disturb any lines of enquiry.'

'What lines of enquiry?' asked Zack, and then that shocked expression came back. 'You don't mean—' He looked around too then, and dropped his voice. 'You don't mean murder?'

I shrugged, trying to look like there could be myriad completely innocent reasons for pufferfish toxin ending up in a cupcake… 'I dunno. Probably not.' Aware that I probably didn't sound terribly convincing, I struggled for something else to say, and suddenly inspiration struck me. 'You know this supposed 'curse'? All these stupid accidents and pranks? Well, I'm thinking that maybe this was just another prank that got out of hand.'

'Really?' Zack looked doubtful.

'I think it's definitely something we have to consider,' I said. 'How many accidents have happened here? Kimi's dog escaping, light bulbs blowing, the generator shorting out, the food-truck stairs breaking, Faith's caravan door getting jammed…' Zack shifted uncomfortably in his seat. He made himself stop quickly, but I'd already spotted it. I recognised the signs… 'I reckon,' I said carefully, 'if we find out who's behind those pranks, we'll find out who's behind the food poisoning.'

Zack avoided my eyes, staring down into his mug and stirring the hot tea with his finger.

'Is there something you want to tell me?' I asked. He looked up before he could stop himself, then away again.

'Course not.' It was his turn to sound unconvincing. Germaine gave a little whine, like she didn't believe him either.

'Zack,' I said, 'if you know something, you need to tell me or the police. If you tell me, I can decide whether it's something they need to know or whether we can forget about it. If you don't tell me and the police find out later – and they always do find out later – then it won't look very good on you, will it?'

He looked at me again, obviously weighing something up in his mind.

'Zack,' I said. 'We're mates, right? We've cooked together. I'd give you a job chopping veg if you ever gave up acting…' He gave a small laugh. 'So you know I'm on your side, right? If you've done something daft…'

He looked defensive. 'Everyone thinks she's this National Treasure, and she acts all motherly to the younger actors on set, but she's a right bloody racist.'

'Really?' I was surprised. Faith's on-screen husband in *Mile End Days* was a big Jamaican guy, and their 'children' were all mixed-race actors. It seemed to me that it would be easy to be prejudiced against a group of people you knew nothing about, but if you were working closely with them, for several years in Faith's case, it would be difficult to keep that up; you surely couldn't help but realise they were exactly the same as you in every single aspect that mattered. 'Are you sure? What makes you think that?'

'I borrowed a phone charger off her and I was on my way to take it back,' said Zack. 'I was outside her trailer and I heard her talking, and she said Kimi and me were the production's 'diversity hires'. She was mouthing off saying that we only got the nod as part of some box-ticking exercise to get funding.'

I looked at him, shocked. That really was a horrible thing to say, and blatantly untrue because both he and Kimi were talented actors. I still couldn't quite believe that Faith would say that, though, despite having had my own doubts about her earlier; but then I'd realised that my own judgement had been clouded by jealousy over her and Tony. That jealousy was still kind of there, but had subsided enough for me to actually quite like the woman. 'So what did you do?'

'I was really upset and angry,' he said. 'I was going to burst in and have a go at her, but I didn't want to make a big scene. Because to be honest, I've been on sets where I *am* the diversity hire, and I didn't want to find out if what she was saying was true.' I reached out and touched his arm, feeling immense sympathy for him. 'I didn't know what to do, but then I felt in my pocket and I still had this tube of superglue one of the crew gave me. Bits kept falling off my stupid sword and I was using it to stick them back on.' I remembered him brandishing the sword the day of the dinner party, striking a heroic pose with it before a big plastic red jewel in the hilt had fallen off.

'You squirted glue in the lock,' I said, and he nodded.

'Yeah. I had some mates back home who had this squat in Tulse Hill years ago, and they tried to stop the police getting in by buggering up all the locks with superglue.'

'So how did your mates get in and out?' I asked, interested in spite of myself.

'They climbed through the windows,' he said. 'It was a third-floor flat and all. Their next-door neighbour used to let them climb onto his balcony then let them out.' He grinned. 'I couldn't see Faith doing that... But look, it was just a daft thing; she was never going to get hurt.'

'Okay,' I said. 'So you were the one who sabotaged Faith's caravan. What about the other things? Did you let Kimi's dog out?'

Zack shook his head. 'Of course I didn't. Why would I? Between you and me, I quite like that dog.' Germaine settled on his feet with an approving grunt. He laughed. 'And this one, too. Maybe I am a dog person after all.'

'You don't know who was behind that, or any of the other pranks?'

'No,' he said, but I was suddenly not so sure.

'Zack…' I said warningly. He sighed again.

'Oh, all right. You might want to talk to Aiko about the dog.'

Chapter Twenty-Three

Zack was due on set, so I went back to the bacon and finished setting everything out for breakfast/brunch-time butties. Then I clipped the lead on Germaine and headed over to Wardrobe to see how Daisy and Mum were getting on.

I'd timed it perfectly, as they had just finished getting their clothes and make-up on, and the two of them looked *amazing*.

'I don't believe it!' I said. 'You're both members of the aristocracy!'

'Too blooming right we are!' said Mum, indignantly adjusting her crinoline. 'Ain't no peasants in this family.'

'Mum was,' smirked Daisy.

'They just didn't want me to outshine Kimi,' I said,

and was mildly offended when both of them guffawed loudly. 'Seriously, you both look lovely. Did you see Jade?' I asked Daisy. She nodded.

'She's playing one of the fairy folk,' she said. 'She's got wings. She had to turn sideways to get out the door.'

We were interrupted by the sound of a wolf whistle. I turned round to see Tony grinning, although he looked a little uncertain when he looked at me.

'Wow, Shirl, look at you!' he said. 'You do know I've always had a thing about older women?'

'Faith does,' I said in a low voice, but I was only messing about.

Mum laughed and hit him (harder than he expected, going by the way he flinched) with her embroidered fan.

'Ooh you're a cheeky one, Tony Penhaligon! Your dad was just the same in his younger days.'

'Now *that* I don't want to know,' he said. 'Daisy, you look really lovely.' Daisy smiled, but she was distracted by the sight of Jade getting her wings wedged into a gap between two trailers and went to free her. Mum looked at the two of us in a way that made it really obvious I'd told her about our kiss.

'I'll give you two some space,' she said, turning away.

'Mum, there's no need—'

'It's fine, Shirley—'

But she was off. We stood and looked at each other.

'Are we *really* okay?' asked Tony, and just like that we were. The ice was broken.

'Of course,' I said. 'It was bound to be a bit awkward, seeing each other today, but it's for the best, innit?'

'It is. Unless you've changed your mind?'

'No. Have you?'

'No, I haven't.' Tony sighed. 'It would have been proper easy, though. I mean, I'm already used to your funny little ways...'

'What funny little ways? Flipping cheek. I'm used to your smell, and I don't even really notice anymore when you wipe your nose on your sleeve...'

'Yeah, whatever.' Tony grinned at me. 'I see you told your mum.'

'And you told Debbie.'

'Callum, actually.'

'Same thing.'

Lucy appeared and began collecting extras, so I let him go, wished Mum and Daisy good luck, and then headed over to Zack's trailer, which was now officially (as far as I was concerned, anyway) a crime scene.

Sergeant Adams was on duty today, sitting on a fold-up chair, guarding the stairs up to the trailer. Germaine bounded over to him and popped her front paws on his knees, making him laugh. He patted her head and looked up at me.

'All right there, young Jodie?' he said.

'I'm good, thanks. They let you out of the station, then?' He was rapidly approaching retirement age and not really up for chasing criminals, so they normally kept him on desk duty but occasionally they let him out for a change of scenery.

'Yeah. Dunno what I done to deserve that,' he grinned, taking a small paper bag from his pocket and offering it to me. 'Jelly baby?'

'I can never say no to a jelly baby,' I said, selecting a red one and popping it into my mouth.

'If you're looking for the DCI, he's on his way,' said Sergeant Adams, shuffling about in his seat. 'And not a moment too soon, either. I needs relieving for a pi— For a bit.'

'I can take over, if you want?' I said, but he shook his head.

'He'd have my guts for garters if I deserted my post,' he said. 'I just 'ope he comes soon, otherwise…'

'Cavalry's here,' said Nathan from behind me. I turned round and he gave me that smile of his, full beam. *Don't swoon, woman!* I told myself sternly, but my self-chastising didn't have much effect. 'Sergeant Adams, whatever dire thing was going to happen doesn't need to happen now, does it? Off you go. We'll be inside.' He stood back and gestured for me to go up the stairs in front of him, as Sergeant Adams leapt up in a far sprightlier manner than I would have given him credit for and dashed off towards the Portaloos. I tied Germaine to the steps (she gave me a look of hurt resignation as I did so) and led the way up.

Inside Zack's trailer, the scene was pretty much how we'd left it. The Scene of Crime team had been over it the morning after Mayhew's death, but at that point we'd been pretty certain it was the fish, so they had been there more to prove that theory than find another cause of death.

We stood at the table and looked at what was left of the food. It was starting to smell, and I thanked my lucky stars that we were in this draughty caravan in October and not in July, when it would have been a sweltering metal box.

'So…' said Nathan, looking at me.

'So…' I said, looking at him.

'What are you thinking?' he asked. I was actually thinking about him swiping everything off the table and onto the floor, then flinging me onto it to make mad passionate love to me, but I could hardly admit that.

'I'm thinking,' I said, playing for time as I desperately tried to think of something that didn't sound like the final scene in a Mills-and-Boon bodice ripper, 'I'm thinking, you didn't tell Zack that it wasn't the fish yet. You don't seem to have told anyone.'

He smiled. 'You're right, I haven't. But I'm assuming that you *have* told him?'

I nodded. 'Yes. The poor bloke was falling apart from the guilt, not just of killing Jeremy but of poisoning his new girlfriend as well. I did tell him to keep it to himself, though. Said we didn't want to prejudice any lines of enquiry.'

''Prejudice lines of enquiry'? Oh *that* sounds good; that sounds really legit.' Nathan grinned. 'No, really, that's a good one. Do you think he will tell anyone else?'

'I don't know. Maybe Aiko. Why don't you want anyone to know?'

'Well, one, I was waiting for the lab results to come back on the fish – they have now; negative of course – and two, I just wanted to see how everyone would react, to see if anyone gave themselves away.'

'How would they do that?'

'Well, look at all this. There's not much food left here, but there is a bit. If I'd slipped the toxin into something, I'd stay quiet until it looked like the pufferfish was going to get the blame for it – which as far as they all know, it has – and then I'd be the first person to suggest that we send the cleaners in to get rid of all the mess, so Zack can have his caravan back.'

'And you think that'll work?'

'No idea. The other thing is to find what was actually

poisoned, and see if we can narrow down who had access to it and was therefore most likely to have done it.'

'Or, like I suggested *ages* ago, we find out what it was that everyone apart from Kimi and Faith, who didn't get sick, ate. Neither of them had the pufferfish, but they also didn't have—'

'The cupcakes,' he said.

'I was suspicious of them all along,' I said. 'No one knows where they came from.'

'Who have you asked?'

'Well, only Zack, Kimi, and Faith, but they were delivered in a weird, secretive way, just dumped on the counter of the food truck when I wasn't looking.' I spotted the box on the table. 'So I reckon we should be testing whatever's in that box.'

Nathan pulled on latex gloves and lifted the lid of the box carefully. We both took a deep breath as he peered inside…

'There's none left,' he said.

'Really?' I was surprised. 'That's odd. There were a lot of them – ten I reckon, or maybe even a dozen. There were seven people for dinner and two of them didn't eat them, so that means they all had at least two cakes each.'

Nathan looked at me and grinned. 'You telling me you couldn't eat two cupcakes?'

I looked at him indignantly. 'No, I couldn't! Well, not

big cupcakes like these, with a ton of frosting on, not straight after a meal.'

'So where are the others?'

We stared at each other. Maybe the poisoner had beaten us to it; maybe they'd already somehow sneaked into the caravan and taken the incriminating cupcakes…

'There's been a uniform on the door twenty-four hours a day since the death,' said Nathan. 'There's no way anyone could have got in.'

'Through the window?' I suggested, remembering how I'd badgered Tony into climbing in through the big one at the back of Faith's caravan. Nathan went over and checked it, then shook his head.

'It's locked from the inside,' he said. 'Even if they'd left it unlocked on the night of the murder, so they could get back in, it would still be unlocked now after they climbed back out.' He looked at me. 'We might be making something out of nothing here. They might have just eaten all of them.'

I shook my head. 'You didn't see them. They were works of art, but they were covered in loads of frosting and icing and glitter. They would have been really sweet – maybe on purpose to cover the taste of the poison. Even without the big meal first, they'd be too rich to eat all of them.' Another thought occurred to me. 'Plus it seems to me that all the cakes would have to have a certain amount of toxin in them, so that everyone got sick and made it look like accidental food poisoning, rather than someone targeting Jeremy—'

'So if the diners had eaten more than one cupcake, and therefore more than one dose of toxin, we surely would have ended up with more than one corpse on our hands.' Nathan looked at me thoughtfully.

'I was thinking about this earlier,' I said. 'The poisoner must have been at the meal, to make sure that Jeremy took the right cake. So they could have taken any leftover cakes with them on the night, when they left. They could have slipped them into a bag. There was probably enough chaos going on to do that unseen.'

'But by your reckoning, there would have been at least five cakes left,' he said. 'They'd need a big bag, like a messenger bag or rucksack.'

'Kimi has a rucksack,' I said, 'A hideous designer number with a tiger's head on it...'

Nathan waylaid a scurrying crew member and asked if Kimi was at the shoot today. The harassed woman gave him an irritated look, before looking at him properly and suddenly becoming all big smiles and helpful attitude. It was certainly useful having a good-looking DCI on the case...

Kimi had finished in Hair and Make-Up, and was

now waiting in her trailer until she was needed. *Probably drinking a bottle of sea water that cost fifteen quid,* I thought. Cornwall was surrounded by water on three sides, and we had lots of Blue Flags, the award given to coastal areas with the cleanest water and beaches. Maybe one of our local entrepreneurs should start bottling *L'eau de Penstowan* and charging a tenner for it.

We approached Kimi's trailer. Germaine was straining at her leash, and if Nathan had been wearing one, he would have been too.

'Hold on,' I said, as we reached the foot of the trailer's steps. 'What are we going to say to her? She's hardly going to admit to poisoning the cupcakes, is she? And she'll have binned them by now.' He raised an eyebrow. 'All right, you're the policeman. What are *you* going to say to her?'

'There's this technique I learned during my CID training,' he said. 'You might not have heard of it, seeing as you were only a lowly uniform…'

'Watch it, DCI Withers,' I growled. He laughed.

'Or maybe you *have* heard of it. It's called 'winging it'. Just follow my lead.' He turned towards the steps, then stopped. 'Oh, and if you manage to leave all the talking to me I will be amazed.' He turned away. 'I'm not holding my breath…'

I gave him a dig in the back as he walked up to the door of the trailer and knocked. Inside, there was the sound of muffled swearing and then silence; Kimi obviously didn't want visitors. Nathan knocked again.

'Miss Takahashi, it's DCI Withers. I'd like to ask you a few questions, please.'

From inside came the sound of frantic movements and a muffled voice again. We exchanged alarmed looks.

'Can you open the door please, Miss? Kimi?' Nathan knocked again. Germaine gave a small yap as, behind us, a very pale-looking Aiko and Princess approached.

'What's going on?' asked Aiko, alarmed. Inside, the sounds of frantic movement increased.

'Walking the dog today, are we?' I said. 'Rather than just letting her out so she could take herself off for a swim?'

Aiko started guiltily. 'I never meant— I didn't think she'd get that far…'

'We think your sister might be in some trouble,' said Nathan. Aiko took a key from her pocket and rushed up the stairs. He took it from her and opened the door.

'Miss Takahashi, we're coming in…'

Inside, was a scene of devastation. Devastation if you were a cupcake, anyway. Kimi sat bolt upright on the sofa, her massive fairy wings making it impossible for her to recline in the slightest. The hideous designer rucksack was next to her on the seat, and two empty cupcake wrappers lay beside it, their shiny gold paper twinkling in the ray of weak October sunshine that came in through the open door. It was already blatantly obvious that Kimi had been eating the evidence, but as if to underline it for the people at the back and anyone who wasn't paying attention, there was a dollop of pink and white frosting on the tip of her nose, and her cleavage (which was on full display in her not-particularly-modest costume) was covered in sprinkles and edible glitter.

'Kimi!' cried Aiko, rushing over to her.

'Mmmpf mmf mmm!' said Kimi, her mouth full of cake. She swallowed. 'What the hell? What are you doing, breaking into my trailer?'

'We didn't break in. Aiko had a key,' I pointed out, thinking, *I hope we were wrong about those cupcakes, otherwise any time now Kimi's going to really experience the evils of sugary snacks…*

'Oh Kimi!' Aiko looked distraught. She sat next to her sister and took her hand. 'You've been doing it again, haven't you?' Kimi looked at her for a moment and opened her mouth to retort, but then burst into completely unexpected tears.

Nathan and I looked at each other, feeling awkward.

'Um…' said Nathan. He looked a bit bewildered; neither of us had been expecting this. 'Miss Takahashi, you're not in any trouble. We just wanted to ask you about the cupcakes…'

'I couldn't help it!' she sobbed. 'They looked so good.

When we left the dinner party after Jeremy's death I had to have one.'

'One?' said Aiko, sternly. Kimi shrugged.

'It was quicker to just tip them all out of the box and into my bag,' she said. 'And I was so upset after watching Jeremy… and I was worried about Princess…'

'You were worried about the dog? That figures.' Aiko angrily let go of her hand and went to stand up, but Kimi grabbed her.

'Of course I was worried about you! But you were safe at the hospital, and you've got Zack. I could tell he liked you the first time I saw the two of you together. Without you, Princess is all I've got…'

Aiko still looked angry, but she shook her head and put her arm around her sister. 'Don't be so silly.'

'I was so upset that I went back to the hotel room and I … I ate a cupcake.' Kimi looked guilty, and for a moment I remembered what Faith had said about not wanting the younger generation of actors to suffer the way she had. They obviously still were – obviously still obsessed with their looks and their weight, not risking putting on even an ounce in case it ruined their careers. And they were probably right; the roles probably would dry up if they got old and fat, or even if they looked like an ordinary woman. Who wants to see an ordinary woman on the screen? *I do,* I thought, *and so do a lot of other female moviegoers.*

'You ate a cupcake the night of the dinner party?' said Nathan, glancing at me.

'Yes,' said Kimi defensively. 'Sam did order them for my birthday, after all.'

'Sam Pritchard bought them?' I asked. She nodded and scrabbled around in her bag, pulling out a small card.

'This was in the bottom of the box,' she said, holding it out. I took it.

Happy birthday to my leading lady on her birthday, love Sam.

I couldn't imagine the director wanting to poison his own stars.

'And you weren't sick after you ate it?' I asked.

'Of course not,' said Kimi, but she looked like she was lying. Aiko sighed.

'She probably *was* sick,' she said, 'but not because of food poisoning.' Nathan looked confused. 'My sister has an eating disorder, Detective Chief Inspector. I thought she was getting better.'

'I am!' wailed Kimi, but the frosting and the scattered sprinkles and the discarded cake wrappers told a different story. I felt guilty now that I'd laughed at all her healthy eating talk and the ridiculously expensive water. She was just a vulnerable, confused young woman who had been thrust into the spotlight, a spotlight that had illuminated and played upon all the insecurities that most of us have; but most of us are allowed a bit of privacy to work through them.

We left Aiko helping her sister to clean up the mess and have a heart-to-heart talk. Nathan was quiet as we went down the stairs, Germaine trotting along behind us solemnly; I think she'd liked the look of Princess and wanted to have a run around with her, but now was not the time.

'Tea?' I asked, and Nathan nodded.

We sat at a picnic bench. It felt a bit warmer today; it was one of those autumnal days when the weather can't quite decide if it wishes it were still summer or whether it should just get on with it and turn into winter. The sun was out, although it was already too low in the sky to give off much heat, but it was still pleasant enough, sitting there in our coats, hot mugs clasped in our hands.

'Poor Kimi,' I said eventually, and Nathan nodded.

'I'd never really thought about how young she is,' he said. 'She reminded me of my sister.'

I looked at him, surprised. 'I didn't know you've got a sister.'

'I don't anymore,' he said. 'Leukaemia, when she was seventeen.'

'Oh Nathan...' I reached out and took his hand. He smiled.

'It was a long time ago. I can go weeks now without thinking about her, and then suddenly something'll happen and some memory will pop up and make me smile.' He squeezed my hand. 'When something like that happens, it makes you think about what's important in life, doesn't it? Stuff like family, and being happy...'

Family, I thought. *And your family is back in Liverpool.*

Chapter Twenty-Four

We were interrupted by a stampede of cast and crew heading for the food truck. It was lunchtime by now, and I hadn't cooked anything. I really didn't want to let go of Nathan's hand, but I had to get to work.

'It's all right,' he said. 'I know you've got a job to do.'

'What about you?' I asked. 'What's your next move?'

He shrugged. 'No idea. Do you need some help?'

And that was how I ended up with a new sous-chef. I'd thought he was joking, but he wasn't; he needed to think and, like me, he found it easier to do that when he was physically busy. I gave him the boring, menial jobs like washing up and peeling veg, and he did them all without complaining. I made a super-quick cheesy pasta dish (pasta and bacon had really proved to be lifesavers on this job), then threw together a chicken and vegetable stir-fry (veg courtesy of my new kitchen assistant). There had been a delivery the day before, which David Morgan had kindly taken in, and when he brought that over I discovered veggie burgers and sausages, so I shoved them in the oven to cook and got Nathan to slice some burger baps and hot-dog rolls in half.

As we worked I told him about my modest flash of inspiration earlier: that if we found out who was behind the curse rumours, and behind at least some of the 'accidents', then maybe we would find our killer. I also told him that Zack had owned up to one of the pranks, and why; and that he'd said Aiko was behind the dog getting loose. Based on what we'd just seen, the relationship between the two sisters was complex, to say the least, and I almost didn't blame Aiko for getting sick of playing second fiddle to the Pekinese and letting her out, not necessarily expecting her to end up in the lake. She certainly seemed to feel guilty about it now.

There was a fair bit of moaning in the queue, but it was relatively good-natured, and within half an hour the warming dishes on the hot buffet counter had started to fill with food.

The food wasn't the only thing that was hot. The food truck quickly got steamy with the heat from the oven and the pans on the hob, and having another body in there with me only added to it. Add to that the fact that body was Nathan, and I was in serious danger of melting – or at the very least, succumbing to a swoon and passing out like a Victorian lady suffering from an attack of the vapours. There wasn't a lot of room in the truck, and we were constantly squeezing past each other to get to something. *I am going to explode with the sexual tension in a minute,* I thought.

But before I could explode, Nathan's phone rang. He grinned at me.

'Sorry, boss,' he said, and took it out. I half expected it to be his superintendent back in Liverpool, but it wasn't.

'Sergeant Adams! Have you run out of jelly babies?' He looked at me and winked, and I felt myself get even hotter. 'Oh, he does, does he? I'm at the food truck. Send him over… No, he can come here.' He hung up. 'It seems my favourite New Yorker is on the war path…'

I didn't want it to be too obvious that I was being nosey (hey, there's always a first time), so I stayed in the truck but loitered by the counter, pretending to check up on the amount of food in the warming dishes. Mike Mancuso had stormed over to the canteen area, obviously not pleased that he'd had to come to Nathan and not the other way around. I dolloped some cheesy pasta on an extra's plate and shoved them out of the way.

'Mr Mancuso,' said Nathan pleasantly. The producer almost growled at him.

'Can we talk somewhere quieter?' he asked. Nathan looked around, almost in surprise.

'I think here's as good a place as any,' he said. 'Please, take a seat.'

Dammit, I thought, as they sat down. Nathan had chosen a table as close to the food truck as possible, but it was too far away for me to hear. I grabbed a tray and went outside, pretending to clear empty plates from the tables. Germaine helped me, gobbling up any bits of food on the floor. She was better than a vacuum cleaner.

'You got some beef with me?' hissed Mancuso. Nathan smiled politely.

'No thanks, I'm not hungry. I had a late breakfast.' At the next table, I hid a snigger.

'What? No, I mean, you got a problem with me? I thought this case was all wrapped up. I thought you said it was the pufferfish, an accident…'

'The cause of death was poisoning by tetrodotoxin, yes.' Nathan looked the picture of innocence. 'Is there a problem?'

'The insurance company contacted you guys and *they* seem to think there's a problem, so yeah. They seem to think this was no accident.'

'Let me guess, they're refusing to pay out? I said, didn't I, that insurance companies will do anything to get out of paying off a claim.'

'So it *was* an accident?'

'I didn't say that.' Nathan was infuriatingly calm. Mancuso, who was going slightly purple in the face, looked like he wanted to hit something – probably Nathan. He took a deep breath and I could see he was forcing himself to chill.

'Look,' said the producer. 'I'll level with you: it don't feel right, carrying on with the shoot with one of my cast members the wrong side of the grass, you get me?'

Nathan looked genuinely confused. 'The wrong side of the…?'

'Jeremy. It feels wrong to keep filming after he bought it.' Mancuso looked at Nathan's polite incomprehension and sighed, enunciating his words clearly, as though my favourite DCI was an idiot. '*After he ate the pufferfish and died.*'

'Oh, *right*, yes. Not heard that expression before. So what would happen if you just closed down until it did feel right?'

'You fall behind schedule, you pay for stuff you ain't gonna need, crew you ain't gonna use, the budget goes way over, the release date gets pushed back further and further, the investors want their money back… You want me to go on?'

'No, you've made yourself quite clear.' Nathan looked sympathetic, but I knew it was about as genuine as Faith's hair colour. 'So you really need the insurance people to pay out, don't you? Does your policy cover murder?'

Mancuso went pale. 'But it was an accident.'

'I told you, I didn't say that. We think it was meant to look like one. As though all the other little accidents that have been happening on this shoot were really just leading up to this big one.' Nathan smiled. 'What do you think?'

Mancuso stood up. He looked suddenly furious. 'What I think is that the police need to get their heads outta their asses and do their job!'

'What a pleasant image that conjures up,' said Nathan. I snorted. Mancuso looked over at me, then back to Nathan.

'I think you need to spend less time cooking up theories with your little girlfriend here and either find the evidence that says this was a murder or admit that it was an accident. I think that if you don't get your ass in gear I'll be reporting you to the authorities!' He suddenly turned to me again. 'Can you hear me there okay? Did you get all that?'

'I'm just doing my job…' I said, holding up my hands in defence. Germaine growled at him.

'Can it!' he growled back, and stormed off. Nathan grinned at me.

'He's not very happy, is he?' I said, sitting opposite him.

'Nope. To be fair, he probably does feel bad about carrying on with the shoot so soon, but without the insurance payout he doesn't have any other option.' Nathan absentmindedly stroked Germaine's head as she sat and gazed up at him adoringly. I supposed she was only copying what she'd seen me do…

'I don't know about that,' I said, gesturing around us. 'Look. No one looks terribly upset, do they? I'm not saying they don't care, but movie people just seem to be obsessed with the whole the-show-must-go-on thing.'

'Maybe…' Nathan mused. 'Anyway, where are we at now?'

'We know it was pufferfish toxin. But it wasn't the pufferfish.'

'So we know it wasn't an accident, no matter how much Mancuso wishes it. We also know it wasn't the cupcakes, because if it had been then Kimi would have been ill the other night.'

'And dead now. Yeah. So we have to find what else everyone but Kimi and Faith ate.' I shook my head. 'Kimi ate everything but the chicken. Faith ate everything but the tofu. Which doesn't help us much.'

'Not really, no.'

'The poison – the tetrodotoxin – how easy is it to get hold of?' I asked. 'You can't nip into Boots and buy it, can you? Where would they have got it from?'

'I've got DS Turner looking into that,' said Nathan.

'There can't be many places you can get it from. I'm surprised you can get it at all. What about the victim? Any gossip about grudges against him, or overheard arguments? Anything that could be a motive?'

'Nothing,' I said. 'I've been chatting with a few people this morning while I've been serving them, and no one had a bad word to say about him. But then they might just not want to speak ill of the dead. Who knows?'

'Okay. Your other theory – about the curse, all the daft pranks and accidents being window dressing for this one big 'accident' – maybe we should look into that,' said Nathan. I nodded.

'Yeah. I mean, we know that Zack messed up Faith's door, and Aiko was the one who let Kimi's dog out, but that still leaves the annoying little pranks like the generator being overloaded and the bulbs smashing, and of course the steps to the food truck being tampered with…'

'I might be able to help you with that.' We looked up and saw Lucy standing nearby with Gino, whose arm was in a sling.

'Gino!' I leapt up. 'Why didn't you say you were coming back?'

'Thought I'd surprise you,' he said, looking at me disapprovingly. 'And I obviously have. There's hardly any food out—'

Lucy shook her head, exasperated. 'There's loads; no one's going to starve.'

'What do you think you could help us with?' asked Nathan. 'Do you know who sabotaged the stairs and caused Gino to hurt himself?'

Gino and Lucy exchanged looks, then she nodded. 'I think so…'

Lucy led us past the shoot's shanty town of marquees and trailers to a quiet spot towards the back of the house. Here the set carpenters and painters were busy assembling props and bits of scenery. One of them, a heavy-set but good-looking man in his late twenties, was sanding down a fake sword like the one Zack had been carrying a few days previously.

He looked up and smiled at Lucy, but his smile faltered when he saw us and disappeared completely at the sight of Gino.

'All right, Luce?' he said cautiously, eyeing Gino with obvious dislike.

'Not really, no,' she said. 'The steps at the back of the food truck… It's just come to my attention that they were tampered with.'

'Sawn through,' Nathan added. 'You wouldn't happen to know anything about that, would you?'

'No,' he said, but his eyes betrayed him. He couldn't stop himself casting a glance over towards the saw that lay propped up next to his tool box.

'Really?' Lucy folded her arms and stared at him. He shuffled around uncomfortably.

'Of course not. I was right here, all the time.'

I sighed. 'It's quite romantic really, when you think about it,' I said. Nathan looked at me, amazed.

'Is it?'

'Yeah! Fighting for the woman you love. Like something out of a movie.' I looked at Lucy; I could see she'd caught on.

'Like a romcom,' she said.

'Yeah,' I said. '*Falling for You* or something.' She snorted. 'If a man did that for me – tried to get a rival out of the way…'

'Hard to resist,' she agreed.

The carpenter looked from me to Lucy to Nathan to Gino, like he was at a Wimbledon doubles match.

'Well … but … all right,' he admitted. 'Yeah. I did it.'

'What did you do?' asked Nathan.

'I sawed through the middle step so that when Gino stood on it, it would break.' The carpenter looked down at his feet, mumbling, then looked up pleadingly at Lucy. 'I only done it because you and him was flirting. I know what his type's like, Luce. I weren't losing you to someone like that.'

'You did it because you love me, I suppose?' asked Lucy.

'Yeah, I did! I do! You know I do. I didn't want to lose you.'

'You idiot. You weren't going to lose me. I wasn't interested in Gino as anything other than a friend,' she said, her expression softening slightly.

'Really?'

'Really.'

'In that case…' The carpenter got down on one knee and smiled what he obviously thought was a winning smile. 'Will you marry me, Lucy?'

Lucy smiled at him. 'Will I marry you? After you got jealous and broke a man's arm for me? When it could have been a lot worse than a broken arm?'

He smiled again. 'Yeah.'

She snorted. 'You're a bloody psychopath. Of course I won't marry you. And you're fired.'

He stood up, surprised and angry. 'What? But I— You can't—'

'Unless you want me to arrest you, I suggest you leave,' said Nathan, inserting himself between the furious carpenter and Lucy, who was as cool as a cucumber. 'On your bike, sunshine.'

The carpenter looked helplessly at Lucy, scowled at Nathan, then grabbed his toolbox and stormed off.

'Oh my God, I love it when you talk like something out of *The Bill*,' I said. Nathan laughed.

'That show is responsible for my entire career,' he said. He turned to Gino. 'Are you sure you don't want to press charges? He caused you a nasty accident, and it could have been even worse.'

Gino looked at Lucy, but she shook her head. 'No,' said Gino, 'we'll leave it. He's a big enough loser as it is.' And with that he took Lucy's hand (with his non-broken arm) and they walked away.

'Okay...' said Nathan. 'Note to self: never try to stop your girlfriend leaving by taking out the opposition.'

I laughed, but it wasn't me leaving, was it?

Chapter Twenty-Five

We slowly strolled back towards the food truck, but we were waylaid en route by Daisy and Mum, who had just finished filming. Daisy chattered excitedly and even Mum had a glow about her, so they'd obviously enjoyed the experience far more than I had.

'Are you done for the day?' I asked. Daisy nodded.

'I am but Nana isn't,' she said. 'Nana's got a proper part!'

'What?' I cried, turning to Mum. She smiled and looked very proud of herself. Some might even call it smug.

'I've got a line and everything,' she said. 'They're going to let me speak.'

'They'll bloody regret that,' I muttered, and Nathan laughed.

'Nice one, Shirley,' he said. She fluttered her eyelashes at him.

'Thank you, Nathan. You can come round for your tea again.'

We all went to the food truck – I thought I should probably make sure the hot buffet was still well stocked, and we were all getting hungry – but when I got there I could hear singing coming from inside the van.

Gino stopped mid-line – something about a big pizza pie – and poked his head out over the counter.

'You decided to come back, then?' he said, but in a good-natured way; he seemed to be in a better mood than he had been earlier.

'Have I been made redundant?' I asked. He smiled.

'Sorry, I can't sit at home doing nothing, even with my arm in a sling. You can help with the washing-up if you want…'

'No, you're all right,' I said quickly, although I knew I would end up feeling bad and helping him anyway. 'In that case, I want some food.'

We all helped ourselves, including Nathan, who was showing no inclination to leave, which was okay by me. Then we found a spare table and sat down. Daisy looked cold in her pretty costume, so I took off my coat and draped it over her shoulders. Mum said she was fine, although it was a bit chilly, but the temperature went up several degrees when Nathan unwound the scarf he was wearing and wrapped it round her neck. I felt myself go all warm inside at such a caring gesture. *That's because he's a good son,* I thought, and immediately went cold again.

'So much for my theory about the pranks,' I said, after we'd filled our bellies with cheesy pasta, Mum had gone to the Make-Up trailer, and Daisy had gone off with Jade to get changed, Germaine bounding after her. I could only imagine the look on the sour wardrobe mistress's face when confronted with my hairy dog next to her precious costumes... 'The only ones we haven't got to the bottom of are the most minor ones, the lightbulbs being smashed and the generator fiddled with.'

'And wasn't the home owner complaining about someone being in his garden?' asked Nathan.

'That's right. It looked like whoever smashed the light bulbs climbed out of the window.'

Nathan looked thoughtful. 'Maybe we should go and have a look at that flowerbed...'

'The footprints were *here,* and then there were some shards of broken glass *here.*' I pointed at the flowerbed in David Morgan's kitchen garden. Nathan frowned.

'Are you sure?' He carefully worked his way around the remaining seedlings and plants, careful not to do any more damage. 'So whoever was in the flowerbed stood about here? And the window was shut, so they must have turned around after climbing out, reached up, and closed it?' I nodded. He reached up to the window above him and frowned again. 'Okay, I know I'm not the tallest man in the world, but look how hard it is for me to even reach the window frame. The window would have to be open at least halfway to leave a big enough gap to climb through, and I don't think I could close it from out here. The ground's lower this side of the window than it is inside, isn't it?'

'I did wonder about that at the time,' I said.

'What's going on?' David Morgan stood behind us, looking annoyed. His expression changed to one of wariness as Nathan turned round and he realised he was addressing a police officer and not just the nosey caterer. 'Sorry, officer, I can't remember your name. Can I help you with something?'

'DCI Withers, sir. I was just following up on the trespassing issue you had here a few days ago. My associate here' – ooh, I was his 'associate' now, was I? That sounded official – 'believed that there could be a link between that and the vandalism of film company property.'

'Oh, right.' Morgan really did look uncomfortable now. 'Look, there's enough going on here. I don't want to add to it by making a big thing about this, annoyed as I was…'

'It's absolutely fine, sir,' said Nathan. I could see he'd picked up on the house owner's nervousness. 'I was just saying to Ms Parker here that our theory doesn't add up. The footprints were in the wrong place. Even if they were closer to the window, I still don't really see how someone could reach up and shut the window from the outside.'

I looked down at Nathan's feet. The prints in the soil were rather larger than those left by his smart leather shoes.

'What size are your feet, DCI Withers?' I asked. He looked down.

'Size eight. Whoever left these prints had bigger feet than me.' David Morgan's gaze involuntarily travelled from Nathan's feet to his own, and then up to my face. He looked surprised (and guilty) to see me staring at him. *Every time,* I thought. *They give themselves away every time.*

'What size are you, Mr Morgan?' I asked. He looked flustered.

'Um…'

'You know the other thing that occurred to me,' I said, turning to Nathan. 'I overheard the lighting guy say he'd set the lights up last thing, just before everyone left for the evening. So who would have had access to them overnight? Mr Morgan? Would any of the crew or anyone else connected with the shoot have been able to get into the house without you hearing them?'

Nathan looked at him, waiting for an answer. 'Mr Morgan?'

David Morgan looked at him for a moment, then gave a kind of helpless but resigned groan.

'Okay. I admit it. Those were my footprints; I put them there. There never was a trespasser.'

'And the shards of glass?'

'That was me too. Oh God, I'm sorry…' We let him compose himself before continuing. 'You haven't met my wife yet, have you Ms Parker? She's a difficult woman, which I have to admit is one of the things that attracted me to her.' He smiled. 'She doesn't let anyone boss her around, not even me. Ha! Least of all me. When I told her we needed to find a way to make the house pay, she reluctantly agreed to hold weddings here. But the film shoot was the last straw.'

'Your wife doesn't like the film people being here?' asked Nathan.

'No, she doesn't. I don't either really, but we need the money. Anyway, she decided to show her displeasure by causing them a few problems – petty, I know, but … it made her feel better.'

'She smashed the lightbulbs?' I asked, and he nodded.

'Yes. They'd been set up and just left there, overnight. She went in there and smashed them so they'd have to change all the bulbs before they started filming the next day. She thought it was funny, but to me it was obvious that it must have been us…'

'So you planted the footprints and the glass to make it look like someone had broken in and out of the house?'

'Yes.' Morgan looked embarrassed. 'I am very sorry.'

'What about the generator?' asked Nathan. He nodded.

'I caught her fiddling about with it that day, pulling leads out of the circuit breaker and messing around with it, so I sent her off and plugged everything back in.'

'But you overloaded it, and that's when it went bang and scared Jeremy's horse,' I said.

'Yes. I was so relieved that he hadn't been thrown. And then that night, my wife was annoyed that they were having a party, because we hadn't agreed to that, so she went back to the generator and turned it off. But I realised what she was doing and followed her, and I managed to turn it back on quite quickly.'

'That's when the lights went out,' I said. 'When I was clearing everything away, and you turned up…' I looked at Nathan, remembering the way he'd stood in the doorway, wet and windswept, channelling Heathcliff as the lights had come back on.

'When I heard that Jeremy Mayhew was dead, I was terrified that it had something to do with the lights going out – maybe he'd fallen in the dark – so when you said it was pufferfish toxin I was relieved.' He looked at us anxiously. 'Will we get into trouble? I admit we were wrong, but…'

Nathan stared at him for a moment, making sure he felt guilty (I mean, he and his wife *had* damaged other people's property) before shaking his head. 'I wouldn't have thought so. As you said, the production company have enough to contend with at the moment, so I would be very surprised if they wanted to press charges against your wife.' He looked serious. 'However, if any more little accidents were to occur, I would not bet on them being quite so forgiving. Do I make myself understood?'

'Yes. Crystal clear. Absolutely.' Morgan reached out to shake Nathan's hand, and then mine. 'Thank you, thank you so much. I am so terribly sorry about all of this…'

'Guv?' Nathan's detective sergeant, a bloke whom I was constantly running into during investigations but whose name I could never remember, loitered nearby. Nathan dismissed Morgan with a nod of the head, then turned to his junior officer. 'Matt. Have you got something for me?'

Matt! I thought. Matt Turner. The one I'd spoken to on the phone when Jeremy had died.

Matt nodded at me. 'All right, Jodie?'

'All right, Matt?' I said. Nathan rolled his eyes.

'Oh good, we're all all right,' he said, with a touch of sarcasm. 'What is it?'

'I got all the stuff about tetrodotoxin you wanted.'

'And you couldn't tell me it over the phone?'

'Well, you know, I just wanted to...' His gaze swept over the house and the organised chaos of the shoot around us. Nathan shook his head, but he looked amused.

'You wanted to have a nosey around the shoot. Fine.' He waited. 'So...? Tetrodotoxin?'

'Oh, yeah, sorry.' Matt took out his notebook. 'Tetrodotoxin is not available to purchase in this country. It's not used at all over here, but there has been research into using it as a painkiller for cancer patients in the States and in Japan. It's also been used as an experimental treatment for lessening cravings and preventing relapses in heroin addicts going through withdrawal, again mostly in the States and Japan, although there are also two private addiction clinics in Switzerland and one in Canada where it's occasionally prescribed.'

'So there's no way anyone could buy it here?' said Nathan. 'What about in the States, or in Japan?' He looked at me, significantly; because of course Zack had previously lived in Japan, as had Aiko and Kimi.

Matt Turner shook his head. 'Nah. You have to be a health professional to buy it. In the States you have to register with the CDC and follow all kinds of regulations. I couldn't find anything like that in Japan, but I reckon it would be the same. They wouldn't sell it to just anyone.'

'So how would you go about getting someone to prescribe it to you?' I asked.

'You couldn't ask for it to be prescribed because it's experimental and really expensive,' said Matt. 'Plus, you'd have to be suffering from cancer or heroin withdrawal. Oh, or Parkinson's Disease – that's another thing they sometimes use it for. You'd probably have to get picked for a medical trial. Here.' Matt unfolded a sheet of paper tucked into his notebook. 'I printed this off the Internet for you, Guv.' Nathan took it from him.

'Okay,' he said. 'We know that it's pretty bloody difficult to get hold of, but someone *did* get hold of it, so now all we've got to do is find a cast or crew member who's secretly receiving treatment for cancer, addiction, or Parkinson's…' Nathan looked thoughtful. 'Off the top of your head, which would you say is more likely?'

'Addiction,' I said promptly. 'You know what movie stars are like… But heroin's a bit hardcore, innit? Celebs normally go for coke or weed.'

Nathan looked amused. 'Do they?'

'They do if you believe the tabloids…'

Nathan let DS Turner go and have a nose around the shoot. It might not have been terribly professional, but it wasn't every day we got a film crew in this part of Cornwall, and Nathan, who had apparently been a real stickler for the rules when he'd first moved here, had now relaxed enough to occasionally let his junior officers have a bit of fun.

We wandered through the grounds of the house, watching the organised chaos of the movie business unfold around us.

'Okay,' said Nathan. 'We know someone had the toxin, even if we don't know yet how or where they got it. The next thing is, how did they administer it to Jeremy and the others? We know now it wasn't the cupcakes, which really seemed like a good fit because we don't know who made them and the toxin could have been added during baking.'

'But it wasn't.'

'No. Was there a chance that it could have been added to the other dishes? The ones you made?'

I thought it over. 'Well… maybe. Zack and Aiko carried all the food over from the food truck to his trailer, so…' I didn't want to admit to the possibility that it could have been either of them. Nathan smiled gently.

'I don't think it would be Zack. Why go to the trouble of buying poison that would make it look like you were the only one who could have done it? No. But Aiko?'

'It can't have been Aiko,' I said firmly. 'I mean, yeah, it could have been her, but why? She likes Zack, so she wouldn't want to incriminate him—'

'Unless she's playing him.'

'That's true, I suppose. But why kill Jeremy? She can't have known him before this shoot.'

'Maybe Jeremy wasn't the target?' said Nathan. 'Maybe she meant to kill her sister, or Faith…'

'Maybe, if Zack told her what Faith had said…' I shook my head. 'No, I don't believe that. In fact, I don't even believe that Faith would say the things he says she did. I think he must have got it wrong.'

'I think we need a chat with both of them,' said Nathan.

Chapter Twenty-Six

As luck would have it, we got our interview with them almost by accident. Our wander had taken us full circle and we were nearly back at the food truck when we heard raised voices coming from Faith's trailer close by. We glanced at each other and quickly headed up the steps.

The door was open, and inside Zack was glaring at Faith as Aiko tried to calm him down.

'Don't invite me in here like we're all friends,' he spat at her. 'Pretending to care, like some mother hen. Wanting to make sure Aiko's well enough to be here!' Aiko didn't look well enough, to be fair, and his anger was making her look even more frail.

'Zack!' I cried out, as Nathan got between him and Faith.

'You need to calm down, son,' said Nathan.

'It's okay,' said Faith, exasperated. 'We need to get to the bottom of this. Come on, tell me. You obviously don't like me, and I have no idea what it is I'm supposed to have done.'

Zack glared at her. 'I heard you in your trailer, talking to someone. Telling them me and Kimi were only there to meet some diversity quota. Don't deny it.'

Faith looked confused for a moment, then her face cleared. 'Oh my God, you thought…? That wasn't me, that was Jeremy.'

'I heard you,' said Zack defiantly.

'Yes, I'm sure you did, because I was repeating what he'd said.' She sat down, and a shaky Aiko followed suit. 'You have to understand, Jeremy was a product of his generation, of his upbringing. He used to say he was proudly un-PC—'

'That's just code for 'I'm a racist',' I said, and Faith nodded.

'I know. Anyway, we shared the same agent, and he'd rung me to ask how the shoot was going, but he really wanted to check up on Jeremy. You know he's got— He *had* this reputation as a bit of a hell-raiser. I told him what Jeremy had said to me about you two on the very first day of the shoot, when we were filming up in Scotland.'

Zack didn't speak, but he looked upset, and I remembered the day of the dinner party when we'd watched them filming. The two men had seemed to get on very well that day, but now he was hearing that it had been an act. Or had it?

'If you'd hung around or, better still, come in and talked to me,' Faith continued, 'you'd have heard me tell Howard that Jeremy had come to me a week later and admitted he was wrong, and that you were an amazing young actor. I can't say you cured him of being a racist, but he was trying.'

'Oh,' said Zack, looking even more upset now. He plopped down on the seat next to Aiko, who reached out to hold his hand firmly.

'I think he was trying to clean up his act in his old age,' said Faith. 'He still had a long way to go, but he'd signed a sobriety clause for this film and he was actually sticking to it.'

'Sobriety clause?' I asked.

'He was a heavy drinker – a recovering alcoholic really,' said Faith. 'One of the many reasons our relationship ended, and why I won't even touch a drop these days. If an actor has an addiction problem, a lot of production companies will get them to sign a contract saying they'll stay clean for the duration of the shoot, but often it doesn't really mean anything; it just means they'll hide the fact that they're wasted. But Jeremy really wasn't drinking. The only thing he'd drunk, as far as I know, was the sake that Mike Mancuso brought to the dinner party, and that was only because Mike poured everyone a glass so we could toast the birthday girls.' She looked wistful. 'He *was* trying. He wasn't a bad person deep down, he just had his demons.'

An addiction problem, I thought. Jeremy had been addicted to alcohol.

'Was Jeremy getting any treatment for his addiction, do you know?' I asked. Nathan looked at me sharply, and I knew he'd realised what I was thinking.

'I don't think so,' said Faith.

'There's medication you can get, isn't there?' persisted Nathan. 'To stop you getting the shakes, to stop you craving alcohol? He wasn't on anything like that?'

'Oh God no, he wasn't *that* bad,' said Faith. 'He wouldn't shake or get ill if he didn't drink. He drank because he wanted to, not because he had to.' She looked from Nathan to me. 'Is that what you think happened? You think he died of an overdose of some kind of medication?'

'But Zack and I got ill as well, and the others,' pointed out Aiko. 'So surely it was some kind of food poisoning?'

'You said the lab had found pufferfish toxin, just not in the pufferfish,' said Zack. All three of them looked at us, confused, demanding answers. Nathan spoke slowly, thoughtfully.

'Yes, it was tetrodotoxin – pufferfish toxin,' he confirmed. 'But it wasn't in the pufferfish you prepared,

Zack. We're not sure how it was administered, but it must have been in something you all consumed—'

'Hang on,' said Faith, her face paling. "Administered'? You mean it was put in the food on purpose? I thought— I thought poor Jeremy had died of food poisoning, or some kind of allergy, but what you're suggesting is that it was deliberate.'

'Murder,' said Zack, turning to me. 'That's what I thought you meant, when you told me about the toxin. Someone murdered him, didn't they?'

Faith gave a sudden jerk and we all looked at her. She swallowed hard.

'Sorry, muscle spasm. Dodgy back.' She made a big show of getting up and stretching, her back to us. *All the better to compose herself before she shows us her face again,* I thought, because her expression had been that of someone who had just had a very nasty surprise or revelation…

'Are you okay, Ms McKenzie?' Nathan inquired politely. She nodded fervently as she turned back to us, a big smile on her face.

'Yes, I'm fine. Shocked, of course. Poor Jeremy.' She gave a dramatic sigh and then looked at her watch. 'I'm so sorry, DCI Withers, Jodie, but I'm due back on set in ten minutes and I have to go through my lines again. You'll let me know if there's any more news on the investigation, though?'

Someone's very keen to get rid of us, I thought. *I wonder why…?*

Nathan smiled. 'Of course. And please, don't worry yourselves about this. We are getting closer to finding the murderer, and they won't act again, not with myself and my uniformed officers around.' I had to hide a smile at that, because the only uniformed officer around at the moment was Sergeant Adams, and I couldn't imagine him scaring anyone.

We left Faith, Zack, and Aiko in the trailer.

'Back on set in ten minutes my ar—' I began.

'Are you suggesting our National Treasure in there is hiding something?' asked Nathan. 'Because I'd be amazed if she isn't.'

'She certainly knows something,' I said. He nodded.

'Oh yes, the whole muscle spasm thing… It's like something suddenly occurred to her, and it was such a shock it actually made her jump.'

'You think she knows who did it?'

'Oh God, yes, don't you?'

I nodded, but I wasn't entirely convinced. 'Yes…'

Nathan stopped and looked at me with a grin on his face.

'Here we go with another 'yes, but', don't we?'

I laughed. 'Yes. I mean, I think you're right, but I think the fact it clearly hadn't occurred to her before means that the murderer's motive for killing Jeremy isn't going to be that obvious. It's not to her, anyway.'

'So it's less surprise at the thought they could kill someone, more at the thought that they'd kill Jeremy?' Nathan looked at me thoughtfully. 'Yes, you could be right there. So what does that mean?'

'Maybe Jeremy wasn't the intended victim. Maybe they meant to kill someone else. Or maybe they didn't mean to kill *anyone.*' Nathan looked at me in surprise.

'Go on...'

'Everyone got sick, didn't they? Or everyone who ate whatever it was that had the toxin in. There's no way the murderer could have known who would eat what. I was assuming that it had to be someone at the dinner, someone who could make sure that Jeremy ate the right cupcake or whatever, the one with the lethal dose in it, but how could they do that without it looking weird?'

'Plus, it wasn't the cupcakes, so they would probably have to slip the toxin into the food at the table, in front of everyone,' said Nathan. 'And I really don't know how they could have done that.'

'No...' I said. Something was nagging at me. 'We still don't know what the toxin was in. But it seems to me that maybe no one was meant to die; they were all just meant to get sick—'

'To make it look like another accident, something else caused by the curse,' said Nathan. 'Yes, that makes sense. But until we know how the toxin was consumed…' He took out the sheet of paper Matt Turner had given him. 'Tetrodotoxin comes in pill form, so the murderer would have had to crush it and sprinkle it onto the food.'

'Which everyone would see, unless it was cooked into it, which we know it wasn't.' I groaned in frustration.

'And if you crushed it up and put it in a drink, it would make it go cloudy and they'd notice that too,' said Nathan. *Cloudy,* I thought, and something lurking in the recesses of my brain stood up and waved at me.

'Not if the drink was already cloudy,' I said. I grabbed his hand. 'We need to go back and check on the crime scene.'

Nathan had called the Scene of Crime officers back to Zack's trailer earlier that day, and they were there now taking samples of every single food item that was left – not that there was much. Jeremy's plate had already been taken, but they now bagged up all of the crockery and the cutlery and chopsticks to test for any trace of tetrodotoxin.

Nathan nodded to the lead officer as we entered, and I made my way to the table.

'These glasses,' I said, pointing to the small sake cups that sat empty among the remains of the meal. 'Were they all empty when you got here? I didn't look before.'

The SOCO nodded. 'Yes, there was no drink in any of them.'

'Where's the bottle?' asked Nathan. The SOCO looked around, then at the list of evidence being bagged up.

'We haven't found one,' he said. Nathan raised his eyebrows and looked at me.

'The sake?'

'Yes,' I said. 'Aiko told me that Mike Mancuso had made a point of buying a bottle of sake, so they could toast their birthdays in proper Japanese style. Only, she wasn't impressed because it was *nigori* sake, which is filtered differently. It's less refined and, more to the point, cloudy.'

'So you could slip a crushed-up pill into it and nobody would notice?'

I shrugged. 'I don't know, but it sounds likely. Kimi wouldn't have drunk it because it's made of fermented rice and she has a rice allergy, and we both just heard Faith say she hasn't touched a drop of alcohol in years after her relationship with Jeremy.'

'So that explains why they weren't ill.'

'One of the things that's been niggling me,' I said, 'is why Mike Mancuso poured a glass of rice wine, with its extremely high alcohol content, to a recovering alcoholic who had signed a sobriety clause, presumably on Mike's own insistence. I mean, he might just be an absolute git…'

'He is,' said Nathan firmly.

'I won't argue with you there,' I said. 'But think about it: he encouraged Jeremy to have a drink. Not only that, he allowed Zack to go ahead with serving the pufferfish, even though as far as everyone but Gino knew, it was risky. I know he said Gino had reassured him, but the fact is, if you're serving something that's toxic it's always going to have the potential to be a disaster, innit? He didn't know it *wasn't* toxic.'

'Okay…' said Nathan, and I could see him working it out in his own mind. 'So say the intention was just to make everyone sick. Why did Jeremy die?'

'Because all the glasses were empty. Faith and Kimi definitely did not drink their sake. An alcoholic, about to fall off the wagon for the first time in a while, is not going to leave two glasses of rice wine undrunk. He probably finished them off for them.'

'That makes sense… But Mancuso poured *himself* a drink. I know he claims he was sick as well, but he surely wouldn't actually drink it, would he?'

'No…' I said, but then Nathan did a mini fist-pump.

'I've got it! He spiked the bottle with tetrodotoxin from … somewhere, and then poured everyone a glass.' Nathan mimed picking up a glass. "A toast to the birthday girls!' And then his phone goes off at some pre-arranged time – either he's set an alarm to sound like a ringtone, or he's genuinely got his daughter or whoever it was to call him, so he says, 'Sorry, everyone, got to take this, start without me', and goes outside—'

'Still carrying his glass of sake—'

'Which he tips out onto the grass while he's on the phone, then goes back in looking like he's drunk it, and then pretends to be ill overnight.' Nathan looked at me. 'You are bloody brilliant, Parker.'

I beamed at him. 'Why thank you, DCI Withers.'

'Ahem…' We were interrupted by the SOCO, who we'd both completely forgotten about. 'That's a great theory, as long as we can get a trace off the glasses. It would be nice if you could find us the bottle…'

'Guv! Guv!' Matt Turner burst into the trailer like an overexcited puppy. He stopped, embarrassed, as he spotted the SOC team watching him.

'Matt, what is it?'

'I've been doing some poking around, talking to the crew, and you'll never guess who has a teenage daughter who just came out of heroin rehab in a poncey Swiss drug clinic!'

'Mike Mancuso,' Nathan and I said together. Matt's face fell and his whole body deflated – funnily enough, just like a pufferfish.

'Yeah,' he said. Nathan patted him on the back.

'Nice work, Matt,' he said. 'You may have just stitched up the whole case.'

'Not quite,' I said. 'We might know the who and the how, but we still don't know the why.' And then my phone pinged, and we knew that too.

Chapter Twenty-Seven

Work on the shoot had all but stopped. Everyone who wasn't on set had their mobile phone on them, and they'd all received an anonymous group message with a link to an internet news site and the words, 'please share', at the same time as I had.

Top story on the site, underneath the lurid headline 'Award-winning Producer in Sex-for-Roles Scandal', was a video, secretly and inexpertly filmed. It was slightly blurred and out of focus, but still clear enough to recognise the man at the centre of it. Mike Mancuso, clad in a loose-fitting bathrobe, sitting on a sofa in a tastefully bland but expensive-looking hotel room. There was an ice bucket with a bottle of champagne in it on the coffee table in front of him. Also on the table was a small heap of white powder. And opposite him sat a handsome young man in his early twenties.

The young man held some pages of a script in his hand. He read from them, pouring emotion into every line; he had real presence and professionalism, which can't have been easy with the sweaty New Yorker sat across from him, his legs open wider than any middle-aged-man-in-a-bathrobe's legs should be. At the end of the reading he stopped, expectantly. You could almost sense his feeling of hope, that his dreams might be about to come true. But underneath that, in his demeanour, in his body language, seemed to lie the unwelcome realisation that it wasn't going to be as easy as that. Or was that just the old cynic in me? Because I had the horrible feeling I knew what was coming next.

'You did good,' said Mancuso, on the screen. 'You got that quality, kid. You could be a big star.'

'Do you really think so?' said the young man. His eagerness was almost heartbreaking.

'I do.' Mancuso shifted, moving his legs further apart, and I really, *really* wished he was wearing underpants. 'But you know, I know a lotta young guys like you – great actors, good-looking guys. Why should I give you the part and not one of them?'

The young man also shifted, but instead of spreading out he looked like he was trying to physically withdraw into himself. 'Well, I-I got great reviews when I played Romeo—'

'Yeah, these other guys got great reviews too,' said Mancuso, inspecting his fingernails, bored. 'That ain't how it works though, is it?' He looked up with a frank expression on his face. 'Come on. You know how it goes. You scratch my back...'

'You want me to scratch your back?'

Mancuso laughed. 'You know what I want.'

The young man was still for a moment, and I thought, *Tell the big fat bully to stick his part where the sun don't shine! Get up and leave!*

But obviously the young man hadn't left, otherwise we wouldn't have been here watching the video. I won't go into details about what followed. Unless you're terribly sweet and innocent (sweeter and more innocent than me, anyway), you can probably guess. The Hollywood casting couch might have suffered a dent with the advent of #MeToo, but the video showed that it hadn't completely gone away after all. Underneath the video was a quote from the 'unnamed source' who had sent in the video:

> *The games played by the powerful men in this industry continue, despite our best efforts. The younger generation of actors and creatives should not have to go through what we did.*

Nathan and I watched the video – or enough of it, anyway – open-mouthed with shock. We weren't the only ones. The whole crew were glued to their phones, many of them tapping away – sharing it, I assumed. Daisy and Jade ran over with their phones in their hands, but thankfully they hadn't clicked on the link (I had instilled in Daisy a fear of cybercrime, online bullying, and hacking that had really come into its own today) and I was able to delete it before they did. There was no way I wanted them to see it.

Mike Mancuso stepped out of the production-office trailer, phone in one hand, car keys in the other. He was obviously planning to get out of there as quickly as he could, away from the shocked, judging eyes of the cast and crew who were even now turning to look at him.

Nathan approached him and I followed at a trot, after asking Jade to call her mum to pick them both up. I might be here a while…

'Excuse me, Mr Mancuso, sir!' called Nathan. Mancuso ignored him, but we could see where he was heading. Nathan reached the car first and stood in his way.

'Mr Mancuso, I think you and I need to have a little chat, don't you?' And there wasn't much that the producer could do, other than agree, especially when Matt Turner emerged triumphantly from the dumpster behind the office clutching an empty sake bottle wrapped in a plastic bag.

Faith opened the door to her trailer. She looked quite happy to see me, but her smile slipped a little as she spotted Nathan behind me.

'Jodie, DCI Withers, you do look serious. I think you'd better come in.'

She sat down and gestured to us to take a seat. I did, but Nathan stayed standing. *Power move,* I thought.

'Ms Mackenzie,' said Nathan, 'we'd like to ask you about your relationship with Mr Mancuso.'

'I didn't have one,' she said. She smiled at me, but there was a hint of sadness behind it. 'You of all people know I have much better taste in men than that.'

'We don't mean a sexual relationship,' I said. 'We mean—'

'You mean, you want to know if I blackmailed him or not?'

Nathan and I exchanged surprised glances.

'Well, yes,' he admitted. 'Although it's really a rhetorical question, because we've just spoken to him and we know you did.'

'Does it still count as blackmail if I never actually asked for money? Or for any type of personal gain?'

'Technically, yes,' I said. 'But you did ask for money.'

She shook her head vehemently. 'No, I didn't. Not once. Did he know it was me? Or was it the video that led you to me? I did tell the website people not to lie about where they got it from if it was going to get them into trouble.'

'I recognised your words,' I said. 'The younger generation shouldn't have to go through what we did...'

'I just wanted him to come clean and admit what sort of man he is.'

Nathan looked at her sceptically. 'Really? A man like Mike Mancuso was never going to admit to something like that, was he? What did you expect him to do?'

'I don't know. I just wanted him to know that we were on to him, and he couldn't carry on that way anymore.' Faith looked a bit vague, and I got the feeling she'd acted before she'd had a chance to really think it through. 'I thought maybe he'd retire, or make some big thing of going into rehab for sex addiction or something. He could have controlled how it came out, made it look like he was really sorry. Hollywood can be very forgiving if you're contrite enough, and rich enough. At least it would have meant people knew what he was like.' She shook her head. 'Maybe I was naive. I never wanted the video to come out, but when I realised what he'd done... I thought, maybe he thought Jeremy was behind it all, and when he realised it wasn't him, I would be next. At least the news site had the decency to blur the poor boy's face.'

'Who is he?' I asked.

'He's a fan. My *Mile End* character, Clara, has a big following amongst the gay community. It's the clothes, you know. And the big heart. Anyway, he had a meeting with Mike about a role, but one of his friends worked in the hotel in London he always uses for his 'casting' sessions.' Faith grimaced, as if the words had left a foul taste in her mouth. 'His friend had heard rumours and he wanted to protect him, so he hid a camera in the room, and… Well, you saw what happened. He sent the tape to me because he was upset and he didn't know what to do. He wanted Mike held to account but he's a no one; nobody would take it seriously. And of course he wasn't physically forced into doing it. I mean, technically it wasn't rape, was it? So I sent it to Mike anonymously and told him that if he didn't own up, I would leak it to the press. The gay community needs their own #MeToo moment.'

'So how did you end up getting a hundred and forty thousand pounds from him?' asked Nathan, clearly not buying her story. But I almost believed her.

Faith almost choked. 'Is that how much he said he'd given me? Cheeky bugger! More like fifty thousand. Sounds to me like he's been lining his own pocket in case it *did* come out.'

'But you're not denying you received some money?'

'Oh no, although it didn't come to me. It was never about money for me. He immediately offered me some to keep quiet, but I said no. He just kept coming back with higher and higher offers.'

'For a man like Mancuso, it would *always* be about money, and it would never occur to him that someone might have different motives,' I said. 'He thought you were playing hardball, trying to get him to offer you more.'

'And he did,' she said. 'He kept going until he got to an amount that I just couldn't turn down. So I got him to pay it into a PayPal account that I'd set up under a charitable trust, and then I paid it into a couple of charities I'm a patron of—'

'A women's refuge and a rainbow youth centre?' said Nathan. She nodded.

'Yes. See, I'm hardly a criminal mastermind, am I? You've obviously been able to trace it already. I was only worried about Mike finding out. I knew he wouldn't go to the police.' She sighed. 'It's such a shame. I love this film. The script, the cast, everything. And it'll all just stop now, won't it?'

I nodded, thinking, *It's the end of the movie, and the end of the investigation, but is it also the end of me and Nathan?*

We sat outside the food truck. It was starting to get late. Nancy had picked up the girls and taken them back to her house for tea, so I sat with Nathan waiting for Mum to get out of her costume. She'd been on set throughout the whole drama, along with Tony, and I didn't have the heart to tell her that her acting debut probably wouldn't make it onto the screen now.

Germaine scouted about in the grass, looking for scraps of food. The crew stood around in groups, some lethargic and depressed about the shoot being cancelled, others talking animatedly about the day's events. Gino whistled cheerfully enough as he packed everything away, but there was none of his trademark singing; it would have been a little inappropriate.

Tony joined us. I smiled at him, knowing that I would never again see him in the Mr Darcy-esque outfit that had caused me so much hormonal bother – although to be honest, now that we'd kissed I didn't think it would have quite the same effect on me anymore. I could look at him now and appreciate that he was a nice-looking bloke, but … he was my mate.

'Proper shocking turn of events,' he said. Nathan nodded.

'I think you might've missed your shot at fame, mate,' he said. Tony shrugged.

'I'm getting used to missing chances,' he said, with a

rueful grin at me. I was glad Nathan didn't notice. His phone rang.

'Not another video, I hope,' joked Tony. Nathan smiled tightly.

'Nothing quite as exciting,' he said, and declined the call. I could guess only too easily who the caller was…

'What have I missed?' asked Mum, sitting down next to me. 'Is it really all over?'

I nodded. 'Yeah, I'm afraid so. Did you see the video?'

'Ooh, the one on here?' She took her mobile phone out. Up to now it had always annoyed me the way she held it suspiciously in her hand like it was about to explode, but now I welcomed her ineptitude with anything more technical than the kettle (honestly, nothing to do with her age, she just always had problems with anything that had an on-off switch). She opened the message and her finger hovered over the link. 'Should I click on this?'

'NO!!' we all cried, and she looked mildly surprised.

'Okay then, I won't,' she said. 'So what's going on? Why is the shoot cancelled?'

Nathan and I exchanged glances. This was likely to take some time.

Mike Mancuso was a powerful man, and powerful men are used to getting what they want, especially in the movie industry. One of the things he wanted was – how to say this nicely – *favours of the more sordid variety* (that's how my mum would probably have put it, had she been discussing it with her friends at the OAPs' coffee morning, probably in a loud stage whisper to show how shocked she was). And he usually got them, too, because most of the people he pursued were desperate enough to agree to almost anything.

This particular young man *had* agreed, reluctantly, but had regretted it immediately. I wondered how many other young men (and women) had been through the same thing, having been convinced by a sexual predator like Mancuso that this was how things worked in the film industry. From what Faith had told me before, it had almost been par for the course in the early days of her career, but that hardly made it okay.

The hidden camera had caught the whole thing, but when it came down to it, even with the video as evidence, what could they do? There was nothing illegal on that video – apart from the white powder, but for all we could prove it could have been icing sugar, or talcum powder. I wouldn't bet on it, though. Mancuso hadn't physically forced the victim to do anything. It was coercion rather than assault, something which ethically was clearly wrong, but legally considered a 'grey area'.

The police, said Faith, did not have a good track record in such cases, and to my eternal shame, Nathan and I both had to admit she was right.

But she was an actor, and she still wanted a career, so she couldn't do anything openly. She'd sent Mancuso a copy anonymously and told him that his days were numbered if he didn't do the right thing and come clean. He'd immediately assumed that the unknown blackmailer had wanted money.

He'd begun to put funds aside from the production budget, not just to pay off the blackmailer but also as a little nest egg for himself if it did all come out and he suddenly found himself without a career. Not that he really needed that hundred grand (although, when the production accountant went through the figures later they would discover it was more like two hundred and fifty thousand pounds that were unaccounted for), but he had thought it was best to be prepared.

Only the production manager had begun to ask questions. Bills were due, and suddenly there wasn't enough money to pay them. The budget was blown and they hadn't even finished shooting. It would all come out. The investors would want their money back, and it was no longer there.

The series of 'accidents' and talk of the curse had been a godsend. If Mancuso could arrange one big accident that would stop filming for a few weeks, maybe even a month, then the accident insurance would pay out, the creditors would be satisfied, and it would give him enough money to pay off the blackmailer once and for all – or time to find them (and do what to them he did not divulge to Nathan, but it couldn't have been good). And with his teenage daughter coming to stay with him in sleepy Cornwall after being released from rehab, along with her medication, the final part of his plan – the tetrodotoxin – had fallen into place. It had felt like fate, lending him a hand. He'd been so sure of the brilliance of his scheme, and so convinced that no one would ever suspect it was anything other than pufferfish poisoning, that he'd carelessly tossed the sake bottle into the dumpster outside his office.

No one was supposed to die. It was sheer bad luck that Jeremy, the recovering alcoholic who had only fallen off the wagon because of Mancuso himself, had drunk more than he was meant to and ruined the plan.

'Well, I don't think much of *him*,' said Mum sniffily as Nathan and I finished the sorry tale, and we couldn't disagree with that, either.

Chapter Twenty-Eight

It was too cold really to be out in the garden at this time of night, but I'd got used to finishing the day sitting on the wall and staring out at the ocean, and I missed it when I couldn't. It *was* too cold to sit on the stone wall, though, so I leant on it and looked out across the sheep field onto which my house backed. I could smell the sea beyond the field (and the sheep as well, to be honest), but it was too dark to see anything other than the odd ripple of the waves in the distance as the moonlight glinted off the sea. The stars were bright overhead. It felt desolate somehow, but still romantic. I felt like I was on the cover of some romance novel, a lone woman staring bravely out to sea – an image that was spoilt slightly by the gastric explosions emanating from a nearby huddle of my woolly neighbours. Surely they shouldn't smell that much, just from eating grass?

'You all right?' Tony stood by the back door of the house, silhouetted against the light from the kitchen behind him.

'Yeah, course,' I said. 'You joining me?'

He pulled the door shut, then came over and leant on the wall next to me. 'Getting cold at night now, innit?'

'Yeah.'

We were both quiet for a minute.

'Have you seen Zack's social media appeal?' he asked.

'No! What's that all about?'

'He's launching a crowd-funding campaign, to finish the film.'

'Really?' I said, pleased. 'That's brilliant! I hope they raise the money.'

'Me too,' said Tony. 'I can't bear to think of Shirley's big-screen debut going to waste.'

'I wish I'd seen it,' I admitted. 'I feel bad about not watching the filming.' He shrugged.

'You were catching a murderer, to be fair.' He shook his head and laughed. 'I have to say, you did miss a right treat.'

'Was she good?'

'You know your mum. She were magnificent. A

proper Elizabeth Taylor. You should get her to do her line for you. Did she tell you what it was?'

'No. Go on!'

'She had to look at Zack, all haughty like, and say,' – he put on a high-pitched, aristocratic voice that would have made Lady Bracknell sound like an extra from *Mile End Days* – "Young man, you happear to have something protruding from your britches."

I stared at him for a moment, and then we both burst out laughing. Then he turned to me.

'You and me, we're good, yeah?'

'Of course we are,' I said. We really were. 'Good as gold. I meant what I said before, Tony.'

'Friends for life?'

'Friends for life.'

We stood in silence again, but it was a rather more relaxed, companionable one.

'I was thinking,' I said, 'if we're still single in twenty years' time—'

He laughed. 'You won't be single in twenty years' time.'

'Well, no, nor will you. But if we are...'

'Let's not plan that far ahead,' said Tony, with a grin. 'Let's just see what happens, yeah?'

'Er...' I turned as I heard *another* voice behind me. Now *Nathan* stood in the doorway, looking awkward, holding two mugs of tea. Tony smiled.

'Oh yeah, I forgot to tell you, you've got a visitor.' He leaned over and kissed me on the cheek, then said softly, 'Don't miss this moment.'

I looked into his eyes; he genuinely seemed to be okay. I was relieved. He winked at me and said, 'I'll leave you to it, then.' He crossed the garden and stopped for a second in front of Nathan. Neither of them spoke, but something seemed to pass between them. Or was I imagining it? It had been a tiring and emotional few days, after all. Then Tony went into the house and shut the door behind him.

Nathan cleared his throat. 'Your mum made us some tea,' he said, holding up the mugs. I sat on the wall, trying not to notice how cold it was under my bottom. He smiled and joined me.

'Sorry, was I interrupting something with you and Tony?' he asked, handing me my tea. I shook my head.

'Nope, nothing at all,' I said. We sat quietly for a moment, inhaling the steam off our tea. He looked up at the sky.

'The stars are bright tonight,' he said.

'Not a cloud in the sky,' I said. 'That's why it's so chilly.'

'Yeah...'

We sipped at our tea. I began to wonder why he was there, even though I was glad he was. I didn't have to wonder for long.

'So, I have some news about that job…' he said, and my heart sank.

'When are you leaving?' I asked. I really didn't want him to go. He opened his mouth to speak but I suddenly thought, *No, don't let him go without at least telling him how you feel. Don't miss this moment!*

'I—' he started.

'Don't go,' I said. He shut his mouth abruptly, then opened it again.

'What?'

'Don't go. We need you here. I mean, *I* need you here. I want you as my partner in crime. I want—' I was already struggling for words, but then in the field behind me one of those blasted sheep farted (seriously, what had they been eating?) and totally threw me. Way to ruin the atmosphere. Literally. 'That was the sheep, not me.'

He laughed. 'I know.' He took a deep breath. 'I came to tell you I'm not going.'

I stared at him in amazement. 'What? But it's a great job, and it's near your parents…'

He rolled his eyes. 'Are you trying to talk me into taking it now?'

'No! No, of course not. I just…'

He put his mug down, then gently plucked mine from my hands and set it on the ground. 'Jodie, I'm not going anywhere. I told my old super that I'm not interested in moving back there anymore.' He smiled and took my hands. 'I put in for a transfer straight after Andrea changed her mind about moving down here, in the hope that if I went back then we could patch things up. Even after I realised that I didn't want her any more, I still felt like an outsider here, like a … what's that word you lot use?'

'Emmet.'

'Ha! Yes, I felt like an emmet, for a long time. And then I met you.' He gazed deep into my eyes, and I thought, *YES! THIS is how I should have felt when Tony kissed me! Tingly!* This was exactly what had been missing. Nathan smiled, and, just as I had been on the day we'd first met when he'd questioned me at Tony's disastrous wedding-that-never-was, I was struck by how absolutely bloomin' gorgeous he was. 'And now, you know what? Liverpool's not home any more. I can't go back, Jodie, because you make me feel like I'm already where I belong,' he said simply.

And then finally – *finally* – he pulled me into his arms. And with the gentle night breeze toying with our hair, the stars above bathing us in their celestial glow, and the sadly unmistakable scent of flatulent sheep assaulting our nostrils, we finally, *finally*, kissed.

THE END

Jodie's tried and tested recipes #3

Japanese *kakiaage*

These Japanese seafood and vegetable fritters are a lot easier to make than they are to pronounce, and they taste great! What, did you *really* think I'd give you the recipe for *fugu sashimi*? I don't want you lot going off, eating poisonous pufferfish and carking it before you've bought book 4…

So anyway, I love Japanese food. Everyone thinks it's all raw fish and karaoke with noodles, but there's a lot more to it than that. Crispy and mildly spiced *karaage* chicken, *ebi furai* – deep-fried prawns in panko breadcrumbs, pan-fried teriyaki tofu… Japanese food is varied and delicious. Well, the savoury stuff is, anyway. I was originally going to find a nice Japanese cake or sweet recipe to finish off my adventure this time, but it didn't end well.

Anyone who's watched *The Great British Bake Off* will have seen several of the contestants use matcha powder, so I went in search of this exotic (and achingly trendy) ingredient. Matcha is green-tea powder, and the Japanese use it for all sorts of things. For starters, they drink it ('tea' in Japan doesn't come with milk and two sugars. Heresy!), and they add it to all kinds of desserts, not just cakes but ice cream and mousse too. So on a trip back to London to visit some friends, I took Daisy to a fancy Japanese bakery (nothing like that here in Penstowan, or even in the cosmopolitan metropolis that is Truro). We chose a layered matcha crepe cake and a matcha cheesecake. Both looked absolutely amazing (and cost a flipping fortune). We both tucked in eagerly. The taste was strangely evocative; it brought back memories of the time I fell off my bike in the park when I was kid, and face planted on the ground with my mouth open, because both of them tasted like eating grass. Happy days.

So, a savoury dish it is, then! These fritters are deep fried in crispy tempura, a light batter that you can actually use to coat loads of different things. You can even do your

Friday fish and chips in it. Or Mars bars, if you're that way inclined (or Scottish).

1. Coarsely chop 7 or 8 medium-sized peeled, de-veined raw **prawns** – you want some nice little chunks, so don't chop them too finely or they'll get lost in the batter, and *nobody* wants to lose their prawns. Cut 1 **carrot** into matchsticks, or you can use **sweet potato**, **courgette**, or even a **broccoli stalk** – the bit that everyone throws away. You could use a mixture of these if you wanted to. Do what you like. I ain't your mum.
2. Thinly slice an **onion** and a **shallot** (or you could use a couple of **spring onions** instead) and combine them with the other ingredients.
3. For the tempura batter, mix 1/2 cup of **plain flour** with 2 tablespoons of **cornflour**. Make a well in the centre and add 1 **egg yolk** and 1/2 cup of **iced water**, and stir until just combined. The traditional way is to stir it with a chop stick, and leave it a bit lumpy, but that goes against the grain for me and I have to beat it until it's smooth. Add the chopped veg and prawns and stir them in until they're just coated.
4. To deep fry, you'll need a depth of around 5cm of **oil** in a saucepan, heated to 170°c. You'll

know it's hot enough if you chuck in a cube of bread and it sizzles (the way my bits do when Nathan kisses me) and quickly turns golden brown (my bits don't do *that)*. Drop 1/3 cupfuls of the mixture in to oil, making sure you get a good mix of ingredients in each one; you don't want a cup full of batter, because it'll just taste like a deep-fried Yorkshire pudding – which actually sounds quite nice, but isn't Japanese. Fry on each side for 2-3 minutes until golden brown and crispy, then drain on kitchen paper while you cook the rest. The first one is usually a bit soggy because the oil is never quite as hot as you think it is. Or maybe that's just me? Anyway, it's a good excuse to eat it while you cook the others, because of course you don't want to serve anyone else something that's under par…

5. These *kakiaage* (and no, I don't know how you pronounce that. I think it's *kaa-key-ah-hay*, but don't quote me on that because it could be wrong and I will deny it) are great on their own or served with a dipping sauce. Nathan likes them with sweet-chilli sauce, but that's probably because it's hot and sweet (and tasty), just like him…

Acknowledgments

These things get harder to write every time! Not because I did it My Way (cue music) or all on my own — far from it — but because I thank the same people over and over again, and quite frankly I owe them so much that it's beginning to get embarrassing.

I'd like to be able to say, 'thanks, you know who you are', but that just won't cut it, because these wonderful people deserve public recognition.

First and foremost, my husband Dominic and son Lucas. You two are the apples of my eye, the ying to my yang, the icing on my cake, and I love you. You have supported me (financially, emotionally, and probably even physically on occasion), and I am more grateful than you can imagine. Dominic, I hope to one day be so massively successful that I can tell you to quit your job and go and play golf all day. But for the moment you might just have to settle for some new balls (as it were). Lucas, I could win the Booker Prize, the Nobel Prize for Literature *and* be chosen for the Richard and Judy / Oprah Winfrey / Reese Witherspoon book clubs*, and you would *STILL* be my greatest achievement.

I am also lucky enough to have the support of some brilliant ladies, all amazing writers themselves, who provide an oasis of calm during turbulent times, a plethora of shoulders to cry on, and a safe space to bitch, moan and vent when the need arises. Oh, and we laugh *ALL THE FRICKIN' TIME* too, which is nice. Carmen Radtke, Jade Bokhari, Sandy Barker, Nina Kaye and Andie Newton, I consider myself blessed to have you in my life.

Ooh and I actually *do* have some new people to thank this time! Thank you to Julie Fergusson at the North Literary Agency, who has been looking after me so brilliantly while my usual agent Lina Langlee is on maternity leave, and thank you to Bethan Morgan and Charlotte Ledger at One More Chapter, who have taken over the reins on Nosey Parker. It's a pleasure working with you.

And the final thanks is also a cheeky request. Thank *YOU*, dear reader (if you're still with me), for reading this book. I appreciate it. If you enjoyed it, please take 30 seconds to leave a star rating or a review, and tell your friends about it. If you hated it, please don't!

**yeah yeah, never gonna happen, I know…*